P

Pr

"Delightful… Lizzy and Darcy may be one of the greatest classic love stories, and Reynolds' spin on the love story reads like a classic."

—Savvy Verse & Wit

"Romance worthy of Austen herself."

—Palmer's Picks for Reading

"Fresh and unique while staying true to the Darcy and Elizabeth I know and love."

—Diary of an Eccentric

"An amazing read that explores the romantic possibilities between two unforgettable characters: I found it thought-provoking and extremely sensual."

—Readaholic

"A poignant love story and… an exceptional read."

—Once Upon a Romance

"Delicious tension between Mr. Darcy and Elizabeth!… Almost—just almost—as good as the original *Pride & Prejudice*."

—The Epic Rat

"The portrayal of Lizzy and Darcy was absolutely fabulous. Both characters were completely on point."

—Books Like Breathing

"An engaging and clever variation… I love how heartbreaking and emotional the story is. Abigail Reynolds is a very talented and gifted author who clearly loves Jane Austen with a passion!

—Austenesque Reviews

"A charming and whimsical read… Reynolds succeeds in delivering a passionate *Pride and Prejudice* detour that is entertaining and honest."

—Bookworm's Dinner

"A story to make any reader who ever loved Darcy love him even more."

—Apprentice Writer

"A tale of 'what if' that if I didn't know better could have been written by Jane Austen herself. What a beautiful story."

—A Bibliophile's Bookshelf

Mr Darcy's Obsession

Abigail Reynolds

sourcebooks
landmark

Published by Sourcebooks Landmark, an imprint of Sourcebooks, Inc.
P.O. Box 4410, Naperville, Illinois 60567-4410
(630) 961-3900
FAX: (630) 961-2168
www.sourcebooks.com

Library of Congress Cataloging-in-Publication Data

Reynolds, Abigail.
Mr. Darcy's obsession / Abigail Reynolds.
p. cm.
1. Darcy, Fitzwilliam (Fictitious character)--Fiction. 2. Bennet, Elizabeth (Fictitious character)--Fiction. 3. Courtship--Fiction. 4. England--Social life and customs--19th century--Fiction. 5. Gentry--England--Fiction. I. Austen, Jane, 1775-1817. Pride and prejudice. II. Title.
PS3618.E967M68 2010
813'.6--dc22

2010027014

Printed and bound in the United States of America
VP 10 9 8 7 6 5 4 3 2 1

To Elaine and Harriet,
with thanks for their enduring and supportive friendship.

Chapter 1

"Missed, damn it!" Bingley handed off his musket without a second glance.

With a frown, Fitzwilliam Darcy accepted an intricately decorated rifle from his loader. "Bingley, is anything the matter? You do not seem yourself."

"I missed the damned bird; that is the matter!" Bingley scowled. Darcy had seen little of Bingley's habitual smiles since his friend had arrived at Pemberley.

"There is no shortage of birds to shoot at." Darcy waited while the handler shooed the spaniel into the brush. A brace of partridge rose obligingly from the trees. He sighted down the barrel and shot. One of the birds plummeted to the ground, and the dog crashed through the brush to retrieve it. "I was surprised your sisters did not accompany you on this visit." It was his only guess as to what might be troubling Bingley.

"I do not care if I ever see them again."

So it was something his sisters had done. Certainly they could be irritating, but it surprised Darcy that they would affect Bingley enough to cause this uncharacteristic fit of ill humour. "Have you quarreled, then?"

Bingley took another shot, hardly bothering to aim, but said nothing until Darcy had his own rifle to his shoulder again. "Do you remember Miss Elizabeth Bennet?"

Darcy's finger tightened involuntarily on the trigger before he braced himself. The rifle recoil knocked him back a step, and his shot went wide. "I remember her, yes," he said brusquely.

"I saw her at Kew Gardens. Did you know she is living in London now?"

Darcy rubbed his shoulder where the rifle had kicked him. He tried to still his racing pulse. Of all the mutual acquaintances Bingley could have named, why did it have to be that one? Darcy had almost put her memory behind him after his last Easter visit to Rosings when he discovered Mr. Collins had left his aunt's employment, thus terminating his only potential source of intelligence about Elizabeth. "No, I had not heard."

"Her father died last autumn, and the estate was entailed away from the family. That idiot cousin of theirs, your aunt's clergyman, inherited. Mrs. Bennet and her daughters moved in with her sister in Meryton, but there was not enough room for all of them, so Miss Elizabeth came to live with her aunt and uncle in Cheapside. She helps them with their children."

"I had not realized there was an entailment." Yet another reason it was fortunate that Elizabeth had returned home from Rosings the previous year to care for her ailing father before Darcy had time to act on his impulse to ask her to marry him. Still, the idea of Elizabeth without a home of her own gave him a tinge of discomfort. He had always imagined her comfortably ensconced at Longbourn. And unmarried. His imagination refused to consider the possibility she might marry another. He watched absently as the handler took the dead partridge from the dog's mouth and dropped it into the game bag.

"She seemed to think I might know about it, and said her sister Jane had written to Caroline and told her the news, but never received a reply. I asked her if Jane was in London as well, and do you know what she told me?"

"I have no idea." He was certain from Bingley's savage tone that it was nothing good.

"A week before their father's death, Miss Bennet accepted an offer of marriage from one of her admirers in Meryton, one who had been thought beneath her consideration, but this way Jane could be in a position to provide for her mother in her old age. My Jane, married to a shopkeeper old enough to be her father." Bingley practically spat the words out.

Darcy shook his head. Bingley should be thanking his lucky stars for his narrow escape, and instead he was still pining over the girl two years later. "I hope it will work out well for her."

"Miss Elizabeth told me she had tried to persuade Jane not to do it, because Jane always wanted to marry for love, but she said she could never marry the only man she would ever love, so it mattered little whom she did marry. I could not help but ask what happened to the man she loved. Miss Elizabeth looked me straight in the eye and said, 'He left one day without explanation and never returned.'"

Darcy could picture it all too easily. Elizabeth had never hesitated to speak her mind, and if her sister had truly loved his friend, despite her appearance of indifference, Elizabeth would no doubt resent Bingley for his abandonment. "I am sorry to hear it."

"Not as sorry as I am. Then she asked me if I happened to see her sister when she had been in London the winter before their father died. Apparently Jane had called on Caroline and Louisa, who never saw fit to mention it to me. Caroline claims she did it to protect me." Bingley's bitterness was obvious.

It was just as well Bingley had no clue as to Darcy's interference in the matter. Darcy was not sure he would trust his friend with the information while he had a gun in his hand.

The loader held out a musket to Bingley, but he pushed it away. "I have lost my taste for shooting."

Darcy had promised himself he would not do this. Not a day had passed since he learned of Elizabeth's presence in London when he had not imagined seeing her somehow, but he knew it was foolishness. Their paths were unlikely to cross, and even if by some chance they did, the degradation of such a marriage would be even worse now than it had been when he had first considered it, that night at Rosings when her playing and verbal jousting had entranced him.

Yet here he was, not a fortnight after his return to London, riding down Gracechurch Street, attempting an air of unconcern as if he were paying no attention to his surroundings. It was not truly an attempt to see *her*; no, he had decided that his preoccupation stemmed from a concern as to Elizabeth's circumstances. If he could see for himself that she was part of a respectable household, he would be able to stop thinking of her constantly.

The street itself did not appear disreputable, despite the warehouses visible just beyond the houses. There were no more than the usual number of beggars and shifty-looking characters. He wondered which house was hers. Was she there, behind one of the windows? Did she ever think of him?

He shook himself out of his reverie, spurring his mount to a faster pace. He had learned what he needed, and now he should go, but instead he stopped at a small flower shop near Bishopsgate. Georgiana would like some flowers.

A street urchin appeared at his side as he dismounted. "'Old your 'orse, sir?"

Darcy handed him the reins. The small, disreputable boy with a smudge of soot on his face no doubt had the privilege of seeing Elizabeth in the neighbourhood, an opportunity unavailable to Darcy. Without much thought he selected a bouquet from the flower girl. Returning to the boy, he fished a coin from his pocket and dropped it in his outstretched hand.

The boy pulled at the edge of his ragged cap. "Thank yer, sir."

"Do you know the house of Mr. Gardiner?"

"Course I do." The boy pointed unhesitatingly up the street to a smallish house with painted shutters and well-tended flower boxes.

It was as if he could not help himself. "There is a young woman who lives there, a Miss Bennet."

The boy screwed up his face in thought. "Pretty bird, wiv dark hair?"

The description could have fit half the young women of London, but it brought only one image to Darcy's mind. "Do you know anything of her?"

"No, sir, but I know the cook's boy. I could find out somefin', if yer wanted me to, sir."

With a certain misgiving, Darcy handed the boy another coin. "Can you meet me here tomorrow? There will be another one of those for you if you can tell me about her."

"For sure, sir. What would yer be wantin' to know about 'er?"

Darcy hesitated. "Whether she is treated well, if she is happy, if she is… engaged or has a young man." He could barely bring himself to say it. "But not a word to anyone that someone has been asking."

"Course not, sir. Yer can count on me!"

"I found out what you wanted, sir." The boy, looking even more disreputable than the day before, barely paused for breath. "She has lots o' sisters at home, and her father's dead. Her ma had five thousand quid in the funds, but she's already spent it, so there's none for Miss Bennet, and no room, neither, so she came to live here. She been here about a year, and didn't go home but once. She writes lots o' letters, but Freddie don't know who to."

Apparently he had picked a very competent spy. "Do the Gardiners treat her well?"

"Seems like. She 'elps wiv the children, gives them lessons and such. No young man she favours, but Freddie says there's one as would like to be, a friend of her uncle's, and Mr. Gardiner favours him for 'er."

Darcy developed a sudden dislike for the unknown Mr. Gardiner. But that was unfair. He should be happy that Elizabeth had the prospect of something better than unpaid employment in her uncle's house, but he could not bring himself to appreciate it. "Anything else?" he asked brusquely.

A knowing grin split the urchin's face. "She rises early and goes walkin' most mornin's in Moorsfield."

Darcy caught his breath. "By herself?"

"By 'erself, sir." The boy was clearly pleased with his initiative.

"Well done." He pulled out a handful of coins, more than the boy deserved.

The boy examined his earnings with wide eyes. "Thank yer, sir! Any time yer need somefin', yer just ask for Charlie. Any time."

Elizabeth pulled her pelisse more tightly around her. It had not seemed so cold when she left the Gardiner house, but Gracechurch Street was well sheltered from the brisk wind that blew across Moorsfield, bending grasses and stems already brown from the frost. Still, she intended to take full advantage of her free hour. She could not complain of unhappiness in her uncle's house; she had always enjoyed visiting them, but it was different to live there. Always before she had known she would return to Longbourn and the countryside she loved. Now her life was in London, and despite the manifold attractions of town, she missed the freedom of her rambles and open land around her.

She nodded to an older couple walking past, one she often saw in the early morning hour. Across a field she could see two horsemen exercising their mounts, and she paused to admire the seat of one of them. As if feeling her gaze, he turned towards her.

Elizabeth froze in recognition. But there was nothing so strange about encountering Mr. Darcy in Moorsfield. After all, he had a house in London. She curtsied an acknowledgment, expecting no more than a nod in return from such a proud man. To her surprise, he reined in his horse and trotted in her direction, followed by the other horseman.

He dismounted and tossed his reins to his companion, who was dressed in a servant's livery. "Miss Bennet," Darcy said.

"It is an unexpected pleasure, Mr. Darcy." The words were not just politeness. Proud and disagreeable as Mr. Darcy might be, he was still a part of the life she had left behind, and his presence was a reminder of better days.

"The pleasure is mine." He looked as if he had no more to say, and she wondered why he had bothered to come to greet her.

"Have you been in London long?" she asked.

"Yes. That is, not long. I was at Pemberley until a fortnight ago."

"It must be very cold in Derbyshire this time of year."

"Very cold, yes."

She had forgotten how difficult it was to engage him in conversation. "It is quite a coincidence meeting you. I saw Mr. Bingley at Kew Gardens only a month or two ago."

The name of Mr. Bingley seemed to rouse him from his torpor, and he shifted from one foot to the other. "So he mentioned. He said you live in London now."

"Yes, I do." Elizabeth wondered what else Mr. Bingley had told him. If Mr. Darcy knew her present situation, she could understand even less why a man of such pride should deign to speak to her.

Darcy rubbed his hands together as if to warm them. "Do you enjoy city life?"

"In some ways. I enjoy living with my aunt and uncle, but

I miss the countryside at home. I walk here whenever I can, but it is not the same."

"No, it is not. It must be agreeable, though, to be settled such an easy distance from Meryton."

"An easy distance do you call it? It is nearly thirty miles." Far enough that Elizabeth could afford to go home only once a year. Even then it was not the same, staying in her Aunt Philips's crowded rooms in town. Longbourn was no longer her home. She had visited Charlotte there precisely twice and did not intend to return again. Unlike her mother, she did not find it painful to see her old friend as mistress of Longbourn, but Mr. Collins could not miss an opportunity to comment on her changed circumstances and lost opportunities, and she questioned her ability to keep her temper if it happened again.

"And what is thirty miles of good road? Less than half a day's journey. Yes, I call it a very easy distance."

It must be easy to consider it such when one had ten thousand pounds a year. She did not wish to think on the home that was no longer hers, though, so she merely said, "It is far enough for me."

She expected him now to depart, but instead he offered her his arm. Did he intend to walk with her, then? She could not understand it. She silently thanked her aunt for her recent gift of new kid gloves. Her old ones had been quite worn through, and she would have been embarrassed to accept Mr. Darcy's arm in them. At least he would see the one item of her wardrobe for which she need not blush.

They walked a short distance in silence, and then Darcy cleared his throat. "I was sorry to hear of your father's death. He was a man I would have liked to know better."

She fixed her eyes on the toes of her boots. "Thank you." If she did not say anything further, he might not notice her distress.

"My own father died six years ago. Life never seemed quite the same afterwards. I still miss him."

Mr. Darcy openly expressing such sentiments? Elizabeth could not have been more astonished had he suddenly started speaking Chinese. Still, she could see he was in earnest, so she tightened her hand on his arm. "There are some losses, I suppose, that one never forgets."

"Yes, I suppose so. But time moves on, and eventually other interests move to the fore."

Elizabeth was startled by the expression in his dark eyes. "I take comfort in that."

"The rest of your family, are they well? Your mother and sisters?"

"Tolerably well, I thank you." She looked out across the fields, grateful for a lightening in the conversation. She was not ready to discuss her losses with Mr. Darcy.

Chapter 2

One time. That was what Darcy had decided. He would meet with her one time, reassure himself of her well-being, and then leave. With any luck, he would discover that her magnetism had faded, dimmed with time, and that her fine eyes no longer cast a spell over him. Then he could forget her, forget the dream that had haunted him since that night at Rosings when he had briefly believed she could be his. One time.

Yet here he was again in Moorsfield just after dawn, waiting for her to appear. For five days he had fought the urge to return to her company, to feel that unique sense of being alive only she could create in him. He had not realized what was missing from his life until he met her, but every day had been the same for him, a repeat of all the other days of his life, wherever he might be, with whomever he might be. He moved through his days like an automaton, not unhappy, but caring about little. Until he met Elizabeth.

All she had to do was look up at him with her fine eyes, an arch smile gracing her tempting lips, each movement of her body light and pleasing. She made him want to respond to her teasing. Even the air around her seemed to sparkle, to taste new and intriguing. He wanted to know what she would say next, what she would do. He felt alive again with her, all of his senses awake and alert, as if he could fly, if he chose. Leaving her was like smothering in thick, murky air, weighed down forever.

He had no excuse this time. He simply could not stay away.

Elizabeth seemed startled to see him. As well she might, he thought. He greeted her, his heart in his throat.

"You are becoming quite a denizen of Moorsfield, Mr. Darcy." She smiled up at him, and his heart beat faster.

"It appears I am not the only one."

Elizabeth smoothed her kidskin gloves. "It is my habit to walk here most mornings. It is my hour of peace in the day."

"I hope, then, I am not disrupting you if I walk along with you."

She raised an eyebrow at him saucily. "So long as you do not continually ask me to read fairy tales and *Robinson Crusoe* aloud, insist on playing hide-and-seek through the house, or refuse to do your lessons, your company will be a pleasant change from my day."

He knew she had no idea how attractive the idea of playing anything with her was to him, but it was best to say nothing of that. "I believe I can oblige you, in that case."

They walked along in silence for some minutes until she asked after his aunt and cousin, and he reciprocated by asking whether all her sisters were still in Hertfordshire, not that he particularly cared what she said, as long as she said it to him.

"My two youngest sisters are still with my mother in Meryton. Mary has gone to care for an aged cousin in Oxford, and declares herself well suited to the situation. Jane is married, of course." Elizabeth fell silent, twirling her bonnet strings around her finger.

He could tell something was troubling her, and it was not difficult to guess what it was. "I imagine you and she are regular correspondents."

"Yes, when she has the time."

"She is busy?"

"Mr. Darcy, her husband is a milliner. She assists him as she can. He provides for my sister, but they are not well-to-do." She crossed her arms as if she were cold and then added with the shadow of a smile, "You may now decamp from my disgraceful company, if you wish."

"Because your family has fallen on hard times?"

She shot a look of surprise at him. "My family was beneath your notice even before my father's death."

She thought he had not noticed her? "Not at all. You and your sister were the most charming young ladies in the neighbourhood. I doubt that has changed. Nor does it make you any less accomplished or amiable."

"I did not know you counted flattery among your skills, sir." Her words were sharp, but her tone was warmer.

He found his ability to reduce her distress to be a heady drug. "Your devotion to your sister when she was ill was touching, and I cannot help but wonder if you are concerned for her welfare now."

"Mr. Darcy, you do not hesitate to speak your mind!" She paused. "Yes, I am concerned for Jane's welfare, but there is little I can do about it. So let us speak of pleasant matters instead."

There it was again, that arch look that he could not resist. It was fortunate that she would never know how much it affected him.

The memories of her pleasant morning walk with Mr. Darcy stayed with Elizabeth through the rest of her otherwise unremarkable day. That afternoon, she found herself watching out the window in hopes that, despite all expectations to the contrary, he might come riding down Gracechurch Street, ready to share another hour of amiable conversation.

Her cousin Matthew pulled at her sleeve impatiently. "Lizzy, we need your help."

With a last longing glance out the window, Elizabeth followed him to the schoolroom table where his sister, Margaret, was frowning over their new wooden puzzle. Elizabeth picked up a piece and turned it first one way, then the other. The coast of France, or perhaps Sweden? The children had completed the frame of their puzzle, but she could not see where this piece belonged. She searched through the other pieces on the table for one that might match the border.

It was difficult to focus when her mind kept travelling back to Moorsfield and Mr. Darcy. He had been there yet again today, without even the pretence of an accidental meeting. She could come up with no explanation but that he enjoyed her company. They shared no common acquaintances apart from the Bingleys and did not move in the same circles. He was amused by her teasing, and even teased back on occasion, displaying a dry wit she had not realized he possessed.

Perhaps Charlotte had been correct when she suggested that Mr. Darcy admired Elizabeth. A not completely uncomfortable sensation pressed at her chest with the thought. Mr. Darcy interested in her, Elizabeth Bennet? She could not credit it. He did not act as a suitor might—he did not wish to meet her aunt and uncle, as she had discovered when she invited him in the previous day. No doubt a simple tradesman and his wife were so far beneath him as to make such an introduction unpalatable.

Elizabeth frowned, sorting through the puzzle pieces. Margaret held out a section to her. "Lizzy, where does this one go?"

She peered at it, rubbing her finger along the smooth edge. "Look here, can you see those letters?"

"L-i-s-b… Is the last one a C or an O? It is half cut off."

"What city would have those letters in it?"

"Lisbon!" Matthew, two years younger than his sister, produced the name triumphantly.

"And where is Lisbon?"

Matthew screwed up his face. "Spain?"

Margaret drew herself to her full height, looking down her nose at her younger brother. "No, Portugal, silly."

No, if Mr. Darcy had felt Jane was an unsuitable match for Mr. Bingley when they were still in possession of Longbourn, how much more unsuitable Elizabeth must be for him now that she was dependent upon the generosity of her uncle! But what then was his purpose in meeting her so frequently? He could not possibly imagine that she would agree to be his mistress. Then again, she had not forgotten how cruelly he had treated Mr. Wickham, though it seemed hard to reconcile the man she was coming to know and such behaviour. Perhaps there had been some sort of misunderstanding.

Margaret crowed with satisfaction as she fit in a piece showing northern England. Mr. Darcy's home would be somewhere on that piece, his much-admired Pemberley, but Elizabeth would never see it. Even if she ever had the opportunity to travel so far, she was not the sort of person he would invite to his home. No matter how much he might admire her, he had never suggested furthering their acquaintance in the society he frequented.

Blinking hard, she turned her attention to the puzzle, trying to make out the pattern, but she could not see the whole of it yet, just a jumble of unrecognizable pieces.

Darcy impatiently rapped on the carriage roof to signal the driver and was rewarded by the crack of a whip and the clip-clop of hooves on cobblestones as the carriage jostled into motion, pulling away from White's. He tossed his hat on the seat opposite him with a scowl.

The day had started auspiciously, a sunny morning with a smiling Elizabeth in Moorsfield. Miss Bennet. He needed to remember to use that name in his mind, or sooner or later he would slip and call her by name to her face. Miss Bennet. Their conversation about Byron and Napoleon was almost as stimulating as Elizab… Miss Bennet's fine eyes, eyes he would never tire of looking into. She had bade him a cheerful farewell at the end, more cheerful than he had felt. After all, once she left him, there would be no chance to see her again before the following morning. And he should not go to Moorsfield even then, lest it raise her expectations. He should wait a few days, if he could last that long.

His club had served as a passable distraction at first. He had played cards with Viscount St. James and Lord Sinclair until he tired of the latter's coarse jokes, and then he engaged in a heated political discussion that resulted in a large bet between two of the members being recorded in the betting book as to the outcome of the next debate in the House of Lords. Darcy stood as witness to the bet and then joined in the traditional round of the finest brandy that followed such bets. He had just taken the first sip when Addington, with a slight sneer, told him the news about Bingley.

What could Bingley have been thinking? After all the months of lobbying Darcy had done to get Bingley a membership at White's, all the favours he had called in on his friend's behalf, he had *resigned* his membership? No one ever resigned from White's. Sometimes they might disappear for years at a time, but they did not resign. What crazy idea did Bingley have in his head this time?

He would find out soon enough. He peered out the window to discover they were almost to Bingley's townhouse. It was not as exclusive an area as Brook Street, but it was stylish nonetheless. The carriage drew to a halt. Darcy opened the side door without waiting for the driver's assistance, strode up the steps to Bingley's front door, and rapped on it sharply.

He was taken aback when Bingley himself answered the door. Bingley's servants always managed to take advantage of him, but this was ridiculous. Bingley stepped back hastily at the sight of Darcy. Something was clearly wrong.

"Darcy. Do you want to come in?" Bingley sounded nervous, and well he might.

"That was my general purpose in calling," Darcy said. "Are you well? I have not heard from you since you left Pemberley."

Bingley ushered him into a sitting room. "I am well enough."

Normally Bingley bore the burden of conversation between them, but today he seemed to be waiting for something. Darcy tried again. "I was concerned for you. I was informed you resigned your membership at White's."

"Oh. That."

"Yes, that! Bingley, whatever is the matter? You are not yourself."

Bingley clasped his hands together, and Darcy could see his knuckles were white. "No, now I *am* myself again. I am no longer trying to pass myself off as the gentleman I will never be."

Darcy felt like rolling his eyes, but controlled the impulse, lest it intimidate Bingley even more. "Bingley, would you please calm yourself and tell me what is troubling you?"

Bingley stood stock still for a moment, and then he heaved a sigh and flopped down into a chair. "I am sorry. I have been avoiding you because I did not want to have this conversation."

Had his friend discovered his complicity in disguising Jane Bennet's presence in London? "This sounds unpleasant. Have I offended you in some way?"

"Not you, at least not in particular." Bingley sprung to his feet again and paced over to the fireplace. "I am leaving."

"Leaving?"

"Leaving London. Leaving the *ton*. Leaving the Season. Leaving it all."

So this was nothing more than one of Bingley's dramatic impulses. Darcy expected he could soothe him out of whatever was bothering him this time, just like always. "Is something wrong? Where are you going?"

"Back to Scarborough. My father's business is still there, and I plan to return to it."

Comprehension dawned in Darcy, along with concern. "A financial reversal? Is there any way in which I could assist? You know you only have to ask."

Bingley snorted. "My finances are as solid as ever. Money cannot buy what I want."

"And that is?" He waited with some dread for Bingley's answer.

"I think you know." Bingley turned to face him, a resolute look on his face. "Have you ever looked around you, Darcy? Really looked?"

"What do you mean?" Darcy helped himself to a chair, since it did not seem Bingley would invite him to sit.

"Our lives. Whiled away at clubs with fortunes lost and won. All the drinking, gluttony, gambling, led by none other than Prinny and the finest of his set. Beau Brummell spending four hours tying his cravat. Then, to show off our privilege, slumming in the rookeries, watching cockfights, and worse, laughing at the ignorant peasants around us. Not to mention the brothels."

Darcy sighed. "Bingley, there are upright men as well."

"Upright men? You mean a man who has only a wife and one mistress, does not risk his entire fortune when he gambles, and drinks his night away, indulges in laudanum until he cannot think, but still he goes to church on Sundays and pays his debts of honour. This is commendable! These are what we are proud to call gentlemen. This is what I have spent my life striving to become. It makes me ill." Bingley smacked his hand on the mantelpiece.

"I cannot defend the behaviour of the young bucks and dandies, or even the Prince Regent. You know I detest the Carlton House set. But we are not all wastrels, and you know it." Sometimes it took a great deal of patience to handle Bingley when he was in one of these rash moods.

"It is true that *you* would prefer a book to a cockfight, and I have never known you to frequent a brothel. But you play at cards with the same men at White's, while you look down on the honest people of Hertfordshire because they lack the breeding of those degenerates. I have heard you mock them with my sisters, and God help me, I listened to you. The *ton* is *fashionable*, and that is more important than honesty, virtue, good judgment, or loyalty. They were not fashionable, so they were beneath us."

If it were anyone but Bingley speaking, anyone but a dear old friend he had seen in other sudden passions over the years, Darcy would have taken offense. "It is the way of the world. No doubt there is more virtue in those people than you can find in the entirety of Carleton House, but what does it matter what we say among ourselves? It hurts no one."

"Did you never see the expression on Miss Bennet's face when my sisters made their little insinuations? Oh, it hurts; you know it does. Do you know why her sister, Miss Elizabeth, took such a dislike to you? Jane told me. Because you said at an assembly that she was not handsome enough to tempt you. I remember your saying it. And she heard it, because you made no effort to ensure she did not. No, I cannot agree that it hurts no one. How would you feel if it were Georgiana who was treated so? Or if she had to marry a shopkeeper to keep you from the streets? Or if she were a kept woman or one of those unfortunate girls on the street? Would you still say that it hurts no one?"

Darcy rose to his feet in an unreasoning fury. "That is quite enough," he said, his voice sharp as a knife blade. "No, do not bother, I can see myself out." He jammed his hat on his head and strode out before he said anything worse.

"Wait!" Bingley raced after him into the hall. "I apologize. I should not have spoken of your sister so."

"No, you should not! Now, if you will excuse me."

Bingley grabbed his arm. "Darcy, I would not have us part like this. I am leaving, and God knows when I will ever see you again. Forgive me for allowing my tongue to run ahead of my judgment."

Slowly Darcy forced himself to relax his clenched fists, and then he removed his gloves one finger at a time. "It is forgotten."

Bingley's bright smile showed itself for the first time since his arrival. "Thank you." He seemed to remember his theme. "You know, better than anyone, how hard I have worked to be accepted among the *ton*, to make myself like them. But that was before I learned that Caroline and Louisa deceived me about Jane Bennet and faced the consequences of that. Now I feel as if my eyes are open after a long darkness."

"I am sorry it turned out badly for you." It was as close as Darcy could come to apologizing for his own secret part in it.

"For me?" Bingley gave a twisted little smile. "I rode to Meryton to see Jane, to see what her life is like, what she has to do each day while we attend our little soirees with people of good birth but despicable morals. Not one of them would sacrifice themselves to help their families. No, they are too busy drinking, gaming, and taking other men's wives to their beds."

"Bingley, I take your point. You need not keep repeating it."

"You thought Jane Bennet was beneath me. You said as much. But she is a better person than either of us."

Darcy would not have accepted those words from any other man, but Bingley was a close friend and clearly distraught. "I should not have said that. I thought only to protect you from a fortune hunter."

"She *loved* me!"

"I cannot say. I did not observe any particular affection in her behaviour towards you."

"I should never have listened to you. I knew better, but I trusted your judgment over my own." He closed his eyes as if he were in agony. "Darcy, do you have any idea what it is like to see the woman you love degraded and be helpless to stop it?"

Darcy drew back as if he had been slapped. Bingley could have no idea of his meetings with Elizabeth, nor could he know that her situation had not troubled him overmuch. Then again, her situation was somewhat better. Were she in

Jane's shoes, he might feel differently. Even the thought of Elizabeth married to some old petticoat chaser was intolerable. He rested his forehead on the palm of his hand, suddenly exhausted. It was nonsense, what Bingley had said earlier, about Elizabeth disliking him. He knew better. "Bingley, I do not know what to say."

"Say that you understand why I must leave this den of iniquity. Why I must ignore my father's wishes to make a gentleman of myself and instead make myself an honest man."

"I understand, even if I cannot agree. But I will be here when you change your mind and can see the good in society again."

Bingley reached out his hand and clasped Darcy's. "You are a good man, Darcy, and a good friend."

If Bingley knew the secret he had kept from him, he might not call him a good friend, but with luck he would never discover it. "You will write, I hope. Remember that Pemberley is not so very far from Scarborough. You are always welcome there."

Chapter 3

ELIZABETH HAD LOOKED SURPRISED to see him again this morning. Darcy's good intentions of staying away for several days had disappeared after a hellish night of hearing Bingley's words resound in his head—not the part about the decadence of his society; that was half forgotten. No, it was the bit about Elizabeth he could not forget. *Do you know why Miss Elizabeth took such a dislike to you?* He was sure it was not true. Elizabeth enjoyed his attentions and his company. But suddenly little things she had said to him in the past came back to him, and he started imagining barbs in her comments. He had to see her again to get that nonsense out of his head. Just in case there was anything to Bingley's comments, he would make certain to sound respectful of her family and neighbours in Meryton.

Of course, that was easier said than done. He could not start out by saying he respected the society in Hertfordshire; she would think that more than odd. Once again he wished for the sort of felicity of tongue possessed by Bingley or his cousin, Colonel Fitzwilliam. After some anxious thought, he said, "How did you come to move to London while your sisters remained in Meryton?"

"My uncle had space for only one, and since Jane was not available, he chose me. A true miscarriage of justice, since by all rights I should have the worst life of all, and instead I have perhaps the best."

Her words shocked him. "The worst? Why should you have the worst?" Especially when she might have been mistress of Pemberley, had matters gone slightly differently.

"Ah, you have found my guilty secret. You see, it is my fault that my family had to leave Longbourn." She said it gaily, but he could sense a tension underneath.

"Your fault? How could it be your fault?"

"I should not tell you this, but I hope I can rely on your discretion." She looked up at him mischievously. "Do you remember Mr. Collins, your aunt's clergyman?"

"He would be difficult to forget."

"I refused an offer of marriage from him. Had I accepted him, my mother and sisters would still have a home at Longbourn, and Jane would not have had to marry where she had no inclination. There, is that not a terrible crime?"

"No, the crime would have been had you married Mr. Collins." Even mentioning the idea left a bad taste in his mouth.

"But Jane is paying the price for my choice. She would have agreed to marry Mr. Collins had he chosen her, since our mother wished it, but he settled on me because everyone expected Jane to… make a different match." She looked away into the distance.

He did not want to think about that, but he did wish to ease Elizabeth's distress. "I wonder if your sister could have been happy with Mr. Collins. Suppose you had the choice of marrying either Mr. Collins or your sister's husband. Which would you prefer?"

"If I must choose one?" She sounded dubious.

"Yes, which would it be?"

"Jane's husband, Mr. Browning," she said promptly. "I would rather suffer indignities than marry a fool."

"Perhaps your sister feels the same way. Would she have wanted *you* to marry Mr. Collins against your wishes?"

"No, indeed, but Jane has a gift for seeing the best in any situation."

"And your gift is to see the amusing side of every situation."

She laughed. "You are quite right. I shall immediately put all my guilt behind me and thank God it is my family suffering in my place."

Once again, Darcy was taken by delight, knowing himself able to bring a smile back to Elizabeth's face. It must have been nonsense, what Bingley had said.

She glanced to one side, then the other, and then said to him in a teasingly covert manner, "Do you know what my worst sin is? If I had the chance to do it over again, I would still refuse Mr. Collins."

"Thank God for that." His words were heartfelt.

She gave him an odd look. "You are full of surprises, Mr. Darcy," she said dryly.

"Speaking of surprises, I called on Bingley yesterday." Why had that slipped out? He had not meant to say it, had in fact determined he should not mention Bingley to Elizabeth at all, but all this talk of Elizabeth married to other men had left him off balance.

"Look! A green woodpecker! I have not seen one here before." Elizabeth pointed to a bare oak tree. "Is Mr. Bingley well?"

Now he could hear the tap-tap-tap and see the woodpecker's crimson crown as he coursed his way up the trunk. Usually he delighted in the sights Elizabeth showed him. She observed details he never noticed, things that brightened the natural world around them, but today he had difficulty summoning enthusiasm. "He is well physically, but in such a mood as I have never seen him. We almost had words."

Elizabeth turned surprised eyes on him. "With Mr. Bingley? I thought him constitutionally incapable of quarrelling with anyone."

By God, she could make him smile, even when his thoughts were dark. "He is set on leaving London society, returning to industry. He has always been a creature of impulse, swayed by his passions, but this was quite unexpected."

Elizabeth knit her lovely brows. "Return to industry?"

"He feels that fashionable society has become degenerate and wants no part of it." He found himself holding his breath, waiting for her to contradict Bingley's assumption.

"Really? I did not have the impression Mr. Bingley objected to gentlemen's entertainments," she said tartly. "He amused himself well at Netherfield, did he not?"

He knew she was speaking of her sister, and that she intended him to notice. "Bingley has not a vicious bone in his body. He is goodhearted and charmed by everyone. He would never deliberately trifle with a lady's affections."

"Only by accident, then?" She gave him an arch look.

He smiled at her teasing, relieved that the moment of tension was past. "Perhaps then. He is, as I said, prone to impulsiveness."

"And you are the opposite."

Except when it came to her. "I strive to be rational."

She smiled slightly, as if to herself. "Indeed. And do you enjoy your rational behaviour, sir?"

"No." Good God, why had he said that? Hastily he tried to undo the damage. "Doing the right thing is not always enjoyable."

"One man's right is another man's wrong."

He took a deep breath. Here was his opening. "Bingley said I offended you when we first met."

She let out a melodious peal of laughter and then put on a mock scowl. "No, indeed. You offended me before we were even introduced."

A tightness wound through his stomach. "I must apologize, then."

Elizabeth shook her head. "Mr. Darcy, we both know you found Meryton society beneath you, and you did not care who knew it. And I would guess you feel the same way today."

No one had ever spoken to him that way before, with such frankness yet amusement, but it hurt nonetheless. First Bingley, now Elizabeth. He put on his best indifferent look. "I am sorry I gave offense. I was not accustomed to country society." Even he could hear how cold and haughty his words sounded.

Elizabeth tightened her hand on his arm. "And now *I* have offended *you*," she said cheerfully. "So in that much we are equal."

He could tell she was just jesting, playing with words as she always did, but the idea that she had ever thought ill of him still festered. "Yet you tolerate my company, Miss Bennet. Or perhaps you would prefer I depart."

"No need for that, sir. You improve upon further acquaintance."

It was like a knot had been released. "With such a beginning, I had no choice but to improve, did I not?"

"And I have no choice but to tease such a perversely rational creature! I despise perfection, sir, and must puncture it whenever I can, since I am so full of imperfections myself."

At least this time he managed to bite his tongue before he told her she was perfection itself. It was reassuring to know he had a trace of self-control left.

Darcy poured himself a glass of brandy, then, remembering Bingley's words about drunkenness, put it down again. After a moment he took it up again and rolled the liquor around his mouth, feeling the pleasant heat of it travelling down his throat. He needed a drink, after such a day as he had.

Elizabeth. He was in too deep with her. He should have seen it coming; after all, this was the same woman to whom he almost proposed marriage back at Rosings. He had lost his head over her then, and he was in danger of doing the same again. No, not in danger. He was well beyond that point.

But it would not do. It was one thing to enjoy her company and flirt with her when no one else was aware of it, but Bingley had spoken truly of the cutting tongues of their social circle. He could not imagine what would be said if they knew he was keeping company with a milliner's sister, even if her father was a gentleman. They would assume she was his mistress. Marriage was out of the question. He would be a laughingstock, and no decent gentleman would so much as look at Georgiana. He could not afford to take any risk with her prospects, not now.

Why, oh, why had he interfered between Bingley and Jane Bennet? It had been done for the best, but if he had not, Jane would be Mrs. Bingley, and Elizabeth would not now be beyond his reach. Truly he was being repaid in the same coin he had given Bingley.

He took another sip of the brandy, but it did not help. He would have to stay away from Elizabeth Bennet. No more jaunts to Moorsfield, no more basking in her smiles as they walked along the paths, her gloved hand fitting perfectly on his arm. No more. No more.

Elizabeth brushed a few stray snowflakes from her sleeves when she arrived at her uncle's warehouse. His clerk, Mr. Johnson, stood to greet her, his eyes cheery.

"Miss Bennet, you brighten a gloomy day with your presence."

She laughed at his flagrant flirtation and blew a snowflake off her glove in his direction. "It is winter, you know, so you must expect the gloomy days."

"I shall not mind them in such company. May I take your wrap?"

"I thank you, no. I am here for only a moment to deliver some papers my uncle left behind this morning. Would you be so kind as to tell him I am here?"

"I fear I cannot oblige you, as he stepped out earlier. I expect him any minute, if you would care to wait, or I can give him the papers when he returns."

"I think I shall wait." If her uncle had brought the papers home in the first place, they were likely confidential. Besides, a few minutes in the company of the amiable Mr. Johnson was always a pleasure.

"But you must be cold. Will you sit by the stove and warm yourself? I would never forgive myself if you took a chill." He gestured to a stool by the stove.

It was pleasant to engage in lighthearted banter with a charming young man. Despite his low station, he made her feel like an elegant young lady, and his quick wit was disarming. She was laughing at one of his stories when Mr. Gardiner returned.

Her uncle spared them a quick glance. "Lizzy, will you join me in my office?"

Surprised at his abruptness, she followed him into the small room filled with account books. "My aunt asked me to bring you these papers."

"Thank you; I had wondered where they were." Mr. Gardiner closed the office door behind him.

"Is there a message you wish me to bring back?" Elizabeth could think of no other reason why he would wish to speak to her privately.

"No, I only wished to say that you should be careful not to encourage Johnson in his attentions to you."

"Attentions? He is just being polite."

"Perhaps, but he is an ambitious young man and knows marriage into the family would further his career more than anything he could accomplish on his own. It would be a temptation to any man. But he is unsuitable; you must know that. He lives in a boardinghouse and has nothing to offer you or any other young lady."

"That does not make him any less amiable, and I think you are leaping far ahead if you take a short conversation as a sign of impending matrimony."

"Do you think he has not thought of it? I assure you, he has. As I said, he has ambitions."

Elizabeth shivered, cold again after the warmth of the stove. It was an unpalatable idea that Mr. Johnson's amiability might come from nothing more than an interest in bettering himself. She said sharply, "Do you think, Uncle, that Mr. Griggs's interest in me comes from any other reason?"

"He is fond of you, Lizzy, and you know it. But in his case, marrying you would solidify his position in the firm, not elevate him beyond his station. He would provide for you."

"I have not agreed to marry him. He has not even made me an offer."

"But he will. We have spoken of it. He respects you, and that you do not know him well as yet."

Elizabeth bit her tongue. She did not care for her uncle's assumption that she would marry as he wished or the implication that he had given his consent without asking her first. But if she must marry Mr. Griggs, she was in no hurry to do so. She preferred her aunt's companionship to his. "It is true that I barely know him."

He smiled warmly. "I shall invite him for dinner one night soon. I do not wish you to be uncomfortable with him."

"Of course." She was in no position to refuse if her uncle insisted. Delay was a better strategy.

Mrs. Gardiner fussed with Elizabeth's sleeve until it puffed out properly. "There, my dear. Now pinch your cheeks to get some colour in them."

Elizabeth felt a sudden pang of missing her mother. Mrs. Gardiner was more tactful and respectful to her when preparing to parade her before a potential suitor, but it was her mother's excesses she was accustomed to. Her mother's antics had always made her laugh, which, of course, was preferable to thinking about the situation. But it brought a smile to her face; she had never thought she might prefer her mother's behaviour to her aunt's. "There, Aunt. I think that is the best you can do with me. You can gild the lily only if there is a lily to gild."

"Nonsense, Lizzy. You look lovely, and Mr. Griggs will be charmed. Come, they must be waiting for us."

Elizabeth followed her aunt to the sitting room, feeling like a mannequin on display.

Mr. Gardiner wiped his face on his napkin. "Oh, yes, our Lizzy is a great walker. I believe she could walk from here to Hertfordshire if we would allow it."

Mr. Griggs laughed a little too long at her uncle's joke. Elizabeth gazed down at her folded hands, disguising her smile. Mr. Griggs was no Mr. Collins, thank heaven, but he had his moments. It was not a punishment to sit with him through dinner, but she found herself laughing at him as often as with him.

Mrs. Gardiner said, "Lizzy often enjoys a morning constitutional."

Mr. Griggs turned to Elizabeth. "Not alone, I should hope. London is full of pickpockets and rogues."

"I often go alone, but I take great care in choosing my locations, I assure you."

"Where do you go?"

"St. Paul's," she said quickly. It was the first place she could think of that was far from Moorsfield. What a horrible moment that would be, if Mr. Darcy ever found her with Mr. Griggs. She would have to introduce them, which would be mortifying. But she was forgetting. Mr. Darcy would not approach her if she were with someone else.

A pleased look spread over Mr. Griggs's broad face. "Ah, paying your devotions, then."

She took a sip of wine to hide her smile. "It is impossible not to feel uplifted by the sight of Sir Christopher Wren's masterwork."

Her aunt coughed, but Elizabeth suspected it was to disguise a laugh. "Perhaps we should leave the gentlemen to their port, Lizzy, dear."

"Of course." Elizabeth stood and curtsied.

In the drawing room, her aunt picked up her sewing. "That went well, I believe," she said.

"Yes." Elizabeth was not certain what else to say. She reached for her mending.

Mrs. Gardiner shook her head. "Not tonight, Lizzy. You do not want to muss your gown."

"A little sewing is hardly likely to leave me disheveled, and I doubt Mr. Griggs would care if it did."

"He values appearances." Her aunt expertly threaded a needle. "You must think of your future, my dear. Mr. Griggs is a good man, honest and hardworking."

"Yes, I know that. He is a good match." The best she was likely to make with no dowry. There were few men who would value a connection to the Gardiners as much as Mr. Griggs, and she could not live on her uncle's charity forever. She felt a pang of guilt, knowing it was a strain for the Gardiners to support another person in the household, especially when Mr. Gardiner was trying to send whatever he could to Mrs. Bennet for her living expenses. It was unfair of her to look askance at an eligible suitor who could relieve some of the burden. As it was, her petticoats were almost worn through because she could not bear to ask her uncle for money, and her shoes were little better.

"For both of you. It would bring him into the family as well as the business. Your uncle plans to make him a partner, you know."

Still, it stung, being married off for her mercantile value. "Not yet, I pray you. I am barely out of mourning clothes."

Her aunt's face softened. "Of course. Take your time, dear, and enjoy yourself a little. There is no hurry. But eventually you will wish for a home of your own, will you not?"

Elizabeth tried to visualize herself as mistress of Mr. Griggs's home. She had never seen it, but she could guess fairly well. Keeping the house, a cap on her head as befitted a married woman, preparing to greet him after a long day of work.

In that moment, Elizabeth suddenly knew what she did want, and it involved dark eyes with an intense look and a scent of leather and fresh air, not the staleness of the countinghouse and a narrow street in Cheapside. When had this happened? Oh, this could not be. She could not afford to give her heart to a man she could never have.

Chapter 4

Georgiana perched on the edge on the fainting couch, her hands gripping the upholstered edge. "Please, Fitzwilliam, I beg of you. Do not make me go."

Darcy drummed his fingers on the armrest. "I know our aunt is hardly pleasant company, but we do owe her a duty as her family. It has been two years since she saw you last. I cannot keep making excuses forever."

"I cannot face her."

"Georgiana, I know she can be harsh, but you must learn to turn a deaf ear to her criticisms. That is what I do. They mean nothing."

"Yes, they do. She will tell me I do not practise enough, I do not draw well enough, I am too slender, or too tall, and everything else in the world that is wrong with me, and then she will tell me how much superior Anne would have been in every way, had she been able to learn. Blasted Anne."

"Georgiana!" he exclaimed. He would have to make an effort to use better language in front of her.

"Forgive me. But why must I always be compared to Anne, when Anne can do nothing at all?"

"Anne's ill health is not her fault."

"Oh, bother Anne's health! It is not ill health, the way she stares at nothing and will never look at you when she talks. There is something not right about her; you know it, too."

Darcy rubbed his hand over his face. "Yes, I know, but it is better if we do not speak of it. She is family, and we must remember that."

"I do not *like* our family!"

Darcy looked at her wearily.

Finally she said, "I am sorry. I know what Mother and Father always said. Family is the most important tie." She did not have to say the rest; they had both heard it often enough. *Be careful with whom you ally yourself. Do not forget you are a Darcy*. "But must I go this year? I cannot face her."

"You are being unreasonable, Georgiana."

"I know." She buried her face in her hands.

Darcy knew she was fighting tears. He hated it when women cried. He never knew what to do. "Come, it is not so bad. Richard and I will both be there."

"She will *know*!" Her voice was agonized.

Darcy froze. "How could she know?"

"I do not know, but she will. She will look at me, and she will know."

He would never understand a woman's mind. He crossed over to her and put his hand on her shoulder. "She cannot possibly know. I made certain of it."

He sat beside her on the fainting couch. Georgiana's distress could continue for a long time, he knew from experience. Nothing he could say would help, and all he could do was wait.

He conjured Elizabeth's image before him, as he had done so many times in the past, and her sparkling eyes and teasing look comforted him. Georgiana would have liked Elizabeth. She would not have been afraid of her. Perhaps Elizabeth could have eased the shadows over Georgiana, as she did for him. But it was too late for that. He would have to learn to make do.

The following morning Elizabeth approached Moorsfield with combined trepidation and anticipation, but Darcy did not appear there that day or the morning after that. Elizabeth told herself it was for the best, and she should not be disappointed. His presence could serve only to add to expectations that would be impossible to fulfill. It meant nothing that he had felt a brief interest in her. For all she knew, he might have left London. He was not obliged to tell her of his plans. By the third day, though, she could no longer pretend to be anything but dispirited by his absence. On the sixth day, she decided to stay at home instead of walking. The disappointment was greater than her pleasure in the walk.

She could not believe she had allowed herself to develop tender sentiments for Mr. Darcy. True, he had not been as proud and haughty during their walks as he had been in Hertfordshire, but there had been no reason why he should be, since it was only the two of them. It was hard to remember why she had disliked him so, apart from his infamous treatment of Mr. Wickham, but she was starting to wonder if there was more than one side to that story. Worse yet, he was starting to appear in her dreams, always with that intense look in his eyes, the one that made it hard to look away.

How ironic that she was now dreaming of the gentleman she so disliked a year earlier! But many things she had never thought could come to pass were now the case. She had thought to live for many years yet at Longbourn.

Her aunt, noticing the change in her habits, asked more than once whether anything was troubling her. Elizabeth, never prone to confidences, denied anything more than a headache. After several days had passed, though, her spirits began to rebel against remaining in the house, and she determined to walk out the following morning.

She set forth after a fitful night's sleep, reminding herself at each step that he would not be there, as if by predicting an ill fate, she could prevent it. It was an unusually fair winter's day, with the sun gilding the brown grass of Moorsfield. She loosened the collar of her spencer and took a deep breath of cool air, with only a hint of the odor of soot that often hung over London. Truly there was more to life than the defection of Mr. Darcy. She would learn to remember that.

A wisp of dark curl hung enchantingly in the air as she bent her head over the pianoforte, laughing at some joke his cousin had made. He longed to be the one beside her. Perhaps his arm would brush against the curl as he turned the page. The mere thought was lightning in his blood.

Then she looked up at him with that delightful purse of her lips that foretold teasing. He could listen to her melodious voice forever, letting it wash over him, so it did not even disturb him when Richard joined in the teasing at his expense. Then she had asked him why he could not recommend himself to strangers, and for the first time ever he answered truthfully, without even a glance at Anne in concern that someone might see something of her in him. "I have not the talent which some people possess of conversing easily with those I have never seen before. I cannot catch their tone of conversation, or appear interested in their concerns, as I often see done."

He waited with bated breath for her reaction, but it did not seem to disturb her. Instead she showed him her understanding, as she said, "My fingers do not move over this instrument in the masterly manner which I see so many women's do. They have not the same force or rapidity, and do not produce the same expression. But then I have always supposed it to be my own fault—because I would not take the trouble of practising. It is not that I do not believe my fingers as capable as any other woman's of superior execution."

She understood. For the first time, someone understood and accepted that he could not master this particular skill. He had never known the relief of being understood, and it flowed through him like a stream bubbling over rocks. He tried to put all his sentiments into the smile he gave her as he said, "You are perfectly right. You have employed your time much better. No one admitted to the privilege of hearing you can think anything wanting. We neither of us perform to strangers."

That was when he had decided to marry her, or more exactly, realized he could not let her go. But let her go he did, and without even a struggle, just a fear of condemnation from his family and peers. At least he could still have his memories.

"Fitzwilliam!" Georgiana hissed in his ear.

Belatedly he reached across her to turn to the next page of music. He forced himself to focus on the present, difficult as it might be with Georgiana sitting precisely where Elizabeth had sat that night, her hands touching the keys Elizabeth had played.

The heavy tread of his uncle's boots presaged an end to the interlude. "Darcy, I wish to speak to you," Lord Matlock said. "Richard, wake your brother. I want the two of you as well."

Darcy gave Georgiana an apologetic glance for deserting her and then stood and bowed his acquiescence. Across the room, Richard shook Viscount Langley's arm. "Henry, wake up. Father wants us."

Henry opened his eyes, shading them against the sun streaming in the window. "Oh, very well."

The earl led them to the sitting room he had claimed for his own during this visit. He poured out four glasses of port and handed one to Henry and then Richard.

Darcy held up his hand, refusing the glass. "It is too early in the day for port for me." Not that he would have minded, but if his uncle wanted to have a family conference, Darcy needed his head about him.

He saw Richard's warning look an instant before his uncle snapped, "Very well, please yourself." But Richard's glass sat beside him untouched. Darcy wished he could think as quickly.

Lord Matlock settled in the largest armchair. "Georgiana is growing up. It is time to find a husband for her."

"She will not be out until next year, and I see little point in looking at suitors before there are any."

"Nonsense. Waiting for girls to decide for themselves is asking for trouble. They haven't the sense for it. If she chooses the wrong man, we can always refuse to give permission, but then she will have a fit of sulks and scare off the men we want. No, it is better to decide these things in advance."

"I am prepared to take that risk."

"That may be, but *I* am not. Henry, you know the inner circles the best. Do you have suggestions?"

"Mm." Henry took a long swallow of port. "Sir Thomas Neville is unmarried, and Georgiana's dowry might be enough to tempt him."

"Absolutely not," Darcy snapped. He would not allow Georgiana to be married to a drunken old sot.

"Too old for your tastes? David Grenville, then."

The earl nodded. "A possibility. He is a second son, but Lord Grenville is a powerful man. A good alliance. Others?"

"A good alliance? Sir John Blakeney, then. His father is Prinny's delight."

Darcy snorted. "And the greatest fop in London, not to mention the greatest fool. I doubt his son is any better."

Henry laughed. "Why do you think Prinny likes him?"

The earl cut in. "He will not do, in any case. The boy is half French, if you recall."

So a fop, a sot, or a fool was acceptable, but not French blood. Darcy was glad he had refused the port. Otherwise he might have been tempted to fling it in his uncle's face.

Richard, as usual, saved him. "I believe this needs further thought, Father. Perhaps we could each put together a list and reconvene tomorrow."

Darcy said, "She is very young. We do not have to marry her off this week, you know."

Lord Matlock drew out a cigar and rang for a servant. "True, but you are not so young. When will it be, Darcy? It is past time for you and Anne to wed. Catherine's health is failing."

"Uncle, I do not plan to marry Anne at all." Darcy braced himself for the explosion.

"You have a duty to her. She cannot care for herself, so you must marry her."

"I will do everything I can to assist her, and I would even agree to be her guardian, but I will not marry her."

Henry muttered, "And who can blame him?"

The earl glared. "What is all this nonsense? Why can you not lend her the protection of your name? You need not spend time with her, only tup her until she produces an heir. You may find your own pleasure elsewhere."

Darcy winced at his uncle's crudity. "An heir? Therein lies the problem. We do not know why Anne is the way she is, but what if her child should take after her? I cannot take that risk with the heir of Pemberley, and *you* cannot afford to have Pemberley and Rosings in the hands of an incompetent."

The earl frowned and puffed on his cigar. "You have a point there. Still, we have no reason to think Anne cannot bear healthy children."

"But she takes after her father. Why would her child not take after her?"

"I see no reason to assume that. True, there was something of Anne's behaviour in Sir Lewis, though not the same extent. Still, Catherine always ruled the roost here. Even ordered him to propose to her."

Henry choked on a sip of port. Richard pounded his back, perhaps harder than the cause warranted.

Darcy said coolly, "Anne seemed healthy enough as a baby. Anne's child might be perfectly healthy, or it might be even worse than she is, as her condition is worse than her father's."

Lord Matlock pursed his lips. "The problem remains, though. Anne needs a husband."

"If she needs a husband from the family, why not marry her to Henry? It has been over a year since his wife died." Darcy took a certain pleasure in needling his uncle.

Henry sat up straight. "Never."

The earl waved his hand, as if it were no matter. "I have plans already for Henry. Lady Mary Howard is suited to be Countess of Matlock. Anne is not."

That was not a name Darcy had expected to hear. Beside him, Richard stiffened almost imperceptibly. Darcy hoped the others had not noticed. He wished he could give Richard another drink. Instead, he tried the next best thing, to distract his uncle. "So Anne is not good enough for Henry, but she is good enough for me. Thank you for sharing that valuation with me."

"Oh, pish-tosh, Darcy. As her husband, you can keep her locked away at Pemberley. You need not even see her. Henry's position would not allow that. If you do not marry Anne, after Catherine dies she will be the target of every adventurer and rogue. Even a footman could take advantage of her and then claim the necessity of marriage. No, she must marry first, but who could we trust outside the family? Once she is married, her husband has complete control of her fortune."

Richard put his hands out in front of his chest. "Do not even suggest it. Lady Catherine would never accept me as her son-in-law. She has always wanted Pemberley."

"She will not gain Pemberley through me. Perhaps we should consider other plans." Darcy had given the matter years of thought. "We need someone whose best interest lies in caring well for Anne. Perhaps a younger son of a country squire, one who is respectable and knows how to manage an estate and has no interest beyond land of his own. You could make it clear that if he mistreats her in any way, the combined might of the Fitzwilliam and Darcy families will be turned against him." If Elizabeth only had a brother, he could marry Anne, and it would solve all his problems. Of course, if she had a brother, Longbourn would not have been entailed away in the first place.

Henry nodded. "Better yet, make certain there is some flaw in the wedding ceremony, so we have the threat of annulling the marriage if needed."

The earl tapped the ash from his cigar. "Excellent idea, Henry. But we must approach this delicately, and I must find such a man."

Henry snorted. "And hire some pretty maids here before he visits, so he can have some consolation for his marriage bed. There isn't a girl worth bedding in this entire house. Why can Aunt Catherine not hire maids who are not a punishment to look at?"

"She does not want the competition," Richard said. "It makes Anne look better."

"Still, it is dull for us. Thank God Georgiana is here. Her figure—now that is worth contemplating."

"Henry!" Darcy snapped.

"Oh, do not worry, Darcy, I will not touch your precious sister. Though I would not mind marrying her myself, if Father did not have other plans for me. Those hips hold promise."

Darcy gritted his teeth. Hell would freeze over before he agreed to a marriage between Henry and Georgiana. "Henry, you are drunk. Save it for your London friends."

The earl raised his glass. "Your health." He took a good swig and then pushed the remaining glass in Darcy's direction. "Darcy, I insist you have some. You need something to raise your spirits. I have never seen such a gloomy countenance."

"I am perfectly well." Darcy was not up to one of his uncle's inquisitions, so he took a tiny sip of the port.

"You should take Henry's point of view, Darcy. You need a girl. That would make you lively again. I saw a girl in the village yesterday well worth bedding." He ran his hands in front of him, demonstrating the attributes that appealed to him. "And she would be willing, for the right price, I would bet on it."

"Darcy has no need of assistance in finding willing women, Father," Richard said. "They are constantly throwing themselves at him."

Darcy understood Richard's warning glance, but the frustration of dealing with his uncle and his aunts took the edge off his habitual caution. "I find this topic distasteful, Uncle."

The earl barked out a laugh. "Distasteful! Oliver Cromwell has been dead for a century and a half, Darcy. What a fine Puritan you would have made!"

Darcy drained his glass of port and set it down hard enough that the crystal rang. "Better a Puritan than a wastrel."

His uncle's eyes narrowed. Darcy steeled himself for a demonstration of the famous Fitzwilliam temper.

This time it was Henry who intervened, stretching his feet out in front of himself and folding his hands behind his head. "Now, Father," he drawled. "Be kind. Can you not see the poor boy is in love?" He smirked at Darcy.

Darcy's heart skipped a beat. "I am not in love!"

Henry's eyes held a look of spiteful glee. "Methinks the gentleman doth protest too much! I have seen you staring out the window at nothing, taking long walks around the park and refusing company, reading love poetry. Such a long face, though. Is it so hard to be separated from your mistress for a fortnight?"

"I have no mistress," Darcy said evenly. Henry could be like a foxhound when he scented blood.

The earl gestured to Richard to pour another round of port. "No mistress? What, did you happen to fall in love with one of the few virtuous wives in England? If not a wife, between your money and your name, you can marry at will, and if she is not appropriate, you can afford her price."

The vision of Elizabeth's sparkling eyes laughing at him, making a mockery of the dull brown of Moorsfield, came before him. "Not every woman has a price," he said, his words clipped.

"Pish-posh." Henry raised his glass to Darcy. "All women have their price. You have not bid high enough yet.

Find out what she truly desires and give it to her. Dangle it in front of her. Or compromise her so she has no choice but to be your mistress."

Rage began to bubble in Darcy's chest. "When I desire to become a rake, I will certainly come to you for lessons, cousin. Until then, pray speak of ladies with respect in front of me."

Henry turned to his father mockingly and pointed a finger towards Darcy. "See, Father? He is in love."

The earl stroked his beard. "I do believe you are correct. Who is she, Darcy?"

"She is no one! There is no such woman."

"She is no one, eh? What sort of no one is she?"

Darcy debated how high the price would be if he walked out of the room that instant. Too high, in all probability. The earl knew his weak point and would needle Georgiana mercilessly for the pleasure of seeing Darcy squirm. "Must I invent a lady to satisfy you, then?"

Henry's smile showed he had scented the blood. "Father, I wager you a thousand pounds I can find her before you do. And find her price."

"And enjoy her before he does? No, Henry, save those tricks for your friends. Darcy is family," the earl said. "Now, Darcy, would you not rather tell us who she is than raise Henry's curiosity?"

Was this how the fox felt when he heard the horns of the hunt? Thank God he had decided to stay away from

Moorsfield. There was nothing for them to find; no one knew where he went each morning. "Look all you like, if you enjoy chasing wild geese."

Richard shot him a warning glance. "Have it your way, Darcy, but I am glad not to be so choosy as you. There is a lovely lady on Drury Lane who has caught *my* fancy. A face that would launch ships and a figure to die for. Unfortunately, she belongs to someone else, but I can wait until he tires of her."

Henry waggled a finger at his younger brother. "Or go backstage between the acts with a pearl necklace, and I wager you will be satisfied. Which theatre?"

"The Haymarket. Mrs. Symons. Stunning chestnut hair, green eyes, and a dulcet voice."

Henry snapped his fingers. "I know the very one! I saw her in *The Country Wife*."

Richard raised his eyebrows. "Last I heard, that play was still banned."

"Nothing is banned if Prinny wants it enough. They did a private performance for him."

Richard helped himself to another glass of port and then took the chair between Darcy and Henry. "Tell me, is it as wicked as they say?"

"Even more wicked, and delightful. The actresses stayed afterwards."

Richard gave a silent whistle. "I should have liked to see such a sight. Or to have enjoyed it myself."

Henry laughed and raised his glass. "Take another lesson, Darcy. Our father has not raised any Puritans."

"So I see." Darcy knew Richard was trying to protect him by playing the rake, but he had no taste for this game. "Yes, I certainly see what you mean."

Chapter 5

THIS WAS THE WORST visit to Rosings Park Darcy could recall, and there had been many unpleasant ones. The only time Darcy ever enjoyed Rosings was when Elizabeth was there. He should have followed her when she left and proposed; then she would be in his bed tonight helping him laugh at all the nonsense.

After a tense dinner, Richard invited him back to his room. The door had barely closed behind them when Richard tore off his cravat and flung it over the bedrail. "Finally. That damned thing has been choking me all night."

Darcy slumped into a richly upholstered chair. It was uncomfortable, like all the furnishings at Rosings. "The conversation, if you care to call it that, was asphyxiating enough. Present company excepted, of course, though I was afraid that if your father mentioned Lady Mary one more time, I might have had to pull you off him. Does he know?"

Richard's valet appeared silently from the dressing room and cast a mildly reproachful look at his master as he picked up the discarded cravat and folded it. Richard turned his back to him, shrugged off his tailcoat into Robbins's waiting hands, and said, "Completely oblivious, as far as I know, and I prefer to keep it that way. It would make no difference in any case."

"Is it certain, then, that she will marry Henry?"

Richard grimaced. "They are still negotiating with her father. And no, there is nothing I can do to stop it. She does not wish to marry Henry, but her father will never consent to allow her to marry me, and she will not act without his consent. So Henry will make her miserable, and I will be the friend who offers her what little solace I can." He began to unbutton his waistcoat. "It was bad enough when the best I could hope for was to partner her for a dance, to allow our hands to touch briefly, and the occasional clandestine meeting. Watching her with Henry… it does not bear thinking on."

"I am sorry. Perhaps the negotiations will come to nothing; it has happened often enough before."

"One can but hope. I have long since resigned myself that she will marry another man, but I would prefer it not to be Henry. Robbins, damn it, where is my robe? A man could freeze to death in here." Richard took the poker and stirred the fire with unnecessary vigour until the flames leapt high.

Robbins came up behind him, holding out the quilted moss-green robe. "Here it is, sir. My apologies."

Richard nodded to him and pulled the robe around himself. "Is there no brandy here?"

Robbins bowed. "I will fetch it immediately." If he was perturbed by his master's unusual ill temper, it was not apparent as he took a bottle from a small cabinet and poured the amber liquid into two snifters.

Richard took the proffered glass and moodily swirled it. "They were in fine form today, both my father and Henry, blast and damn them both. You were fortunate to get off so lightly when you refused to marry Anne."

"It was quite enough for me. I do not know how you tolerate it."

Richard shrugged. "You should not allow them to bait you so. Tell them what they want to hear, and that will be the end of it. What does it matter if they think you have mistresses on every street corner? I say what they want to hear, and do as I please."

"If your damned brother had not tried to besmirch Georgiana, I might have done so as well. If he so much as looks at her, I will call him out."

"He only does that to annoy you. She is not his sort; he prefers women who are well versed in bedroom arts."

"Charming," Darcy muttered beneath his breath. "Will you warn me, Richard, if Henry decides to go lady hunting?"

Richard paused to look at him. "So there is a lady."

"No, there is not; but there is a lady I have shown interest in, and I cannot allow him near her."

"So there is *not* a lady, yet there is. How puzzling."

"I have decided not to see her again." There it was again, that familiar wrenching pain in his gut.

"Who is she?"

Richard was the one person he could tell. "You have met her. Miss Elizabeth Bennet. She stayed with that parson, the grovelling one, when we visited here two years ago." It was a relief to speak her name.

"Yes, I remember her well! Charming girl, if a bit outspoken. I might have fancied her myself, had she any money to her name."

Darcy narrowed his eyes. "She has even less now. Her family has been dispossessed after her father's death, and she is living on the charity of relatives."

"Poor girl." Richard took a long swallow of brandy. "How do you come into it, then?"

"I came into it, so to speak, years ago. She bewitches me. I once even thought of making her an offer. But I put her behind me, until we happened to meet again recently."

"She will not accept your protection? A pity; it sounds as if she would be better off than she is now."

Darcy choked on the wine in his mouth. When he could speak again, he said fiercely, "I do not want her as my mistress. I respect her too much for that."

Richard shook his head slowly. "You are far gone, my friend."

"*That* is not news." And he hated himself for it.

"Why not marry her, then? If she would be willing to tolerate all your insufferable relations, that is."

"Do not be ridiculous."

"Why is it ridiculous? *I* cannot have the woman I love, but you can. I would give anything for your opportunities." Richard made no attempt to mask his bitterness. "You are the most fortunate man in England. You need please no one with your marriage. You should seize the opportunity."

"It is not that simple."

"Certainly society will laugh behind their hands, but do you really care? You have enough money to do as you please."

"The family. Georgiana. My duty to them."

"You owe a duty to my estimable father and brother? I cannot think why. If Lady Mary would agree to defy her father, I would marry her in a second and care not a jot for the wrath of my family. I have begged her to do as much for years. When you are on your deathbed, will you be comforted by knowing you did your duty to your family and left the woman you love to suffer alone in God knows what kind of circumstances? Good God, man, think on it."

Darcy dug his fingernails into his palms "I think on Georgiana. It would harm her prospects to no end."

"Her prospects among whom? The likes of John Blakeney and Thomas Neville? By God, if it were my choice, I would not allow her to marry any of them. Let her have a peaceful life as a spinster. She would never want for anything, and no man could mistreat her."

Darcy shook his head. Richard was starting to sound like Bingley. "You talk as if there are no decent men to be found, but you yourself are proof it is not true. And I know others."

"Of course there are. It is just the things I see… most of the young men who surround other heiresses, I would not want them near Georgiana. I would marry her myself before that."

"I have heard worse ideas than that." Some of them that very afternoon.

With a bitter chuckle, Richard clapped him on the shoulder. "Darcy, you have had too much to drink. That was a joke. I could no more bed Georgiana than I could my own daughter, if I had one. Go to bed. Perhaps you will think more clearly in the morning."

Darcy took the hint. His footsteps echoed down the long corridor, lit only by the candle in his hand. The upstairs servants were all abed already, resting for another day at Lady Catherine's beck and call.

At least he could spend the hours of darkness in the silent haven of his rooms. After the tension of the day, he craved the release of solitude. He was no sooner in the door of his rooms than he shrugged off his topcoat, tossing it carelessly over the back of a chair. His cravat had been choking him all evening, and his hands tore at the knot. He took a deep breath when the snow-white cloth finally hung loose over his shoulders. Then he realized he was not alone.

There was a girl in his bed. She sat up when she saw his gaze, the sheets dropping away to reveal that she was wearing nothing at all apart from long blond hair.

This was the last thing he needed. Darcy averted his eyes automatically. "Miss, I fear you are in the wrong room. I will step into the dressing room so you may clothe yourself and go." He wondered whose bed she was supposed to be in—no doubt Henry's or his uncle's.

"I was told to come to you, Mr. Darcy, sir," she said. "Will you not come to bed?" She looked uncertain, and even younger.

He silently cursed his uncle, the infuriating, interfering old codger. "I have no need of your services," he said, his voice clipped. "You may go."

The bedsheets rustled as he turned to take haven in the dressing room, but before he could escape, the girl was standing in front of him, every inch of her body revealed. She put her hands on his chest. "I can please you, sir. I will do anything you wish. Anything at all." The girl sounded as if she were saying lines she had memorized in advance.

As an effort at seduction, it was a poor one, which was fortunate, because he was no more invulnerable to a naked woman's form than any other man. But although he might be tempted to forget his cares in her arms, it would not work. She was not Elizabeth.

Besides, the girl did not hold her body the way a woman who wants to gain a man's attention would. He realized she had no idea what she was doing. His uncle must have thought a virgin would tempt him. How little he knew his nephew. Gentlemen in town might pay a high premium to take a girl's virginity, but the mere thought left a sour taste in Darcy's mouth. He had never been interested in bedding women unless they were willing and eager, not frightened girls barely out of childhood whose lives would be ruined by the experience.

Good God, she was probably younger than Georgiana. Younger than his sister. She could even *be* his sister, and him never the wiser—his father had spent enough time at Rosings, and had no doubt sampled the local wares. He shook his head to clear it. "Put on your clothes and go."

Her frightened eyes filled with tears. "Please, sir. I promise I can please you."

The only way she could please him was magically to turn into Elizabeth. He rummaged in the wardrobe and found a handful of coins. He placed them in her hand, carefully not looking at her naked form. "There. You will not suffer for it."

"But my lord said he would have me whipped if I did not satisfy you. He will know if I leave."

Damn his uncle to everlasting perdition! "You can spend the night in my dressing room, then." His uncle had no doubt told his valet to stay elsewhere. "I will tell Lord Matlock you were most satisfactory." He laced the words with disgust.

"You will? Oh, thank you, sir. You are the kindest gentleman ever to walk the earth." She grabbed at his hand and kissed it.

He snatched his hand away, picked up the worn dress, and thrust it at her. "Go, then."

She clutched the dress to her body and hastened to the door he indicated. Just before she scuttled behind it, she said fervently, "I will always pray for you, sir."

He sank onto the bed and covered his face in his hands. What a world, where a young girl was offering her prayers, the only thing of value she had, in thanks because he had not violated her body. Poor child, to have her innocence sold.

Richard's words about Georgiana came back to him. Was this so different from what his uncle wished to do, to auction Georgiana off to the gentleman who could give the family the most prestige? Darcy's attempts to secure Bingley for Georgiana and bypass the marriage market had failed, and she would be coming out in a few months. Richard was right; there were few gentlemen of his acquaintance who would make her anything but miserable.

But he was expected to find a man of good fortune for Georgiana, regardless of such a man's temperament. Elizabeth, too, would likely have to wed whatever man her uncle chose, in order to have a home. And the poor girl in his dressing room, sold by her family as well. All for what? He longed for Elizabeth's presence beside him, her fine eyes embracing him and offering comfort. What would she think of him, had she seen this scene?

In truth, Elizabeth probably would have barely spared him a thought, and instead worried about the girl, whose lot was far worse than his and who must have been terrified. He would have to make certain she was returned to her family safely the next day. Elizabeth would have liked that. Elizabeth, who was out of his reach forever, because she was beneath him. "Damn it all to hell!" he ground out, punching his hand into the pillow hard enough to send a few downy feathers floating off. He wished it had been his uncle's face instead.

He needed sleep, but instead his veins were running with anger, and there was a frightened child on the other side of the door, not to mention his uncle to deal with in the morning. What was he to say to him? Or was it Henry who had arranged this surprise?

Better to know the truth of it before dealing with them. He knocked peremptorily at the dressing room door before opening it. The girl looked frankly terrified to see him. Her eyes were red rimmed. Did she think he had changed his mind?

"I wish only to ask you a question," Darcy said hurriedly.

"Yes, sir?"

"Who arranged for you to come here?"

She seemed pleased it was so simple a question. "My lord Matlock, sir."

"How did he find you?"

She bit her lip, just as Elizabeth did so often. "I don't know, sir. One of his men came to our cottage and talked to my father, then he told me to go with the man and do what he said."

"Does your family lack for money?"

She glanced from side to side, as if in doubt as to what answer he wished for. "No more than most, but our cow died."

Was a daughter worth the price of a cow, or not even that much? "How old are you?"

"Fifteen next month, sir."

"What will happen to you when you go home?"

This time she did look away, and he could see her fight for composure. "I can't go home, sir. I'm to go with my lord."

"God in heaven!" He had saved the poor girl for only one night. "What if I take you back to your home?"

"I cannot go back. I cannot show my face there again, not after tonight."

So much for his great charitable impulse. It was already too late for her. Tomorrow night she would no doubt be in his uncle's bed and subject to rougher usage than she would have found with Darcy himself. He might have even done her an ill service by refusing her. He could at least have given her a gentle introduction to womanhood and prepared her for what was to come. But the thought of her with his uncle sickened him rather than tempted him. He turned on his heel and returned to bed, but sleep was a long time in coming.

Henry smirked when Darcy entered the breakfast room. "Good morning, cousin. Did you sleep well?"

"Very well, indeed," Darcy said. He would give them no reason to blame to girl.

His uncle waved a pastry in the air. "See, Darcy, I told you. I knew it would do you a world of good."

"It has certainly changed my outlook."

"So she was good company, then?"

"She was quite satisfactory," Darcy said coolly. To his own surprise, he added, "So satisfactory I think I shall take her with me when I leave." It was better than abandoning the poor girl to their mercies.

Lord Matlock barked a laugh. "There you go, boy! Just what you need. She will clean up nicely, I think."

Darcy was saved from the danger of making an intemperate response by the entrance of Lady Catherine.

She surveyed the room regally. "Who will clean up nicely?" she asked suspiciously.

Henry did not miss a beat. "The new mare Darcy is considering buying. Good brood stock."

Lord Matlock choked on a bite of pastry, and his subsequent coughing spell, with Lady Catherine's constant advice on how to make it cease, caused the subject to be dropped.

The sky was grey as the coach finally clattered along the road to London. Georgiana had blankets across her lap to keep away the cold that filtered in through the sides of the coach, her hands ensconced warmly in a fur muff.

"I hope you do not mind leaving Rosings early," her brother said.

"Mind? I could not be more delighted. I was starting to think of stuffing my ears with cotton, since all I ever did was agree with everything our aunt said." Georgiana burrowed deeper into her blankets as she heard the rapid tattoo of raindrops hitting the carriage. "Even London will be a pleasure after this."

Darcy smiled, but it looked forced. Georgiana wondered what had made him suddenly decide to leave today instead of next week, but he had a shuttered look on his face when he announced their departure, and she had been too intimidated to ask, especially once Lady Catherine started in on him. Then there was the mystery of the girl who was sitting up with the coachman. Darcy had muttered something about needing a new kitchen maid, but London was full of girls searching for positions. The girl herself said nothing, but seemed to look to Darcy for protection, while he seemed annoyed by her presence. When her brother was in one of those moods, it was best not to ask questions.

"Georgiana, have you thought about the sort of gentleman you wish to marry?" he asked abruptly.

Georgiana started. "No," she said hurriedly and then realized how ridiculous it sounded. "Not much, that is. Not too old, I hope, but not so terribly young either."

"You will be coming out next winter. Surely you have more thoughts than that."

"I assumed you would pick someone suitable, a credit to the family, and ask me if I liked him." She would never dare choose based on her own sensibilities again, not after the last time. "Do you have someone in mind?"

He shook his head, his lips in a straight line. "There are many men I would *not* wish you to marry, but no one in particular I would choose. That is why I wish to know what you would prefer."

She pursed her lips. He seemed to want an answer, but what could she say? "Someone kind, I suppose. Someone not so very sophisticated, not someone who would want to entertain constantly. Someone like, oh, Sir Robert Sutton, were he twenty years younger."

He laughed, a startling sound in the tension. "I believe Lady Sutton might object to you marrying her husband."

"I did not mean *him*, but someone like him."

"I know, sweetling. It is just an amusing thought. But a fine example. He is a good man, trustworthy and reliable."

"Yes," she said, relieved he had found the words for her.

"Sir Robert and Lady Sutton seldom go to town."

"I would not mind that." In fact, she would much prefer it that way. "But I know I must marry someone worthy of a Darcy." A country squire was unlikely to meet that standard.

He muttered something under his breath. "Georgiana, as long as he is honest and responsible, you may marry whom you wish. I care not about his family or prospects, as long as he is respectable."

She did not know what to say. Perhaps he was not well, and it was a fever speaking. Was that why they left Rosings so abruptly? Suddenly it all came clear, and she stiffened. "Has Lord Matlock already chosen someone? Someone you would not wish me to marry?"

"If he has someone in mind, he has not told me. In any case, he is the last man I would trust to choose a suitable husband for you." He sounded angry.

She pushed her hands deeper into her muff, clenching them together where he could not see. "Oh," she said weakly.

The corner of his mouth turned up wryly. "As it turns out, I do not much like our family either, it seems."

She had never heard her brother talk that way before. Lord Matlock must have said something truly awful. Her brother was so good to her; she had never actually worried much about marrying, since she was sure her brother would have very high standards for her husband.

He was looking out the window, as if fascinated by the pouring rain, his mouth a line of discontent.

She hated seeing him so unhappy. "Is something the matter?"

He turned back to her. "No. I was merely thinking I would not wish to be sitting outside in this weather."

That sounded more like the brother she knew. She gave him a hesitant smile. "Yes, we are fortunate to have our cozy carriage."

"Oh, blast and damnation!" Darcy took his cane and knocked it sharply against the roof of the carriage. The carriage began to slow.

What was it now? She had thought he would like what she said, and instead, it seemed to have made him angrier. He almost never swore in front of her. She was afraid to ask why they were stopping.

When the carriage drew to a halt, Darcy opened the door and swung out before the footman could assist him. Georgiana heard him exchange a few muffled words with the driver, and then the carriage rocked a bit. Why would the driver be coming down, out here in the middle of nowhere?

The door squeaked open again, and to her great surprise, the new maid clambered in, looking quite lost. Darcy was right behind her, his head bent to prevent it from hitting the top of the carriage. "You may sit there," he said brusquely, pointing to the empty corner of the ladies' seat.

"Thank you, sir," the maid said through chattering teeth. The poor thing was soaked through.

Darcy said, as if in explanation, "She has nothing but the clothes she is wearing."

The poor girl. No wonder her brother had stopped. She would catch her death of cold out there. Georgiana shook off the top blanket on her lap and held it up. "Here, let me put this around you. You must be freezing."

"You are very kind, miss." The girl pulled the blanket close around her.

Darcy signaled the driver again, and the carriage clattered on. He looked more content, the lines of worry in his face easing. He leaned his head back and closed his eyes. Once his deep breathing indicated that the carriage's rocking had put him to sleep, Georgiana rummaged through the blankets to find the hot brick at her feet. Her brother would not have approved of giving it to the girl when she needed it herself, but he would not know.

She handed it to the shivering girl. "You can warm your hands on this."

Her hands darted out of the blanket to take the brick. She held it close to her under the blanket, and Georgiana could see the relief in her face as she felt the warmth. "Thank you, miss."

It was her chance to indulge her curiosity to find out why her brother was bringing the girl. "What is your name?"

"Mary, miss. Mary Abbott."

"Have you been at Rosings long, Mary?"

"No, miss. I live—I lived in the village with my family."

"Have you been to London before?"

"Never, miss. They say it is terrible crowded and full of pickpockets and thieves."

Georgiana smiled. "It is indeed crowded, but you need not worry about pickpockets on Brook Street, where we live. It is very different from Kent, but quite pleasant and safe."

"Is that where I am to go?"

"You do not know?"

The girl looked down. "My father made the arrangements."

It occurred to Georgiana that if Mary's family lived near Rosings, chances were good she would never see them again.

A servant could never afford to travel so far, nor would she have the comfort of letters, unless by some miracle she knew how to read and write. Georgiana had never thought much about where the maids in London came from. She knew her brother made certain all their servants were well treated, but she knew nothing of their circumstances. She felt an odd protective urge towards the girl. "You must still be cold. Here, take this wrap as well," she said.

"But miss, then you will take a chill."

"Nonsense, I am quite warm," Georgiana lied. The relief on Mary's face was all the reward she needed.

Darcy awoke from a sweet dream of Elizabeth to the sound of Georgiana's light laughter as the coach rattled over the cobblestone streets of London. "Have you seen something amusing?" he asked.

"No, we were just talking."

At least Georgiana was talking to someone outside the family. Even if it was a kitchen maid, it was progress. The girl looked happier, almost saucy, quite a change from the frightened child of the previous night. Still, as soon as they reached the townhouse, Darcy was relieved to leave the girl in the custody of his housekeeper. With misgivings, he noticed Georgiana looking after her retreating form. He had not thought of having to explain his actions to his sister. He hardly knew how to explain them to himself.

"Fitzwilliam?" Georgiana asked shyly.

"Yes?"

"Could Mary be an upstairs maid?"

"Mary?" He realized he had never asked the girl her name. "I doubt she is prepared for such a role."

"She could learn, could she not? She is quite mannerly and pleasant."

"We shall see." He did not like to refuse Georgiana anything, though he would personally be happier if the girl stayed out of his sight in the kitchens. "You have taken quite an interest in her, it seems."

"It must be so strange for her, coming from the countryside. London can be overwhelming." She sounded almost wistful.

He was definitely seeing a new side of Georgiana. He had always assumed she would want a fine house in town and a noble husband. Apparently he had been wrong about that, as he had been about many other things. Georgiana was happier talking to a kitchen maid than among the riches of Rosings. She would like Elizabeth, too, with her lack of pretensions. Elizabeth would be a far better sister to Georgiana than any lady of the ton. But his family would never stand for it.

Suddenly he knew his decision was made. Careful alliances be damned. "Georgiana, dearest, do you remember when I wrote to you of Miss Elizabeth Bennet?"

Georgiana looked up, her cheeks still rosy from the cold air. "The one who was impertinent to Lady Catherine?"

He smiled in recollection. "The very same. I saw her here in town recently. Perhaps I can introduce you to her. I think you would like her."

She looked at him in surprise, but with a smile. "I would like that."

Chapter 6

It was a challenge for Elizabeth when Mr. Griggs called. She knew her duty to her family, but it was hard to be charming when she wished he were someone else. She must put Mr. Darcy from her mind and learn to think of the challenges facing her family and how she could relieve them by marrying Mr. Griggs. Especially as weeks had gone by without seeing Mr. Darcy, but that was just as well. His intentions were unlikely to be honourable. Perhaps that was why he had vanished; he had realized she would not accept such a role.

The thought was amusing in its own way. If she really wished to assist her family, becoming Mr. Darcy's mistress would do more than marrying Mr. Griggs. He would presumably be generous, and she could pass that generosity along. It was such a ridiculous conceit that she could not help smiling, grateful that Mr. Griggs lacked the ability to read her mind. He would hardly be pleased by her train of thought.

Or perhaps he would think her practical. In the sort of society Mr. Darcy frequented, mistresses were a normal part of life, and there was nothing unusual about them appearing in public with their protectors, as if there were no shame attached to their status. Truly, many gentlemen seemed to treat their mistresses better than their wives.

She could never disrespect herself so, though. Despite the guilty appeal of the idea of being with Mr. Darcy, she could never accept the idea that he would eventually marry another woman and go home to her at night, that her own children would be baseborn, while another woman's would carry Mr. Darcy's name. A chill went through her. What was she doing even thinking of this? For once and for all, she must forget him.

"Mr. Griggs, would you care for some more coffee?" she said, her voice steady and warm. When Mr. Griggs proposed, she would accept him and learn some of Jane's philosophy of seeing the best in her situation.

Darcy stomped his feet on the bare ground, trying to keep the last bit of warmth from leaving his toes. He had been waiting at least an hour for Elizabeth, just as he had the previous day and the day before that. An hour was a long time to spend wondering why Elizabeth had failed to come to Moorsfield yet again.

The first day he had waited with an unusual sense of contentment and the knowledge that he was finally on the right track, dreaming of the expression that would be on Elizabeth's face when he made his offer. The second day he was impatient. Today he was worried. Was she ill? He thought it an unlikely time of year for her to travel, but she might be away. He refused to think of reasons why she might have decided to stay away from Moorsfield. It had been but a month since he saw her there last. Surely she could not have become engaged in so short a time.

If she did not come tomorrow, he would call on her directly. His pride revolted at the idea of accepting the hospitality of a tradesman, but for Elizabeth, he would do more than that. He would have to meet them eventually in any case, though he hoped Elizabeth would limit her contact with them once they were married. She would have a position to maintain, after all.

But he needed to see her. He had felt somehow unclean ever since that night at Rosings, and he knew instinctively that Elizabeth was the cure. He could tell her of his revulsion at his uncle's behaviour, though he would certainly leave out the details. She would understand. With Elizabeth by his side, he would be able to face his uncle and refuse to tolerate his insinuations.

But it was long past the time she usually walked there. He collected his horse and rode back to town via Gracechurch Street, hoping he might catch a glimpse of her somehow, but fate was against him.

A sudden longing for her presence seized at him as he rode past her house. Where could she be? Could she indeed be ill and unable to walk to Moorsfield? There was always illness in London, illness and death.

It would not do. He must know, even if he could not see her. He thought for a moment and then looked for the flower shop he remembered from his first trip to Gracechurch Street. It was still open, despite the season. He dismounted and entered the establishment, requesting their finest bouquet. It was still not as fine as Elizabeth deserved, and he was sure the clerk overcharged him, but it was no matter.

Now he needed a messenger. Back on the street he spotted two young girls in ragged clothing. They were laughing together, but stopped as soon as they noticed his interest. In clipped tones, he said, "There was a boy here a few months ago. His name was Charlie."

"You want 'im?" The taller of the two eyed him calculatingly.

He placed a coin in her chapped hand. "Where is he?"

She darted across the street to the entrance of a dark alley. "Char-leee!" she called in a shrill tone. "There's a mort what wants you."

The boy emerged, rubbing his eyes. He straightened in recognition when he saw Darcy. "You wanted me, sir?"

Darcy drew him aside. He had no desire to be overheard. "Can you deliver these flowers to Miss Bennet without telling her who sent them?"

"Anythin' you want, sir. What if she asks who sent 'em?"

"Tell her..." What could he say that would make her go to Moorsfield the next day? He could not ask for an assignation.

"Tell her they are from an admirer. But give them only to her, you understand?" He hoped she would understand.

"Right, just to 'er."

Darcy handed the boy the nosegay and ducked under an awning. How low had he sunk, skulking in the shadows to catch a glimpse of Elizabeth? But it had been weeks, and if something was wrong, he needed to know immediately.

He watched the dumb show as Charlie knocked on the door. The servant who opened it disappeared after a few words. Darcy held his breath.

There she was, her delightfully arched eyebrows raised in query. The boy offered her the flowers. She hesitated a moment, took them, and said something. Whatever Charlie responded made her laugh. Darcy wished he could hear the sound of it. They conversed for another minute or two, and then she retreated inside.

Charlie crossed the street whistling and made his way indirectly to Darcy. The boy had the makings of an excellent spy; his meanderings would distract any following eyes. His grin as he approached showed he knew his talents as well.

"She took 'em, sir."

"What was it you said that made her laugh?"

"I said what you told me, sir, and she asked if they were from Mr. Griggs, and I told her no, they were from a *handsome* gentleman. That's when she laughed. She asked what you looked like, sir, but I didn't tell her nothin', just like you said."

"Who is this Mr. Griggs?" Darcy said the name with distaste.

"Works for her uncle, he does. Wants to marry into the family."

Darcy would not give in to the fierce desire to know more about his unseen rival. The boy knew too much about him already. "Did she say anything else?"

"No, she were real proper, sir."

Darcy dropped a coin in the boy's open hand. "Mind you, not a word to anyone."

The boy grinned, displaying missing teeth. "Nobody keeps a secret better than Charlie, sir."

Tomorrow. He would see Elizabeth tomorrow.

Elizabeth sniffed the flowers. They had little scent, as was common for hothouse flowers. They must have been expensive. It would be too extravagant an expenditure for her uncle's clerk, and the boy had said it was not Mr. Griggs. There was only one other possibility, one who would not think twice about the cost of a bouquet, but he had disappeared without a word more than a month earlier. Why would he reappear now, when she had finally reached the point where he no longer filled her thoughts constantly? She did not know whether the idea was more pleasant or painful.

If the flowers were not from Mr. Griggs, she did not wish to have to explain them to her aunt. Quietly she went upstairs to her room, where she began to arrange them carefully in the ewer of water. She would have to remember to bring up more water that night. Still, they brightened her room. Her fingers stilled on a stem as reality came pouring in.

She should not have accepted the flowers. If Mr. Darcy wished to see her, all he had to do was knock on the front door, but instead he had sent a silent message. He must have looked for her at Moorsfield, but she rarely walked there anymore. All it did was remind her of pain, of how Mr. Darcy had proved to be just the same as Mr. Bingley, fickle and playing with her affections when it suited him. Now he was back and wanted to be sure she knew it. The flowers were not a gift. They were an invitation to an assignation.

Elizabeth felt sick. He had played her like a puppet, deliberately engaging her affections and then leaving her to become desperate enough to do whatever he wished. But his ploy would not succeed.

She dropped the last flower, unwilling to touch them anymore. Did he think she would sell herself so cheaply? He had played her for a fool, and that was the one thing she could not forgive.

For once, Elizabeth did not feel the cold as she walked towards Moorsfield. Her sensibilities were too troubled. She had decided at least a dozen times that she would not meet Mr. Darcy, but here she was in the dawn's first light. She could not even explain why, except that staying at home and awaiting his next move was intolerable. She would rather give him his answer to his face, and if, despite all appearance, his intentions were honourable, she owed it to her family to accept him. No, who did she think she was fooling? She hoped desperately for such an outcome, and not for her family's sake.

She reached the last row of houses, her heart already pounding. She had not anticipated the stirring she would feel when she saw his figure, standing tall and straight like one of the trees rising in the middle of Moorsfield. Surely he could mean her no harm. Perhaps she should give him the benefit of the doubt.

There she was, pausing at the edge of the field, her lilac dress looking like a flower out of season. Darcy felt a wave of relief flowing over him, the disappearance of the terrible tension that had caught him in its grip. The last few days had shown him the truth. None of his reasoned arguments could satisfy him. He *needed* Elizabeth, to hear her musical laughter and see the enchanting light in her eyes, her quick movements and the fragrance of lavender and roses he had come to associate only with her. His feet were in motion before his mind realized his action. There would be no effort today at making it look like an accidental meeting. Soon it would no longer matter, because he would have the right to meet her whenever he wished.

Now she was before him, only inches away, her dark eyes staring up at him as though uncertain of something. He tightened his hands into fists to keep himself from touching her. "You came," he said in a voice just above a whisper, and then, recalling himself, added more properly, "Miss Bennet, it is a pleasure to see you again." She could have no idea how much of a pleasure it was for him.

"Mr. Darcy," she said, sounding almost breathless. Something was different about her, something in her manner that he could not define.

"I have not seen you here these last few days. I hope you have not been unwell."

"No, I was not unwell, merely… but you, sir, were also not here for some time."

He wondered what she had started to say. "I was away and returned only recently."

Her lips quirked up in a smile that matched the sudden brightness in her eyes. "Or perhaps you were enjoying late nights at Almack's or the opera and could not face the dawn."

"No! No, indeed. Late nights could not have kept me away." He realized almost immediately that he had betrayed himself, but he did not care. "I was at Rosings Park, with my family."

Elizabeth cast her eyes downward and began to walk. He offered her his arm, half afraid she would not take it, but after a moment she glanced up at him shyly and tucked her hand into his arm. He smiled with relief and placed his other hand over her gloved fingers.

The intimacy was making her uncomfortable, he could tell. This had never happened before in the many times they had met. What could it mean? Had she met another man after all? Reluctantly he removed his hand and guided her down the walk, his mind racing. It could make no difference in the outcome, since she was in no position to refuse him, but the idea of Elizabeth looking on another man with favour made his stomach churn.

They walked in silence, a far cry from the comfortable conversations they had enjoyed previously, until he could stand it no longer. "Miss Bennet." The words seemed tied in his throat.

She raised an eyebrow. "Yes?"

He took a deep breath and then said in a rush, "You must know my sentiments towards you. It can be no surprise when I tell you how ardently I admire and love you. These months, nay, years, since our first meeting have never been sufficient to erase you from my mind, even for one day. You bewitched me at Netherfield, but at Rosings I knew it was love, that my feelings for you were driven by the utmost force of passion. No other woman has ever inspired such sentiments in me. Your presence, your voice, your eyes—you are the air I breathe, and I can no longer deny it."

Her eyes had grown wide, but there was a soft look in them. He moved slightly closer to her, and she did not pull away. His gaze dropped to the lips that had so often tempted him, that had formed so many delightfully teasing words, that he longed to claim for his own. And soon he would. She wanted him to kiss her. He could tell by the way she tipped up her chin, her body swaying towards his. It took every ounce of control he possessed not to take advantage of the moment, but they were in public, and he knew there were eyes upon them. But as soon as he had her alone, then he would taste her sweetness.

There was a copse not far ahead. It would have to do, for he could not wait long. He steered her down the path along the hedgerow. Now he covered her hand with his own again, this time tightening his grip possessively, and he felt a gentle squeeze of his arm in response.

It was all he needed. Dizzy with delight, he said, "You cannot know how much relief it brings me to finally say these words to you. I have fought it for so long. My mind would not allow the inclination of my heart because of the many obstacles that stood between us. The objectionable connections of your family, the effects on the consequence of my own family of any alliance between us, stood forever as an insurmountable barrier. I could not accept such low connections, even more so, given the behaviour of certain members of your family. What would society say? I could not overcome it. That last evening when you were in Kent, I finally knew my struggles were in vain, and I resolved to make you an offer when the opportunity might present itself."

A soft smile came over her face. "So long ago as that? You are tardy, sir."

"Longer even than that, had my judgment not fought my inclination with such force."

"I had no idea. I thought then that you disliked me."

"Disliked you? Of course not." He was sorely tempted to show her just how far from dislike his feelings were. "But you departed unexpectedly, and I took it as a sign that I should heed my misgivings. I regretted it more often than I can say. When I saw you here, it was as if no time had passed. Now your situation is different, and the distance between our ranks yet further, an alliance even more inconceivable, yet I cannot imagine a life where I cannot be with you whenever I wish, to hold you close and tell you of my love, to show you the ardour I feel." He stopped the flow of words before he went even further beyond the realm of propriety than he already had. More quietly, he said, "Please tell me you will relieve my misery." He could no longer resist. He cupped her cheek in his hand—that incredibly soft skin he had imagined so often—and turned her face towards his.

Elizabeth looked disturbed, no doubt at his presumption, but he was certain that would change. And then it was done, just the merest touch of his lips to hers, the briefest sensation of warmth, softness, and sunlight. As he drew back, he closed his eyes to savour the sensation and was caught completely off guard by a flash of burning pain across his face.

He stared in shock at Elizabeth, his hand involuntarily moving to his injured cheek. In his astonishment, the only thought that registered in his mind was that it was a blow intended to injure.

Her eyes were filled with tears as she cradled her hand against her chest. It must have hurt her, as well. "How dare you?" she said, her voice trembling. "How *dare* you? Have you no shame? I should have expected it, after all I had heard of you from Mr. Wickham, not to mention your arrogant behaviour towards my family, but I allowed myself to think better of you. I was a fool."

"Mr. Wickham?" The hated name stood out from her unexpected tirade as he flinched from the fury in her eyes. "What did he tell you?"

"Nothing but the truth! How you cheated him of his inheritance, of your insufferable pride, and I saw for myself your complete disdain for the feelings of others, especially those who were *below you*. Well, now your intolerable pride will have to be your consolation, for I will not!" Her voice grew too choked for her to continue, and tears poured down her cheeks. She shook her head silently, a look of horror in her eyes. Before he had even guessed her intent, she gathered up her skirts and fled, running as swiftly as if the Furies of hell were in pursuit.

Elizabeth stared straight ahead. There was no place to hide, no place where she could take time to compose herself, as if time would help! Instead she had no choice but to make her way down Gracechurch Street, fighting to hold back the tears that were no doubt still evident on her cheeks. She knew she was an object of interest, that the Londoners on the busy street would be wondering about her reddened eyes. She had never missed the privacy of the countryside more. At home she could have fled to her special corner of the churchyard, under the ancient oak tree, and cried until she had no tears left.

She hurried up the steps of the Gardiners' house, hoping not to meet anyone on the way, but the odds were against her. She was no sooner in the door when she heard her aunt speak her name with concern. She shook her head without stopping and raced upstairs, past the nursery where her young cousins called, "Lizzy! Lizzeeee!" Not till she reached the dark, dusty storage room on the top floor did she stop. She closed the door behind her and leaned back on it, her breath coming in short gasps.

Her worst fears were realized. She had been so happy when Mr. Darcy began his avowal, so full of hope that a proposal of marriage was to follow, that she had let all her reservations fly from her, at least until his words of disdain for her family and background forced her to conclude that his intentions were not the honourable ones she had hoped for. His words still rang in her ears—*But now your situation is different, and the distance between our ranks yet further, an alliance even more inconceivable*. So inconceivable that he expected her to be his mistress, and he showed his disregard for her reputation—the reputation he clearly thought she had left behind with her father's death—so far as to kiss her in a public field. And she had not stopped him. Her fury at her own foolishness was almost the equal of her anger at his presumption.

She wiped the back of her hand across her face. She should have recognized his intent long before, when he refused her invitation to meet her aunt and uncle. She *had* known it, but she had not wished to admit it to herself, for then she would have had to give up the pleasure of his company for the brief moments when she could again imagine herself as Miss Bennet of Longbourn.

There were footsteps on the stairs. Elizabeth swallowed hard and opened the door. Margaret stood there, balancing on the balls of her feet, a concerned look on her face.

"Lizzy, whatever is the matter? Are you hurt?"

Elizabeth wished for the innocence of childhood when pain was the result only of injuries. "It is nothing, dear. I merely twisted my ankle." It was the best she could do on the spur of the moment.

Margaret's brow furrowed. "But you ran up the stairs!"

"I did not wish anyone to see I was crying. Is that not silly of me?" She gave a shaky laugh. "Pride makes us do the most foolish things."

The most foolish things, indeed.

Darcy squinted into the dark mirror in his bedroom. The mark still showed, an expanse of red across his cheek, even after the furious trip across London. No one had dared stand in his way. He poured cool water from the porcelain ewer into the basin, dipped his handkerchief into it, and wrung it out. Carefully he placed the cloth against his face. It would not do to have the entire household gossiping about what sort of trouble the master had found himself in. He had more than enough on his mind without that.

More than enough. His eyes narrowed at the thought of Elizabeth. How dare she? Did she not realize he was paying her the highest compliment he could? Apparently she was far more foolhardy than he had ever conceived. To believe Wickham—well, he supposed the man could be cunningly convincing, but then for her to pretend to enjoy his company and still believe such lies? Was it all a deliberate attempt to humiliate him?

He turned away from the mirror. He did not want to look at himself anymore. Instead, he paced the narrow confines of the room, his footsteps muffled by the exquisite Persian rug. Past the window, past the door, and back. Past the bed where Elizabeth would never lie in his arms. The wrenching pain brought him to a stop. He leaned his forehead against the wall, feeling the pattern of the wallpaper pressing into his skin. She had made a fool of him. That was the one thing he could never forgive.

His fury warred with the deep ache in his chest. Her treatment of him was nothing short of despicable, the words she said burnt into his heart, never to be forgotten. He never wanted to see her face again, never hear her name, only to forget that he had ever known a woman named Elizabeth Bennet.

The heaviness of his life slipped back over him. He would never again experience the joy and freedom only her eyes could bring him, and now even his memories of her were tainted.

Elizabeth was determined to think no more of Mr. Darcy, but the harder she tried to avoid thoughts of him, the more they intruded. He had clearly thought she would agree to his insulting offer. He had likely thought his offer generous, in offering her some degree of independence. She had hoped for a proposal of marriage. Elizabeth felt she could never wash the shame away.

He had spoken to her of love. Remembering those words brought tears to her eyes.

For the next week, she stayed within doors as often as possible, venturing out only when accompanied by her young cousins or her aunt. But one day, on returning to her room, she spotted a folded paper on her small vanity.

She picked it up. It was fine, heavy paper and sealed on the back, with her name written on it in a firm, masculine hand. How had it come to be there? She would have known had it come in the post. Who could have placed a letter in her room? Only a member of the family or one of the servants, and none of them would employ such a subterfuge. Perhaps someone had bribed one of the servants to put it there. Suddenly she knew who it must be from.

All the humiliation of that morning returned in a rush, the humiliation and the hurt that Mr. Darcy, the man whose companionship she had come to enjoy, would think her capable of agreeing to such a proposition. Darcy would never have made such a suggestion to Miss Elizabeth Bennet of Longbourn. Indeed, he had never said a word when her father was alive, because he had known she would never agree. Now, in her reduced circumstances, he thought her easy prey. And in truth, it was only her uncle's generosity that stood between her and a genteel poverty.

At such a point, what would her principles matter to her? If she had flirted with every available gentleman as her mother had wished, she would likely be married by now, but she had insisted she would never marry without affection and respect. Brave words, but all they had done was to make her more vulnerable to the predations of Mr. Darcy. And he would not be alone in thinking her susceptible. Another man might not take no for an answer. Her reputation was all she had, and reputation could be ruined in the matter of a minute.

She touched the letter. Half of her longed to read it, hoping for more words of love, but it could contain nothing respectable. The mere fact of reading it would ruin her reputation if anyone knew it, and someone in the household already knew of its existence. Perhaps that was what he hoped for, to damage her reputation enough that she had no choice but to accept his offer. The thought made her feel ill. There was only one thing to do.

The butler handed Darcy a card. Mr. Edward Gardiner. He frowned, not recognizing the name. He was in no mood for yet another person begging a favour. Gardiner, though—that was Elizabeth's uncle's name. What would Elizabeth's uncle want with him? Perhaps it was some sort of message from Elizabeth. After all, she had no means to reply to his letter.

"Show him in."

Simms bowed and returned a moment later with a fashionably dressed gentleman a few years older than Darcy. He did not look as if he came from Cheapside. He also did not look friendly.

"Mr. Darcy? We have never met, but I believe you are acquainted with my niece, Miss Bennet."

Darcy motioned him to a seat. "I have that honour, it is true."

"My niece came to me last evening in some distress. She told me she had found a letter addressed to her that she believed you had written. Having some care for her own reputation, she did not open it." The implication was clear that he felt Darcy did not care about Elizabeth's reputation. He drew the letter out of his waistcoat pocket and tossed it onto Darcy's desk.

Darcy flipped it over. Still sealed. She had never read it.

"Do you deny, Mr. Darcy, that the letter is yours?"

"No, sir, I do not. I admit my means of communication may have been irregular, but Miss Bennet had, under false information, made some slanders against my character, and I felt the need to inform her of the truth of the matter. That is all the letter contains." The injury he had felt when Elizabeth flung her accusations at him still hurt more than her blow ever could. That all this time she had been believing Wickham's lies! And still did, by all appearances. As his initial anger with her had faded, the injury of knowing she believed ill of him had grown. The letter had been his only hope to relieve himself of that burden.

Perhaps he could still let her know the truth, albeit indirectly. "Please read the letter, and you will see it contains nothing more than a defense of my character."

Mr. Gardiner stood and drew himself to his full height, but made no move to take the letter. "Mr. Darcy," he said in tones that could only be called scornful, "you attempted to solicit a respectable young woman, the daughter of a gentleman, to be your mistress. Under the circumstances, I fail to see how you could expect me to have any concern for your character. You have insulted my niece and our entire family. You have no character, sir."

"What?" Darcy cried in disbelief. "Is that what Elizabeth told you?"

"She is Miss Bennet to you, and yes, that is what she told me when I pressed her for the full tale behind that letter. You saw her as unprotected now that her father is dead, but it is not true. She is by no means unprotected."

All the fury and disappointment he had felt at Elizabeth's refusal surged to the fore. "I did nothing of the sort! I made her a proposal of marriage, and while I misjudged her sentiments towards me, I fail to see how that can be construed as an *insult*."

"A proposal of marriage? I am not a fool, sir!" Mr. Gardiner said incredulously.

"It is the truth. I cannot explain why Eliz—Miss Bennet would tell you such a thing. And now I *insist* on your reading that letter, as I believe you will find it quite consistent with *my* story."

Mr. Gardiner looked at him distrustfully, but took the letter and broke the seal. As he read it, Darcy paced across the room, stopping by the window to look blindly out at the small garden behind the townhouse. How could things have gone so catastrophically wrong? He could not imagine Elizabeth making up such a story, but when he reviewed her behaviour, especially when she struck him, he realized it was what she truly believed him to be saying and why she refused him with such fervour.

He tried to remember the exact words he had used to her, but it was a vague blur. He had told her of his ardent love and the force of passion that drove him to this uncharacteristic action, how despite the degradation such an alliance would bring him—was that it? Could she have thought he was explaining why he could not marry her and proposing an alternative? He could not recall if he had mentioned the word marriage before she had stopped him, but how could she have thought it of him? He was no rake, everyone knew that, but who could say what lies Wickham might have told her?

The facts were obvious. Elizabeth thought him no better than his uncle, and so lacking in morality as to make such a proposition. It was painful to think she held him in such disdain. Excruciatingly painful.

Mr. Gardiner cleared his throat. "It appears I owe you an apology, Mr. Darcy. I do not claim to understand how such a misunderstanding could occur, but I am also convinced that my niece reported to me the facts as she understood them."

Darcy kept his back to him, fearing his thoughts would show in his face. "It is quite simple. She stopped me before I had finished speaking my piece, and her opinion of me is so low as to cause her to put a different interpretation on my words than the one I meant. Now I hope you will excuse my breach of manners, but I must ask you to leave, sir." He could not continue this conversation. He needed to be alone to nurse his wounds.

He heard the rustle of clothing as Mr. Gardiner turned to leave. "Of course, Mr. Darcy. Is there any message you wish me to convey to my niece?"

For a wild moment he thought of asking her to reconsider, but he realized the hopelessness of such a course. Such disdain might be lessened by knowledge of the truth, but it could not be converted to love. "No. There is no message." At least he managed to say those few words in a steady tone.

"Good day, then, sir."

Darcy did not move until he heard the click of the door closing, and then he slumped his head against the wall, his eyes stinging. Not since his father's death had he shed a tear, not even in private after the double betrayal at Ramsgate. He would not shed one over Elizabeth Bennet.

"He said what?" Elizabeth's voice rose in disbelief.

Mr. Gardiner sat back in his chair, looking reluctant to have this conversation at all. "You heard me quite well, Elizabeth."

A knot formed in her stomach. "But that is not what happened. He spoke at length about why he could not marry me, because of the degradation such an association with our family would cause." The memory of Darcy's words still hurt, especially when he spoke of his ardent love.

"Since I was not there, I cannot speak to how such a misunderstanding might occur, but I assure you, his mind was set on marriage. I read his letter, and it was clear that he thought you had refused to be his wife."

It could not be. She could not have so misunderstood him. "What was in the letter?"

"The bulk of it contained a history of his dealings with Mr. Wickham. I am afraid we were sadly misled in our belief in that young man's character."

"But—" She stopped herself before asking the question. She herself had wondered as to the veracity of Wickham's story. If her uncle believed Darcy's story, it would be for good reason. Her throat tight, she asked, "What was his reaction when he learned of my misapprehension?" How could she have made such an error? How could he have said such things about her family in a marriage proposal?

"The intelligence clearly occasioned him pain. He must have had quite an attachment to you." Mr. Gardiner shook his head as if deep in thought. "I asked if he wished me to give you a message, but he declined. I hope you did not have an attachment to him. I would be sorry to see you hurt by such a man."

Stricken, Elizabeth said, "Thank you, Uncle." She tried to maintain some dignity as she left the room.

A silver platter sat on Darcy's desk, piled with the day's post. Darcy picked up the top one, broke the seal, and tossed it aside to be discarded. Why could they not leave him alone? The last thing he wanted was to attend balls and soirees, but the invitations kept coming, even when he did not reply. He dropped the second letter on top of the first. More of the same.

His hand froze on the third letter, whose sender was identified as Mr. E. Gardiner. The image of Elizabeth's uncle flashed before his eyes, bringing back all the pain of that day.

He had received him in this very room. What could the man want now?

Carefully he ran his finger under the seal. For a moment he paused, fearing what it might contain, but then he unfolded it. It was very brief.

Mr. Darcy,

My niece has asked me to express to you her most sincere regrets for her misapprehension.

Yours, &c.
E. Gardiner

He set the paper down, smoothed it, and then rested his head on his hands. He did not want to think of Elizabeth expressing her regrets. He could not afford to soften his heart towards her. She had told him what she thought of him, and that was that.

Besides, there was no reason to assume Elizabeth had said anything of the sort. Had not that boy said her uncle was eager for Elizabeth to marry? No doubt he had come up with the scheme himself, in a last effort to recover the opportunity Elizabeth had lost, but it was too late. Far too late. Some things could never be forgotten.

She thought he was no better than his uncle or his cousin Henry, willing to do whatever was needed to satisfy his carnal desires, with no care for the price she would pay. He had told her he loved her, for God's sake. How could she think he would degrade her in such a manner? Henry might be willing to pretend to such an affection to obtain a woman, but how could Elizabeth think it of him? She did not know him at all, and what she did know, she held in disdain.

He could still marry her if he chose. The letter was all but an invitation from her uncle to ask for her hand. What would that accomplish, though? She would be a caged songbird who would not sing in captivity. Instead of lightening his spirits, she would be a living reminder that her heart was out of his reach. If he were the man she thought him, he might have done so. That would still be better than his cousin Henry, who would have used that stolen kiss to ruin her reputation so she had no choice but to cleave to him in whatever situation he chose. But he was not such a man. She did not want him, and that was the end of it.

He stood up slowly, as if his joints pained him, then crossed the room and carefully fed the paper into the fire. He did not return to his desk until the last ashes crumbled and fell through the grate.

After a month, Elizabeth knew he would not return. If he had not responded to the letter her uncle sent on her behalf, it meant he could not forgive her. He had said that his good opinion, once lost, was lost forever. It was her turn to bear the burden of it.

It was time to let go of the past. Her aunt had commented on her low spirits more than once, and although Elizabeth had avoided answering any questions, she did not doubt that her uncle had confided her secret to his wife, and they were both watching her carefully. She owed it to them, as well as to herself, to change her ways.

She needed to acknowledge that Miss Elizabeth Bennet of Longbourn was no more, and in her place was an impoverished young lady with a patchwork education and no prospects. Her younger self had cherished romantic notions, but now it was time to act the part of a sensible woman. She shook her head, recalling how horrified she had been by Charlotte's practical decision to wed Mr. Collins. She herself could never have married such a foolish man, but she could admit now that there was some truth to Charlotte's philosophy. Marriage to a sensible man, even without affection at first, could lead to better things, and it would safeguard her future and her family. She could no longer afford to be cavalier about that. Love, after all, had not served her well.

She was resolved to look only forward. With that in mind, she began to offer warmer smiles to Mr. Griggs. If the range of his education was smaller than she was accustomed to, she could respect his dedication to his work and willingness to learn. If his conversation lacked sparkle, he did not lack honesty. If sometimes when she smiled at him a vision of dark hair and dark eyes rose before her, it meant nothing. She was fortunate that a man as eligible as Mr. Griggs was interested in marrying her. So she reminded herself daily, and when a certain melancholy about the situation would overcome her, she learned to closet herself in her room until she could regain her composure.

The butler entered Darcy's study. "Mr. Darcy, there is a young *person* here who says he must speak to you. He will not tell me his business, but he is most insistent that you will want to see him."

"Does this young person have a name?"

"He said to tell you he is Charlie from Cheapside. He is quite disreputable, sir."

Cheapside. Elizabeth. Even the word could still give him a twist of pain, but he had to put that behind him. He dragged his mind back to the present. He knew no one else from Cheapside. "Send him away." As the butler bowed and turned, Darcy remembered the urchin on Gracechurch Street. His name had been Charlie, had it not? "Simms, I have changed my mind. Send him in."

"Very well, sir."

Darcy drummed his fingers on the desk. Finally the boy crept in, hat in hand, wide-eyed as he took in his surroundings and then straightened at the sight of Darcy. He was more skin and bones than ever.

"Well, Charlie from Cheapside, how did you find me?"

"I followed yer 'ome one day from Moorsfield, sir. Thought it might be useful to know someday."

An enterprising sort, indeed. "And what brings you here today?"

"It's about Miss Bennet, sir. There's that gentleman what's courting 'er. He's at 'er house most days."

It could mean nothing to him if Elizabeth favoured another man. She would never be his, in any case. If only he could convince himself it was none of his business. If only the idea did not tie his stomach in knots. "Is he well-to-do?"

The boy cast his eyes around the room. No doubt he had never been in such a fine house. "Not like Mr. Gardiner, but 'is family keeps a servant."

One servant. At least Elizabeth would not have to scrub and clean. That thought was not bearable. Still, she would not be without household duties. She should have been mistress of Pemberley, with dozens of servants at her command. "Does she look on his suit with favour?"

"It's her uncle what wants the match, but she don't avoid his company, if that's what yer mean, sir. But Freddie says she ain't 'appy, and she cries sometimes when she thinks no one is lookin'." Charlie watched him closely.

"Is he respectable?" As if it made a difference.

The boy shrugged. "Respectable enough. He likes his bits o' muslin, though, he does."

Darcy did not allow his expression to change, though he doubted it fooled the boy in the slightest. "And how, pray tell, did you discover that?"

"Followed him a few times, too. I'm good at it."

Darcy did not doubt it. It was fortunate for England that Charlie chose to work on his behalf rather than Napoleon's. "Does she still walk out to Moorsfield in the mornings?"

"No, sir. She don't walk out alone at all now. But I could find out when she goes out wiv the children, if yer want, sir."

Just what he did not need—more temptation. "That will not be necessary." He opened the desk drawer and took out a few coins. Charlie's hand was already out for them. Darcy rang for Simms, who appeared instantly. No doubt he had been waiting outside the door.

"Simms, take this young man to the kitchens and make sure he eats a good meal before he leaves." It was a long walk back to Cheapside.

Darcy tried to return to the newspaper he had been reading, but his heart was not in it. He could think of nothing but the news the boy had brought. He went to the sideboard and poured himself a glass of brandy, but did not touch it. Why did Elizabeth cry? Did she dislike the man? He would not admit the satisfaction the idea gave him. Or did she merely miss her family? Or perhaps it was because she no longer dared to venture on her walks.

No, that was ridiculous. Elizabeth Bennet had never lacked for courage, and it would take more than a few misplaced words from him to cause her to change her habits. And if she disliked her suitor, she would find a way to laugh him off, even if her uncle favoured the match.

He froze, the glass halfway to his mouth. Elizabeth had not laughed off *his* suit. She had cried, made accusations, and slapped him. Of course, she had believed him to be making a different proposition entirely, but still, if he thought about some other man suggesting that Elizabeth should be his mistress, he would have expected her to make a joke of it and perhaps a cutting remark. She would not let such idiocy hurt her. Why had he provoked such a reaction in her? If her opinion of him was as low as her words indicated, surely it could not be worsened by thinking he would take a mistress.

He tossed back a sip of the brandy faster than the fine liquor deserved. As it warmed his throat, he remembered the look in her eyes just before he began his proposal, when he could think of nothing but kissing her and would have sworn she felt the same. Could it be possible that she had cared for him, had in fact wanted him to kiss her? Was that why his words had hurt her, if she had indeed misinterpreted them?

"Simms!" Darcy called before he could think better of it.

"Sir?"

"That boy. I will see him again before he leaves."

"As you wish, sir." Simms disappeared down the hallway.

Darcy wrapped his hands around his drink. A little hope was a dangerous thing.

Chapter 7

Even in his state of eager anticipation, Darcy paused before knocking at the door to Georgiana's rooms to enjoy the sound of his sister giggling. He had so rarely heard it since Ramsgate that it was still a pleasure, albeit one that was becoming more frequent as her spirits became lighter. At times he could picture the girl she used to be.

But time pressed, so he rapped on the door. Mary, the girl from Rosings, opened it. Although her curtsey was quite proper, the saucy manner in which she glanced over her shoulder at Georgiana was hardly deferent; it was clear she had been involved in whatever had amused his sister.

Georgiana's cheeks were rosy and her eyes had sparkle to them. Perhaps the past was finally starting to lose its grip on her. "Fitzwilliam, will you not join me?" She gestured to the chair.

"For a moment only. I came to ask the pleasure of your company on a walk."

"Now? I had not intended to go out today, but I could, if you wish it."

The girl was hovering almost protectively behind Georgiana. Darcy waved his hand in dismissal, and with another curtsey, she scurried from the room. He said, "I think it is too pleasant a day to spend indoors."

He could tell from her slightly puzzled look that she saw something unusual in his demeanour. "Very well. Should I ask Mrs. Annesley to join us?"

"Not today, I think." He looked around the room, noticing her companion's absence for the first time. "Where is Mrs. Annesley?"

"Mary and I were talking, so I told her she could have the afternoon to herself. I hope you do not object." The worried tone had returned to her voice.

"Of course not. She is your companion, and it is your choice. Though if she is unsatisfactory in any way, I hope you will inform me."

"Not at all! She is everything that is kind and proper. But sometimes I prefer to be with someone closer to my own age. I am so glad you decided to bring Mary here for me."

He blinked in surprise. "For you?"

"Is that not why you brought her here from Rosings, because you thought she would be good company for me?"

"It was not my intent, but if it pleases you, then I am happy."

"What was your intent, then?"

Not a question he wished to answer, but it was a good sign

that she dared question him again. If it was the girl's influence, he could not complain. "Her situation at Rosings was difficult, and it seemed best to remove her from the environs."

"Because of her father, I suppose. Was it Sir Lewis, then? Mary says her mother never told her, apart from that he was a gentleman."

It was a measure of Darcy's distraction that it took him a moment to understand her meaning. Seeking to recover himself, he said, "I seriously doubt it was Sir Lewis. He was not one to notice a pretty face." He hoped she would not question his statement. He had tried since Ramsgate to acquaint Georgiana with some of the less innocent elements of life, since naïveté had not served her well, but there were some things he was not prepared to explain to his younger sister. At least he had an excuse to break off the conversation. "Shall we walk out in a quarter hour, then?"

"Certainly."

He had escaped unscathed there. Perhaps that was a good omen for the rest of the day.

Young Matthew Gardiner leaned out over the water of the Serpentine. He pointed excitedly, almost overbalancing in his enthusiasm. "Look, a giant fish! Right there!"

"That is indeed a big fish," said Elizabeth gravely, holding tight to the hand of his younger brother, Andrew.

Margaret huffed. "That is nothing compared to the fish Father caught when we visited Longbourn. It's just a baby."

"No, it isn't," Matthew cried.

An argument of this sort could go on for hours if there were no distraction. "Shall we look for the swans?" Elizabeth asked.

Matthew pouted. "I want to try to catch the fish, just like Father."

"You would need a rod and tackle for that, I fear." Elizabeth tugged gently at his hand, and he followed grudgingly.

Margaret stood on her tiptoes. "I think the swans are down there."

Elizabeth shaded her eyes as she looked down the length of the Serpentine. She could not see swans, but Margaret's eyes were sharper than hers. She stiffened as a movement on the path along the lake caught her eye. Surely it could not be! It must be some other gentleman of the same height, the same proud stature, the same long stride.

But it *was* him, with a fashionably dressed young woman on his arm. Something twisted in Elizabeth's chest. His love had not lasted long; he had already replaced her in his heart, and with a lady for whom he did not have to skulk in Moorsfield.

She could not bear to meet him. "Come, children. We must go now."

"But we haven't seen the swans yet," Margaret protested.

Elizabeth busied herself retying Margaret's bonnet strings, giving her an excuse not to look up. "Let us walk through the gardens, then, and see the swans afterwards."

"Please, Lizzy, can't we see them now instead?"

Out of the corner of her eye, she could see the couple approaching. It was too late to flee. Instead she put her back to the path, gazing steadfastly into the water. "Where did your fish go, Matthew? I cannot see it."

Matthew and his brother needed no further excuse to go back to the reeds by the water. Elizabeth closed her eyes with relief. Mr. Darcy might still see her, but he would not have to acknowledge her. She strained her ears for his familiar tones, but heard only a light feminine laughter and footsteps on the gravel path.

The footsteps paused. Mr. Darcy's voice floated past her, sending a shiver down her arms. "Just a moment, my dear," he said softly and then called out, "Miss Bennet!"

There was no avoiding it. Elizabeth turned slowly and curtsied. "Mr. Darcy." She fixed her eyes on his cravat. It was safer than looking at his face.

The couple approached closer. "Miss Bennet, may I have the honour of introducing you to my sister?" he asked.

Elizabeth breathed a sigh of relief. His sister, not his betrothed or his wife. "It is a pleasure to meet you, Miss Darcy."

"Not Miss Bennet of Hertfordshire? My brother has told me so much about you."

He had told his sister about her? Elizabeth's mouth opened, but it was a moment before she could force any words out. "I am all astonishment."

"Indeed. He told me of your musical talent and how much pleasure he found in listening to you perform."

"He is far too kind," Elizabeth said.

Darcy finally allowed himself to breathe more easily. He had found her. Poor Georgiana had been sweet about being dragged all over Hyde Park without an explanation, since young Charlie could not provide any information as to where in the park his quarry might be. Darcy wondered what his sister might be thinking, faced with the blushing Miss Bennet who would not look him in the eyes.

Naturally it must be difficult for her. He was at least prepared for the moment. But how was he to determine her feelings if she hid her face from him? He could see little of her but the rim of her bonnet.

He had to say something. "It is a fine day for a walk in the park." Hardly original, but unexceptionable.

She still did not raise her eyes, though she seemed comfortable enough looking at Georgiana. When she spoke, it was in a strained voice. "We are fortunate to have such a warm day so early in the spring. But you must excuse us; I promised to take the children to see the swans."

"Perhaps we could accompany you," he said. Was she trying to avoid him or merely looking for a graceful escape from an embarrassing situation?

"Oh, yes!" said Georgiana stoutly, much to his surprise. "I have not seen the swans since last summer." It was so unlike her to speak up in company that he knew she must be doing it for his sake.

Finally, finally she looked at him, with the barest trace

of her teasing look. "We would be honoured, of course, but you must understand the children are not always the easiest of company."

"I love children," Georgiana announced. Darcy gave her a sideways glance. She was going to expect some serious explanations from him later.

Elizabeth said, "Very well, but you have been warned! Come then, Margaret, and you boys as well. No, leave the stick there, if you please, Matthew."

Darcy offered Elizabeth his arm, waiting an anxious moment until she took it. Georgiana, bless her heart, was engaging the young girl in conversation, but he was starting to take a serious dislike to Elizabeth's bonnet, because again it hid her face.

They walked in uncomfortable silence for a few minutes, broken only when Elizabeth stopped to point out to the children two deer among the trees. The boys immediately raced towards them, but the deer fled at the sight.

"Your cousins have a great deal of energy," Darcy said.

"Yes, they do." She kept her eyes on the ground.

Did she ever look up anymore? This would not do. He would have to say something, or he would never know what she was thinking. "I hope my presence does not make you uncomfortable."

"Uncomfortable is perhaps the wrong word, sir. It would be more accurate to say…" She trailed off into silence.

"To say what?"

A small smile played over her lips, but she still did not look at him. "Perhaps mortified. Or embarrassed. Chagrined. Abashed. You may take your pick. They are all true."

"If the choice were mine, it would be none of these."

"What would you have me say, then?" She absently stroked the dangling ribbon of her bonnet with one fingertip.

Entranced, he followed the movement of her hand with his eyes. "Whatever the truth might be, even if it is that you would wish me elsewhere."

She seemed fascinated with the gravel pathway. Did her silence mean it was true? Was he nothing but a painful reminder of an embarrassing episode? Finally, just as he was about to give up, she said softly, "I have missed our conversations, Mr. Darcy."

"As have I." It was something, at least, and it made his heart leap. "You were very patient in listening to me."

"You ascribe to me more virtues than I possess." She glanced over her shoulder towards the boys, as if to ensure they had followed.

"I have no doubt about your virtues." From the crimsoning of her cheeks, he suspected she understood that he spoke of more than just the virtue of patience, but his patience was less than hers, for he could not stand to be in doubt any longer. "You used to look at me on occasion as we talked. Perhaps I have grown a hump or a wart upon my chin."

She turned her head towards him with just a trace of her old arch look. "No, you look quite unchanged."

"My valet will be devastated. He spent weeks persuading me to change the knot of my cravat."

This time she did laugh. "You seek to trap me, sir!"

"Not to trap you, no. But in some ways I *am* quite unchanged." His eyes held hers, and his heart began to pound because of what he saw there. Caution, but also awareness, and perhaps a hint of sadness. Now he knew she had not forgotten his declaration of ardent love.

She was the first to look away, seeming to seize the excuse of a cry from the youngest Gardiner boy. She hurried to the child's side. He held his hand out to her, displaying a scrape on the palm. Elizabeth took the boy's hand and examined it with great seriousness before pronouncing that she thought it would heal with time.

Darcy looked on. It was foolish to be jealous of a child no more than six years of age simply because Elizabeth held his hand and focused her attention on him. He forced his feet to take him down the path to Georgiana, who was looking at him inquisitively.

"Miss Gardiner and I have been discussing her history studies," Georgiana said. "She has a great enthusiasm for the subject."

Darcy appreciated Georgiana's choice of subject. He had little experience dealing with children, but even he could manage to ask about schooling. "Do you have a favourite period in history?"

"Oh, yes, sir. The Romans." The girl launched into the topic with fervour.

Even without looking, Darcy could tell Elizabeth was approaching them. She stopped beside her young cousin. "Margaret, I imagine Miss Darcy and Mr. Darcy have more to do today than to listen to ancient history."

Darcy said, "On the contrary, Miss Bennet. Your cousin is a delightful conversationalist."

"You have chosen her favourite subject, sir, and I doubt you have had the chance to say more than a word."

"It is a favourite of mine as well." He hoped she realized he was not speaking solely of history.

Margaret's face lit up, and she pointed towards the water. "Look, there are the swans! Are they not beautiful?"

"Very beautiful," Darcy agreed, looking only at Elizabeth. Her presence and the sense of hope it gave him were intoxicating.

The boys raced to the bank of the river, each vying to get closest to a swan. The elder one triumphantly picked up a white feather from the rocks at the edge, holding it just out of his brother's reach. The younger one, with a determined look, made a leap for it.

"Andrew!" cried Elizabeth, rushing towards the boy an instant before he toppled into the water.

Darcy was closer, though. The boy was in no danger in the shallow water, or would be once he thought to stand up, but his freckled face screwed up in dismay as he flailed. Darcy touched Elizabeth's arm briefly to stay her and then waded out into the water and fished the boy out. He carried him to the bank and set him down. Darcy asked, "Are you injured, lad?"

Elizabeth was there before he could reply, brushing Andrew's dripping hair from his forehead. "There is no need for fear, you are quite safe, my dear."

Andrew hiccupped. "I fell in," he said, quite unnecessarily.

"Indeed you did, and now you are quite wet. That is an adventure to remember." Elizabeth managed to elicit a smile through the boy's tears. "You must thank Mr. Darcy, Andrew."

The boy mumbled his thanks, and Elizabeth straightened. "It was very good of you, sir. I am sorry to put you to the trouble. I fear you must be uncomfortable."

"It was nothing," he said brusquely. Any discomfort he felt had nothing to do with dampness. "The water barely reached over my boots."

"Yes, I can see you are quite dry indeed," Elizabeth said archly, gesturing towards his chest where the evidence of water could not be denied. "Your poor valet may be even more devastated when he sees you now."

He glanced down. The front of his tailcoat was wet where he had held the boy. He brushed off a few drops of water, but it made no difference to his appearance. "It is no matter." It was not. A stain on his coat was a small price to pay to see Elizabeth teasing him again. He would have happily jumped into the Serpentine himself if he thought it would make her smile. "But this young man is soaked through. Our house is but a short walk from here. We can find him some dry clothes and a warm fire there."

Elizabeth's eyes widened. "We could not *possibly* impose on you."

"Nonsense. I insist. Do you not agree, Georgiana?"

"Of course!" his sister said. "You cannot take him all the way to Cheapside like that. He would catch his death of cold, and I would *never* forgive myself."

Darcy wondered when Georgiana had developed her sudden talent for dramatics. "You would not want my sister to worry, would you, Miss Bennet?"

She gave him an amused look that said she was fully aware he had trapped her after all. "Well, then, I suppose we must accept your kind offer."

Elizabeth looked down Brook Street to the townhouse Mr. Darcy had indicated. "Your house is indeed very close to Hyde Park," she said.

"Very convenient." He looked a bit smug.

"Almost too convenient," she teased. "I might wonder if you persuaded poor Andrew to jump in the lake."

"No, indeed," Darcy said, "though had I realized it would have such an outcome, I might have tried."

Elizabeth smothered a laugh at his brazen answer. "I must ask you one question, sir."

"Anything."

"How did that letter come to appear in my room?"

"The same way I knew you would be in the park today."

"Indeed?" Her words were a challenge.

He smiled indulgently. "Yes, indeed, but a gentleman never reveals his sources."

They stayed but an hour at the townhouse, long enough for Andrew to be hurried off by a servant, his clothing dried and returned to him still warm from the fireside. Both Darcy and Georgiana attempted to persuade them to lengthen their visit, but to no avail, as Elizabeth insisted the Gardiners would worry if they did not return soon.

Darcy was content. The meeting had gone far better than he hoped. Elizabeth seemed more natural with him by the end of the visit, and as her smiles and laughter returned, his spirits rose with them. There was no chance for them to speak privately, but perhaps that was for the best at this stage.

He walked them out to the street where a hackney cab, summoned by his footman, awaited them.

Elizabeth lingered on the steps. "Mr. Darcy, I must thank you for all your kindness today. Were my aunt and uncle here, they would add their gratitude to mine."

"There is no need for thanks. I am grateful for such pleasant company."

An impish smile hovered about her mouth. "You will not even allow me to thank you, then?"

He pretended to consider the matter. "No, I think I shall not. You must save your thanks until next we meet."

She gave him an amused look. The hackney driver coughed pointedly, stamping his feet on the board. Darcy opened the door, and the children hurried in, impatient with the grown-up conversation. Elizabeth lingered a moment as if she would say something else, but then she took his offered hand and stepped into the carriage. "I thank you *anyway*, sir," she said.

"It was my pleasure entirely." He kept his eyes fixed on her, determined not to lose a minute of his opportunity to see her. The driver cracked his whip, and the horses took off at a brisk walk.

Georgiana was waiting just inside the door. She tugged his arm until he followed her to the sitting room, where she closed the door behind him. "Well, Fitzwilliam?"

"Well, Georgiana?"

"Would you care to explain to me why you staged that encounter? Could you not have simply called on her?"

Darcy sank onto the cushioned sofa embroidered with wildflowers. "I have not seen Miss Bennet in some time. We quarrelled, and I did not have a chance to make amends. A spontaneous meeting seemed safer."

"That meeting was no more spontaneous than Napoleon's march on Russia!"

"But somewhat more pleasant, one would hope."

"She is charming, naturally. Ought I to wish you joy, then?"

"Premature, my dear. Quite premature." He was not about to tell Georgiana just how badly their last meeting had gone, but by the time Elizabeth left that day, she was smiling at him again, and she understood his intent. "But perhaps someday."

Chapter 8

Elizabeth's giddiness lasted through the rest of the day. She could not forget her meeting with Mr. Darcy for a moment, even if she had not been subjected to repeated recitations of the entire adventure by the children. She was aware of a whispered conversation between her aunt and uncle when he came home that afternoon and of the sharp looks Mr. Gardiner gave her afterwards. She could not miss that Mrs. Gardiner penned a letter of thanks to Miss Darcy and Mr. Darcy for their kindness to the children, since her aunt made a point of writing it in front of her and read it aloud when she finished it.

But Elizabeth had little time to reflect on it until bedtime. She tiptoed into her room and set the candle on the vanity before the small mirror, careful not to awaken Margaret, who had recently graduated from the nursery to share her room. With a sigh, she lowered herself onto the stool before it.

Why had he reappeared now, months after their last contact? At first she had thought it an accident and schooled herself to be satisfied that they could have a civil conversation, but then he revealed he had planned it, and how had he known? One of the servants, obviously, but which one? She must be careful what she said and did.

She pulled out hairpins, setting them in line on the vanity, ready for the morrow. Her heavy twist of hair fell down onto her shoulders. What would Mr. Darcy do if he could see her now? She imagined his hand running through her curls, to rest on her shoulder. Would he kiss her then, as he had that day in Moorsfield?

Moorsfield. They had always met there. Would he look for her there and not find her? Or had his source told him that her uncle did not permit her to walk out alone anymore? He had indicated he expected to see her again. Perhaps he meant to seek her out as he had today.

She held her hand in front of herself, in the light of the candle, remembering the pressure of his fingers on it as he handed her into the hackney. She had even imagined she felt the warmth of his hand through her glove, but that was impossible. Not that it made a difference, since she had felt warm all over from his look, and he had not touched her at all with that. Mr. Griggs never elicited those feelings from her.

She picked up her hairbrush and ran it slowly through her hair. The look of Mr. Darcy's had said that it was not over between them, but how and when would she see him again?

Would it be days or weeks or months again? Perhaps she should have said more to encourage him, but her embarrassment over her past behaviour was too great. Now she could do nothing but wait. She touched her fingertips lightly to her burning lips, wishing it could be his touch.

Mrs. Gardiner's letter left with the morning post, and a reply arrived that very afternoon. "Quite a prompt response for so slight an acquaintance," Mrs. Gardiner said as she broke the seal.

Elizabeth waited in a torment of impatience as her aunt read the letter. She knew better than to press Mrs. Gardiner, but she was certain her aunt must have read it through at least three times before she said a word.

Finally Mrs. Gardiner folded it, set it on the tray, and turned an inquisitive gaze on Elizabeth. "You must have made quite an impression, Lizzy. We are invited to dine with the Darcys on Tuesday next."

"At their townhouse?" Elizabeth's heartbeat threatened to drown out her every thought.

"Where else?" Her aunt knitted her brows and examined Elizabeth, looking her over from head to foot. "That dress will not do. We must think of something else, since we are unlikely to find a *modiste* who can prepare a new dress so quickly."

"There is no need. My Sunday dress is still serviceable and will do once again." It was an automatic protest against any money being spent on her.

"Nonsense. You must make the most of this opportunity to create a good impression. If you can catch Mr. Darcy's eye once more, it would be a fine thing."

"Somehow I doubt Mr. Griggs would agree with you."

Mrs. Gardiner took Elizabeth by the arm and walked to the corner of the room where they could speak more privately. "Mr. Griggs is not a fool. He will be disappointed, but he would not expect you to pass up such an opportunity as this. He is a good match, but he will not begrudge you a brilliant one."

Elizabeth's lips quirked. "You are very quick to marry me off to a man you have never met."

"Lizzy, you know I only want the best for you. Think of what you could do for your family as Mrs. Darcy."

The use of that name took Elizabeth off guard, and she said more frankly than she might have otherwise, "I would not need that inducement to accept him."

Her aunt's eyes softened. "You care for him, then?"

"I think he is a good man." Further than that she was not prepared to go.

Mrs. Gardiner rubbed her hands together. "Well, then, we must prepare. It occurs to me that my new blue silk dress could be altered to fit you without much difficulty."

"But you have wished for that dress for so long!"

"Your happiness is more important to me. And, if you marry Mr. Darcy, there will be benefits to all of us, and I can easily obtain another silk dress."

No arguments Elizabeth could make would prevail.

The next few days were quiet in the Gardiner household. The younger children were relegated to the care of their nursemaid, while Elizabeth, with some assistance from Margaret, put finishing touches on the blue silk dress. It was finer material than she had worn before, even when she lived at Longbourn.

Mr. Griggs did not pay his usual calls, leading Elizabeth to believe her uncle had spoken to him. It almost frightened her how ready her aunt and uncle were to believe that Mr. Darcy needed but an opportunity to propose. The wish was so close to her own heart that she could barely stand to think on it.

Their toils were interrupted one afternoon by a loud pounding at the front door. It did not presage well for a visit from a well-mannered person. Elizabeth assumed it must be a vendor of some kind and paid little attention to the manservant who left to answer the door. She continued her careful stitching of the fine fabric until she heard the servant clearing his throat.

"Miss Lydia Bennet," he announced.

Elizabeth rose in surprise and embraced her sister, who seemed disinclined to reciprocate.

"Where is my aunt?" Lydia demanded, without even a greeting.

Elizabeth frowned at her lack of manners. "Margaret, would you inform your mother we have a guest?" She waited until the girl's footsteps had faded away. "What brings you to London? This is quite a surprise."

Lydia flounced across the room and settled herself on an embroidered settee. "Lord, how dirty Cheapside is! I don't know how you stand it. Why could our uncle not purchase a house in a more fashionable part of town?"

Elizabeth's lips tightened. "Perhaps you would like some refreshment. I imagine Bates will be bringing some shortly. But tell me, how is our mother? Is Jane well?"

"They are all well, or at least well enough. Mama is ill, but then again, she always is."

"Ill? What ails her?"

Lydia shrugged. "Some fever or other, no doubt."

Mrs. Gardiner bustled in, much to Elizabeth's relief. "Lydia, my dear! What brings you here?"

Lydia grimaced, then rummaged in her reticule and pulled out a crumpled letter. She held it out. "From Jane," she said, as if it explained everything.

Mrs. Gardiner took the letter and broke the seal, her lips moving as she read the close-written lines. She shook her head once and then passed her hand over her forehead as if she were suddenly extremely weary.

Elizabeth had not truly worried until she saw the expression on her aunt's face. "What is the matter?" she cried. Without concern for her manners, she reached for the letter, but Mrs. Gardiner pulled it away.

"No, Lizzy. This is a matter I must discuss with your uncle."

Mrs. Gardiner's skirts swished as she hurried out the doorway.

Elizabeth rounded on her sister, ignoring the sullen expression that boded no good. "If you do not tell me what has happened, it will go hard with you!"

"It is all a tempest in a teapot, and you may keep your superior ways to yourself! You're just jealous. No real man has ever looked twice at you."

If only she knew! But Elizabeth knew better than to breathe a word to Lydia about Mr. Darcy, who had looked more than twice at her. "If you will not tell me, I will apply to our uncle directly." She swept out of the room.

Despite her words, she knew better than to interrupt her aunt and uncle when they were conferring, so instead she went to her room and began to move some of her possessions aside to make room for Lydia's belongings. They would have to share the room, and even the bed, since there was no other place for a visitor, not since Elizabeth had come to live there. She would lose the little bit of privacy she had, that precious hour after Margaret was asleep when Elizabeth was free to dream her dreams. She paused at the thought of Mr. Darcy, her summer nightgown in hand. Perhaps it might not be so long until she left the Gardiners' house. The idea did a great deal to restore her good spirits.

After half an hour, her worry and curiosity became too strong to bear, and she sought out her uncle in his office. His grim face and her aunt's red eyes bore testament that whatever the letter said was even more serious than she had believed.

"Sit down, Lizzy," her uncle said heavily. "This matter concerns you as well."

Visions of her mother or Jane ill danced before her eyes. "Please tell me, Uncle. Lydia refuses to say a word."

"And well she might!" her aunt exclaimed, wringing her skirts in her hand. "The foolish girl—"

Her uncle said, "There is no point in denying the matter. Your sister has succumbed to the blandishments of a young man who now denies knowledge of her, and she is to pay the price."

"Not with child?" Elizabeth's hand travelled to her own stomach, as if to forfend the disastrous news from being contagious.

"I wish I could say she were not. How many times I told your father to rein in her spirits and break her of her free ways! But it is too late now." Her uncle sat back in his chair. "Lydia must stay here until after her confinement. There is nowhere else for her to go."

"And the child?" Elizabeth asked steadily.

"We will raise it as ours," he said, with a glance at his wife, "although the timing is poor. But this is not the only news. Jane begs for your return to Meryton, as she is close to her own confinement, and your mother in poor health. She does not trust Kitty or Mary to watch over her, and, if I read between the lines correctly, Jane herself may require assistance. It is the best solution, although we shall be sorry to lose you. We can ill afford to add Lydia to our household as it is."

Leave London and return to the crowded rooms in Meryton? Now, when Mr. Darcy had returned to her life, against all odds? Elizabeth closed her eyes for a moment, trying to wish it away. Apart from Jane, there was nothing for her in Meryton any longer. But it was the end of all her plans and wishes, in any case. With Lydia's disgrace, any possibility of marriage to Mr. Darcy would now be at an end. How quickly a dream could die! "When do you wish me to leave?" she asked, her throat tight.

Her uncle glanced down at the letter. "Jane expresses some urgency."

"Then I shall go tomorrow." It was for the best; the longer she stayed in London, the greater the chance of seeing Mr. Darcy again, and she could not bear it, not now. She stood, while she still maintained her composure. "I must start my packing."

"Lizzy," her aunt said gently. "I hope you will return to us when… after Lydia no longer needs to stay here."

Her kindness brought tears to Elizabeth's eyes. "Thank you. For everything." She fled before she started to sob.

Elizabeth folded her shift with great care and laid it in the trunk. Even Lady Catherine could have found no fault with the neatness of her packing. Her concentration on it allowed her to pretend Lydia was not there, lounging on the bed and complaining.

"I still do not see why I had to leave Meryton. I could have worn my dresses loose, and no one would have known the difference. There at least I could have some freedom." Lydia huffed a sigh. "My uncle says I will not be allowed to leave the house. For months on end! Can you imagine?"

"He is quite right. You have caused enough damage." Elizabeth kept her voice even, but she longed to slap Lydia.

"Why should you care? You are not the one imprisoned here, with no entertainment at all." Lydia flounced over to a chair.

"It is better than you deserve. If you have no care for your own reputation, you might at least think of what this is costing the rest of us. Do you think our aunt wishes for another baby to care for now, when she is not yet recovered from her last?" Elizabeth did not dare begin on the subject of what Lydia's misbehaviour had cost her.

"They are our family, and it is only right that they should provide assistance." Lydia discovered Elizabeth's gloves and immediately put them on, holding out her hands to admire them. "These are lovely. Wherever did you get them?"

"They were a gift." Elizabeth longed to rip them off Lydia's hands.

"I have none so fine. Mr. Browning says I can choose a new pair of gloves only twice a year. Can you believe that?"

"You are fortunate he allows you any."

"Nonsense. He is Jane's husband, after all. He has so many, and it would not hurt him to part with a few pairs!"

"It is his business." No wonder Mr. Darcy had hesitated to ally himself to her family. Elizabeth slammed the lid of the trunk closed. "I am going out, and when I return, I do not wish to hear another word from you."

She had to escape, even if only for a few minutes. She found her bonnet and tied it on with shaking fingers before hastening out the door and down the street. At first she had no goal beyond distance from Lydia, but soon she found her feet leading her towards Moorsfield. After all, why should she not go there now? Her uncle would understand this one disobedience.

The fields were green, no longer brown stubble as they had been last autumn when she met Mr. Darcy there. The first primroses bloomed in the hedgerows, casting a light fragrance on the air, but Elizabeth hardly noted it. She followed the path along the hedgerow until she reached the copse, the same one where Mr. Darcy had kissed her.

Out of breath, she leaned back against a sturdy oak tree. The rough bark pressed uncomfortably into her shoulders, but she did not care. If anything, the slight pain was a relief. She closed her eyes as a hot tear trickled down her face.

How could Lydia have been so reckless? To risk not only her own reputation, but that of her entire family! Foolish, foolish girl. Mr. Darcy had the right of it that day when he spoke of the objectionable behaviour of her family. Lydia had certainly met the worst of his expectations.

She shook her head slowly from side to side, trying to comprehend the new reality. Why did it have to be now, just when her hope had been raised again? A week earlier she would have been leaving a possible future with Mr. Griggs, a loss that seemed far more bearable. Now she would be fortunate if she had even that much to return to.

She needed to remember herself. She was not the only one affected; her aunt and uncle would be bearing a substantial burden for years to come because of Lydia's misbehaviour. Elizabeth would need to be strong for them. The least she could do was to make herself of use to them before she left. She could speak to Margaret and impress upon her the importance of helping her mother, of taking charge of the baby when the nurse was not available. She was old enough for that and knew enough of the world, child though she was. If and when Elizabeth returned to London, she could offer to take on more responsibility for the younger children, especially Lydia's baby. Her aunt would need all the assistance she could get.

Having a few plans made her feel better. As long as she avoided thoughts of Mr. Darcy, she would manage well enough. And she had spent many weeks thinking he was lost to her; this should be no different, she decided, refusing to acknowledge that then it was because of his choice, and now it was out of both of their hands.

It was foolish of Darcy to come to Moorsfield; he knew full well that Elizabeth's uncle had forbidden her to walk there alone. But at least this way he could know she was nearby; he could ride down Gracechurch Street and breathe the air she breathed every day. In Moorsfield it would be easy to imagine her hand pressing on his arm, to remember the silvery music of her laugh, to think about how they might walk that way again soon. He did not intend to wait this time. Mr. Gardiner would dine at his townhouse, and it would counteract his memories of their only meeting to date; then, the very next day, he would call on Mr. Gardiner and ask his permission to court his niece. No one would accuse him of doing it secretly this time.

He was so caught in his reveries that he almost thought the figure was his imagination, the figure standing by the old tree, in the place he thought of as theirs. He hesitated to look again lest he disturb the illusion and then shook his head firmly to rid it of such foolish fancies. It must be another woman wearing colours Elizabeth favoured, another woman her height, with a light and pleasing figure like hers. But his body recognized the truth, and almost without volition he hurried towards her.

It *was* her. Her eyes were closed as she leaned back against the tree, like a slumbering wood nymph. The tangle of wild roses just beyond her could neither touch her beauty nor draw him like a moth to the flame as only she did. Was she there because she was thinking of him?

Her eyes flew open as he approached and took on a look of surprise. "Mr. Darcy!" she exclaimed.

The mere sound of her voice speaking his name was enough to send a wash of feeling through him. "I had not dared hope to see you here today, Miss Bennet."

A delicate colour rose in her face. "I did not know you still visited Moorsfield, sir."

"I have not in some time, but today I felt an urge to come here." His eyes continued to drink in the sight before him.

Her lips twitched in a smile. "At least your source could not have told you of my presence this time, since I did not decide on a destination until I walked out the door."

"I had no knowledge of your whereabouts, except to hope you were nearby. Perhaps some greater power drew us both here." He could not believe he had spoken his thought aloud. It was like the day in Hyde Park all over again, when his mouth kept insisting on letting out a stream of words that should have been kept within. He half expected his forward behaviour would drive her away, but she did not seem troubled by it then or now and almost seemed as if she were laughing silently, sharing the joke with him.

With an arch look, she said, "Perhaps it was the power of springtime, or of early roses in bloom."

She had saved the moment neatly, and he should be grateful for that much. "The power of new beginnings, perhaps," he said. He tied his horse to a tree and held his arm out to her. She hesitated for a moment and then with a certain air of decision, she wrapped her hand inside his elbow.

He was astonished to see she was not wearing gloves.

Astonished and delighted, since it meant he could feel her touch more through the layers of fabric, and he could hold her unprotected flesh against him. He had always loved to watch her hands, her tapering fingers always in motion, never still, as other women's so often were, but he rarely had opportunities to see them freely, unhidden by her gloves. As pretty as her kidskin gloves were—he could still see the pattern of embroidery on them, as he remembered so many details about her—they could not compare to the true beauty of her hands. He had seen them only when she played the pianoforte and when she removed her gloves to partake of refreshments, but he had studied them on those brief occasions, admiring the smooth curves of her skin, marked only by a tiny, crescent-shaped scar on the back of her forefinger. He had wondered, even back at Netherfield, what had caused that scar. Now he could see her hand closer than ever before, and he was flooded with a desire to kiss that small bit of puckered skin that only highlighted the perfection that was Elizabeth. But his sense of propriety won out, that and a fear of frightening her away. A moment too late he realized he should not be staring.

"What, Mr. Darcy, are you such a stranger to the sight of a woman's hands that it creates such amazement? Or perhaps it is shock and dismay at being found in the company of such an inelegant and immodest lady?" she asked tartly.

Only Elizabeth would have spoken to him so. Any other woman of his acquaintance would have blushed and pretended nothing had happened, but not Elizabeth, and he loved her all the more for it. He thought for a moment before responding gravely, "Perhaps I am struck dumb by the loveliness of a particular hand."

She laughed as if he had made a particularly good joke. "Oh, well done, sir; a fine recovery. As for a lady's protestations of immodesty, it is wisest to pretend you did not hear them, is it not?"

"Elizabeth, it would bring me nothing but delight if you never again wore gloves in my presence." He could tell by her sudden interest in the grass that he had gone too far. Her sparkling eyes had seduced him once again into saying what he should not. She had not reprimanded him for calling her by name, though, and surely that must be a good sign. But he must not press his luck too far. With a quick movement he stripped off his own gloves and stuffed them in his pocket. "There, Miss Bennet, now we are equals, and you may think as ill of me as you choose."

It must have been the right thing to do, because she looked up at him, really looked at him, as if she could see all the way to his soul. "You need not fear, sir; I shall tell no one of the gross impropriety of your behaviour. Your reputation will remain unsullied."

He would have laughed, if he were not held captive by the depth of her dark eyes. "You are all kindness, Miss Bennet. I am glad to know I can rely on your discretion."

Her face lit up with amusement at his words, sending a flush of happiness up his spine. If he did not break her gaze, he would not be able to stop himself from kissing her. Somehow he managed to tear his gaze away, but he felt the loss so keenly that, with great daring, he placed his own bare hand on top of hers.

She gave a smothered gasp, but said nothing, which was just as well, since he could not have possibly heard anything over the sound of blood rushing through his ears. Elizabeth's warm skin against his palm was like an electric sensation, and he was elated at her lack of protest. Beyond elated, especially when their fingers, as if under their own power, intertwined.

He could not misunderstand this signal. Flooded with exultation and anticipation that, after all they had been through, she would someday be his, he almost blurted out the words of a proposal. For once, good sense stopped him, or perhaps it was the memory of last time he spoke those words to her without thinking. No, he would do it properly this time. There would be no mistake as to his intentions, but nothing, not even those dark memories, could dim the euphoria he felt.

Although she said nothing, the pressure of her fingers clasping his was all the reassurance and happiness he needed. It was a moment too precious for words, in any case. He wondered what she was thinking. This touch must be more intimate than she would have received from a gentleman before. Her cheeks were flushed, and he had no doubt his were the same.

Elizabeth wished the moment would never end, but she knew it was unfair to raise Darcy's hopes any further. Still, finding the strength to say what she must was a Herculean labour, especially when she was so exquisitely aware of his fingers clasping hers. Now was the moment for her resolution to be executed, though, while her courage was high.

"Mr. Darcy, as much as I would not wish this interlude to end, there is something I must tell you, something you may not be happy to hear."

His face grew pale, and his grip on her hand tightened. "Are you already promised to someone else?"

His question was so unexpected that she might have laughed, but for the gravity of the situation. "No, it is nothing of that sort. I travel to Hertfordshire in the morning, and I do not know when, or if, I shall return."

His pallor turned to a look of concern. "Is someone ill?"

"No, but there is dreadful news, and I cannot conceal it from you." She took a deep breath. "My youngest sister has compromised herself in an unmistakable manner, one which will have lasting consequences. She will take my place at my uncle's house, in hopes that gossip will not follow. But Meryton is a small town, and secrecy there is impossible."

"I am grieved—shocked," Darcy replied in a low voice. "But what of the man responsible for her state? Is it certain he will not do the proper thing?"

Tears welled to her eyes as she imagined what he must think of her. "I do not know the particulars, save that he denies knowledge of her. She has no money, no connections, nothing that can tempt him. She is lost forever."

"What has been done, what has been attempted, to preserve her honour?"

With a hollow feeling deep inside, Elizabeth withdrew her hand from his arm. The least *she* could do to preserve the family's honour was avoid causing any further embarrassment. "Nothing can be done; I know very well that nothing can be done. How is such a man to be worked upon? Who could defend her honour? My uncle, with five children of his own? My brother, Mr. Browning, who has never held a weapon in his life? It is in every way horrible."

Darcy's lips thinned. "What is his name?"

Horror washed through her. She had not thought he might take her words as a reproach. Even if she could never be his wife, she could not bear it if he were hurt or killed. "No! You must promise me you will not! Promise me!"

"Do not fear for me. Though I would be willing, there are more powerful tools at my disposal than a pistol. Is he in the militia? A word with his commanding officer—"

She shook her head, guilty for the relief that he would be safe. "I do not know his name or his situation." She wrapped her arms around herself and shivered, although the day was warm.

His voice softened. "Come, you are not well. Allow me to escort you to your uncle's house."

She knew what that meant. He must have finally recognized the impossibility of their situation. "Very well," she said quietly.

To her surprise, he held out his arm, a challenging look on his face. She hesitated. Nothing good could come from more intimacy. They were destined to part when they reached Gracechurch Street, but if a few minutes more was all she could have of him, she would make the most of it. Deliberately she took his arm and was rewarded by a smile on his lips and a promise in his eyes. His warm hand once again found hers as he drew her closer to his side.

She put all thought of the future from her mind and concentrated on the present, on the strength of the tall figure beside her, the fine weave of his coat sleeve beneath her fingers, the scent of new leather and horses that accompanied him, the deep timbre of his voice as he asked if there was anything he could do for her present relief. She hardly knew what she said in response, so caught up was she in the moment.

Too soon they were at her uncle's door. Darcy was slow to release her hand, slow enough that Elizabeth feared the neighbours would notice the novel sight of an elegant gentleman's attentions to her. It did not matter what they saw; soon enough she would be far from Cheapside and their gossip.

Darcy's fingers tightened on hers as he bowed over her hand. "I wish you a pleasant journey, Miss Bennet."

"I thank you, Mr. Darcy, and… may God bless you." She held his eyes for one long moment and then hurried up the stairs and into the house.

Darcy did not move. He could not tear himself from the sight of the door that had closed behind Elizabeth. He knew she would not come out again, but he wished to be as near to her as he could. He could not stand there all day, so he turned on his heel and strode back the way they had come, until he reached the edge of Moorsfield, where Charlie stood guard over his horse.

The boy grinned impishly as Darcy paid him for his labours. "Thank ye, sir. Always happy to be of service."

Darcy nodded and took the reins, but as he was about to mount, the boy's words echoed in his ears. He turned back decisively towards Charlie. "Would you be interested, then, if I had further employment for you, a position that would require some weeks of your time, as well as your discretion?"

Charlie's face lit up. "Of course. What is it ye want me to do?"

"I will explain it to you at my house. Can you come there yet today?"

The boy cast a practised look at the sun. "You can count on me, sir."

Chapter 9

Charlie looked more out of place than ever in Darcy's study, making Darcy wonder briefly about the wisdom of his idea. "You seem to be a clever lad. Do you learn quickly?"

"Very quickly, sir," the boy said stoutly.

"Good, for you must learn a great deal about millinery."

His face took on a comical look of surprise. "Millinery, sir?"

"Yes, millinery," Darcy said dryly. "I have no doubts about your spying skill, but this requires specialized knowledge."

Charlie looked smug. "I won't let you down, sir."

"Very good." Darcy rang the bell. He had told Mary to expect his summons, so she appeared promptly. "Mary, I have a special task I wish you to undertake. This young man needs to learn about millinery. Can you take him in hand and teach him?"

"Millinery, sir?" Her tone was an unconscious echo of Charlie's. "Sir, I don't know much about it."

"No, but you are far more expert than I, or any other man, I doubt not. Take him around to shops and teach him which ribbons are fine and which are not. Can you do that?" Darcy noticed Mary eyeing the boy's rags. "Find him some respectable clothes first, and clean him up."

Mary looked at him as if he had lost his mind, but she curtsied and said, "Very well, sir."

"You will need to make some purchases, I imagine, lest the shop owners wonder at your presence." He rummaged in his pocket and held out several shillings. She took the coins gingerly, with a sidelong glance at the boy. "I do not want to hear other members of the household speaking of this matter, do you understand?"

"Yes, sir." She seemed even more confused.

"Thank you, Mary." He waved them out of the room. Settling back in his familiar leather chair, he tapped his fingers against his lips thoughtfully.

Mrs. Bennet greeted her newly arrived daughter from her sickbed with expressions of delight Elizabeth had not expected. Apparently she had grown in her mother's favour during her long absence, or perhaps it was simply the novelty of a change.

She kissed her mother's cheek, feeling the heat of a low fever in it, yet grateful it was no worse. She settled herself in the hard-backed chair beside the bed, anticipating a long litany of complaints regarding her mother's health and nerves, but to Elizabeth's surprise, Mrs. Bennet asked first how the townsfolk had greeted her on her arrival.

Elizabeth brushed a speck of road dust from her skirt. "I saw only Mr. Daniels at the posting inn, and he enquired after you quite civilly."

"That is the best we may hope for, I suppose. Lord, Lizzy, how did this calamity come upon us?"

"Do you speak of my unfortunate sister?"

Mrs. Bennet waved her handkerchief weakly. "What else? Your uncle's clerk was about to offer for Kitty, I am sure of it, but now he will have nothing to do with her. Why did my dear Lydia have to be so foolish? I have told her a thousand times that a man will not buy the cow when he gets the milk for free. I am sure she could have landed a fine husband had she kept her wits about her."

Elizabeth blushed at her mother's crudity. "Lydia said no one here knew of her condition."

"No one *knows*, it is true, but there are always rumours, and Lieutenant Ralston, whom we all thought so charming, has boasted of his conquest. Apparently he had no intent to wed her; he thought her portion too small. If only they had married, how lovely it would have been!"

"There is no point in thinking of what might have been," Elizabeth said briskly. "Perhaps it will all be forgotten in a few months."

"Do not tell me not to think on it! If only *you* had married

Mr. Collins as I told you, none of this would have happened. We would still be at Longbourn, and Lydia with us."

It might be true, but poverty and disgrace were a preferable outcome. Elizabeth reached down and plumped her mother's pillow. She wondered how she would bear living in these crowded quarters with the constant litany from her mother.

The conversation continued for nearly half an hour. Afterwards, Elizabeth realized her mother had not once mentioned her nerves. It was almost as if she were a different person from the woman who had been mistress of Longbourn. Her understanding was no deeper than it ever was, and her silliness could not be denied, but there was some change, a practicality Elizabeth had never recognized in her mother before. She wondered whether her nervous complaints had ceased because there was no one to attend to them, or perhaps because she no longer lived with a man who alternately mocked and ignored her. Having contemplated marriage to Mr. Griggs, a man she did not love, had taught Elizabeth to consider her parents' marriage in a new light.

The following morning dawned with mist softening the rough edges of Meryton and dampness masking the sour odor of too many people living in too small a space. Elizabeth had slept restlessly, sharing a bed with her mother, whose tossings, turnings, and mutterings did not bespeak a refreshing sleep. Still, her mother's body was no longer hot to the touch, and her breathing sounded less raspy, so Elizabeth determined it would be safe for her to leave briefly to seek out Jane.

It was already late enough that many villagers were astir, and several stopped to greet Elizabeth, slowing her progress. Eventually she made her way to Mr. Browning's shop, where she had often taken her custom in her younger, more carefree days, but then Jane had been by her side. Now, as she pushed the shop door open, causing a small bell to tinkle, she found Jane behind the counter, sorting through a bin of coloured threads.

Jane's face lit up at the sight of her sister, and she hurried to embrace Elizabeth. Elizabeth's eyes burned with tears of happiness to be with her beloved sister again. Jane's slim figure was unrecognizable with pregnancy, but nothing could disguise her beauty.

"Oh, Lizzy, I am so glad you are returned!" Jane drew out a handkerchief from her pocket and dabbed at her eyes. "I have missed you so. Mama has been frantic with worry over Lydia." She glanced over her shoulder, as if to make sure no one had overheard.

Elizabeth gripped Jane's hands. "I am sorry you have been left with so many burdens, but now I am here to share them. And you? Are you well?"

"I have no complaints. I am a little weary of swollen hands and feet, and I tire more easily than I would like, but it will be over soon enough. It will be so much easier, now that you are here. I will not fear my confinement so much, knowing you will be there."

Elizabeth wondered who would have helped Jane through her delivery otherwise. Kitty, perhaps. Their mother might do more harm than good.

The bell jingled again as an older townswoman entered the shop. Jane immediately turned her attention to the new customer, patiently showing her the buttons and trims she requested. Elizabeth, uncomfortable seeing Jane in this role, wandered about the shop as if examining the notions. The shop was cleaner and tidier than she recalled, with more light, despite the cloudy skies outside. A ginger cat sat in a corner, licking herself daintily. When Elizabeth drew near, the cat skittered away to crouch under a table and became preoccupied with some phantom cat-interest in the corner, her ears back and tail lashing. Her antics entertained Elizabeth until the customer departed.

When Elizabeth could once again claim her sister's attention, she ran her fingertip along the edge of a satin ribbon displayed on a side table. "Jane, Mr. Browning knew what he was about when he asked you to marry him. I recognize your touch here. The shop is more inviting, and the ribbon was never this fine before."

Jane, one hand on her lower back, settled onto a stool beside the counter. "Thank you, but it is not all my doing. I arrange the wares, but Mr. Browning is responsible for the choice of goods. He has expanded the notions, as you see, and we carry more fabrics and hats, but that is because we have a new seamstress and have invested in more merchandise. We have been fortunate."

There was a thump from the back corner, and the cat reappeared, proudly carrying a squirming mouse in her mouth.

"And you have a useful cat," said Elizabeth. "But the shop must have become more successful to allow the greater investment."

Jane shook her head. "Mr. Browning found an investor. He was correct; better merchandise has improved our custom."

It was a shock to hear Jane sound like a shopkeeper. It was not just her words; her new status showed in her appearance as well. Although she was as lovely as ever, Jane wore a less ornate hairstyle and a simpler dress. Still, she seemed content enough. Elizabeth wished she shared Jane's gift for finding happiness in trying situations. Now that her own hopes had been dashed once more, she found Meryton stifling.

Noticing the dark circles of fatigue under Jane's eyes, Elizabeth said, "Perhaps I can assist you, now that I am here."

"Oh, Lizzy! I could never ask you to work in the store!"

Yet Jane did not hesitate to take such labour on herself. Elizabeth forced herself to laugh. "I am not afraid of hard work, and it will give me an excuse to be away from Aunt Philips's rooms. And this way I can see to it that you rest occasionally."

The relief on Jane's face was reward enough. "I cannot say the assistance would be unwelcome, but are you certain, Lizzy?"

"Of course," Elizabeth said stoutly. Her courage would rise to meet the occasion.

Elizabeth had never realized how hard shopkeepers worked until she took Jane's place in the shop, nor had she given a thought to how shops were run. It looked simple when one could just stroll in and buy what one wished. It was another matter completely to keep the displays always neat and free of dust and soot, to keep the fire burning, and to perform the endless little sewing tasks, not to mention writing out bills by candlelight after the shop had closed. She had not realized the magnitude of Jane's sacrifice for her family's sake, but Mr. Browning paid the apothecary who cared for Mrs. Bennet, helped with her bills at the butcher and greengrocer, and provided Kitty—and Lydia before her—with pretty trinkets from his stock. Elizabeth had to admit his generosity could not be faulted, but she could not forget how much Jane might have been spared had she herself chosen to accept Mr. Collins. Elizabeth did not mind paying the price herself for her decision, but it was hard to see Jane suffer for it.

She was relieved when Mr. Browning announced that he had made arrangements to take on a new apprentice. Elizabeth hoped he would arrive before Jane's confinement, so that she could spend more time with her sister during that time, but either Mr. Browning chose to keep that information to himself, or perhaps he did not know.

Elizabeth's solace came from seeing Jane's greater comfort as a result of her labours. Elizabeth's long walks in the early morning to her favourite haunts prepared her for the even longer days inside the shop with hardly a breath of fresh air.

In occasional free moments, she wrote letters to her aunt and cousins filled with amusing details of life in Meryton.

She tried hard to keep Mr. Darcy from her mind, but without success. Her busy days could distract her, but each night thoughts of him returned to her as she lay waiting for sleep to come, and memories of their last walk, his fingers entwined with hers, created both joy and sadness. She did not know if she would ever see him again, a thought that caused many a wakeful night where she would press her hand against her cheek trying to regain that magic moment. Then her mother would complain that Elizabeth was disturbing her rest, and she would try to stay as still as possible until sleep finally took her away.

How could he maintain an interest in her now, with her situation so drastically beneath his? She knew that he should give her up rather than risk scandal and disgrace, but his interest in her had persisted so long already, through so many setbacks, that she could not give up hope completely that somehow he would find a way. She would have no answer, though, until he either appeared or until she gave up any hope, and the waiting was agonizing.

A fortnight after her return to Meryton, she received a letter from Mrs. Gardiner. Elizabeth opened it eagerly, scanning through it until a familiar name jumped out at her.

Mr. Darcy called a week ago, no doubt in search of intelligence about you. Lydia's behaviour could not be trusted that morning, so I dared not admit him. Bates tells me he asked when you might return to London. He is a little forward, I must say; but perhaps in this circumstance it is understandable. Once this is behind us, we must make a point of inviting Mr. Darcy and his sister to dinner.

Elizabeth read the paragraph several times over, as if in hope of finding new information. Surely it must be a good sign that he had sought her out once more. A hot surge of hope rushed through her. How could she possibly bear the uncertainty?

As Jane's time drew nearer, Elizabeth spent more time at the Brownings, usually assisting in the shop so Jane could rest. She did not mind the work so much when it made the laggard hours go more swiftly. She developed a certain respect for Mr. Browning, discovering that his mind was sharper than she thought, albeit his education and manner of speech were sometimes lacking. She had once again judged only on appearances.

It was painful when old friends and acquaintances shopped there, though. Some were overly sympathetic, some were condescending, and a few pretended not to know her; but none could be completely neutral. Elizabeth knew she would find it equally difficult to be waited upon by someone she considered an equal, and understood the sympathetic acquaintances; but the others made her wish she could speak as freely as when her father had been alive.

When such customers came in, Elizabeth took to retiring to the back of the store, where there was always plenty of extra sewing work to be done. She told herself it was not so different from embroidering in the sitting room at Longbourn. She still had much to be thankful for and was determined to follow Jane's example and make the best of her reduced circumstances.

Charlotte Collins was among the few old acquaintances Elizabeth was happy to see at the shop. Charlotte had made an effort to keep their friendship alive, although Elizabeth still refused to visit Longbourn when Mr. Collins was present. Her spirits lightened when Charlotte came into the shop one sunny day in search of new scarlet ribbons.

They chatted about mutual acquaintances and village gossip for some time while Charlotte was choosing her ribbons. "Lizzy, what think you of this one? Will it suit my bonnet?"

"Oh, yes," Elizabeth said in her old teasing way. "Its glory will strike Mr. Collins blind when he sees you wear it."

Charlotte laughed as Elizabeth cut the length of ribbon and rolled it up neatly. She held it out, but Charlotte did not immediately take it. Instead, her gaze seemed fixed on Elizabeth's hand. Charlotte lightly touched the chapped skin of her fingers. "Oh, Lizzy, I am so sorry."

Elizabeth fought the impulse to snatch her hands away. "It is nothing. Please do not think on it again."

Charlotte held her gaze for a moment and then took the ribbon and put it in her reticule. She bit her lip and said, "Sometimes I fear that I supplanted you."

"Nonsense! You are not to blame for the entail." Elizabeth

was sure that if Charlotte had her way, Mr. Collins would have been more generous in his dealings with the Bennet family, but he had his petty revenge to extract.

Charlotte leaned towards her and spoke in a low voice. "Do you ever wish that you had accepted Mr. Collins?"

Elizabeth blinked, surprised her friend would even ask the question. "Of course not! I am glad he has made you happy, but I would prefer to scrub floors night and day, if it came to that. You were right that I should have thought more practically of my future in those days, but not *that* practically!"

Elizabeth was relieved when Charlotte laughed. "I fear you could never be that practical, Lizzy."

Mr. Browning emerged from the storeroom at the sound of their merriment. Charlotte glanced at him and said, "Perhaps we could walk together tomorrow morning, Lizzy."

"I would like that." It meant a great deal to have a friend there, and it helped her forget that had she only been slower to anger, she might be living in the elegant house on Brook Street with Mr. Darcy instead of working in a shop. The familiar sense of longing for his presence flooded her, but she reminded herself she must not think of him. She must learn to be content with the life she had.

Chapter 10

Once Charlotte took her leave, Elizabeth took up a half-trimmed bonnet, held it this way, then that, and then chose a new violet ribbon to edge it. She hummed quietly to herself as she set to work, sitting in the corner by the window where the light was best. The ginger cat, as was her habit, curled up by her feet.

The bell tinkled again, but when Elizabeth looked up, she saw Mr. Browning moving towards the door, so she did not rise. A gentleman entered, doffing his hat, followed by a young lad.

Elizabeth's hand stilled, her needle halfway through the ribbon. For a moment she did not believe her eyes, but she would never forget the figure he cut, his decisive step, the swing of his frock coat. He had not noticed her yet, off in the corner. Her mouth dry, she stole the opportunity to look her fill. The light filtering in the shop window seemed to throw his profile into sharp relief. Belatedly she rose to her feet.

Mr. Browning bustled forward to meet him. "Mr. Darcy! What a pleasure to see you in Meryton again, sir!"

Darcy handed his hat to the boy at his side. "Thank you. You received my letter?"

Elizabeth almost dropped the bonnet in surprise. Mr. Darcy writing to Mr. Browning? She could not imagine he patronized local stores to any extent when he had visited Netherfield, and that had been long ago, in any case. He had never given any hint of a connection when she had spoken to him about her worries for Jane, all those months earlier.

"Indeed I did, sir, and is this the young man you mentioned?"

"Yes, this is Charlie. Perhaps you would like to speak with him for a few minutes to judge whether he will suit."

"Oh, that won't be necessary, sir. Your recommendation is all I require. I am sure he will be completely satisfactory."

Darcy cast a sidelong glance at the boy. "He has never been outside London and is not accustomed to small towns."

Darcy's recommendation? Elizabeth could not miss the implication of the words. She had told him about Jane, and then Mr. Browning had found an investor. It could not be a coincidence. Had it been for her sake? Her heart knew the answer, though he had told her nothing of it. Mr. Darcy, dabbling in trade, for her sake.

The boy's gaze wandered around the shop until he discovered her, and then he tugged at Mr. Darcy's sleeve and whispered something. Darcy's head turned in her direction. When their eyes met, a shock went down her spine. Her feet seemed rooted to the floor. The first sight of his slight smile brought her a happy thrill, though, and she thought he must be able to see her heart in her eyes. Perhaps it would all turn out well after all.

Darcy's pulse hammered. He had not expected Elizabeth to be in the shop; his plan had been to call on her once he had disposed of Charlie. Seeing her form lit by filtered sunlight took his breath away.

Mr. Browning must have noted his loss of interest in their conversation, for he said, "Mr. Darcy, did you make the acquaintance of my wife's sister, Miss Bennet, when you visited Netherfield? She has been assisting me in the shop. I am sure she will appreciate a set of strong young hands to help here."

Darcy frowned. Elizabeth was *working* in the shop? How could her family permit it? Helping with her young cousins and being dependent on her uncle's good will had been troubling enough, but working as a shopgirl, where any casual passerby could demand her attention and she would have no recourse but to respond—it was completely intolerable. It took all his self-control not to take her by the arm and drag her out of that place.

Elizabeth said quietly, "Mr. Darcy and I are indeed acquainted." She seemed subdued, and her cheeks were scarlet.

Mr. Browning rubbed his hands together. "Ah, very good,

very good. Mr. Darcy, perhaps you would like Miss Bennet to show you some samples of our wares."

Darcy had to say something. He could not simply stand there as if frozen by Medusa, but he could find no words. Her presence, compounded by his discovery of her activities, robbed him of the ability to think.

Elizabeth, apparently taking pity on him, said, "You might find something Miss Darcy would like, although our goods cannot compare to those in London."

Her melodic voice woke him from his stupor. He said gravely, "When it comes to beauty, I do not think London offers any advantage over Meryton."

If anything, her cheeks became a deeper red. "What would you like to see? We have some silk shawls, or perhaps a bonnet?"

How could he possibly allow Elizabeth to wait upon him? It was impossible, yet he could not leave without speaking further to her. "I have something quite particular in mind." He hoped she would understand his emphasis. "But perhaps that can wait; I need some fresh air after sitting in a carriage all morning. I recall, Miss Bennet, that you know all the finest walks in the area. Perhaps Mr. Browning could spare you for an hour."

Mr. Browning smiled broadly. "Of course, Mr. Darcy! As long as you like."

Elizabeth hid a smile. It was fortunate that *she* did not object, since Mr. Browning seemed determined to give Mr. Darcy whatever his heart might desire. An odd sensation trickled through her at the thought that she might be his heart's desire, but she wondered who the boy might be. There was something familiar about his gamin features. Perhaps he was a distant Darcy relation, or one not so distant, but on the wrong side of the blanket. She bit her lip in a rush of jealousy, but she could not imagine that Mr. Darcy's pride would allow even an illegitimate child of his to work in a shop. She had seen his horrified look when he realized her position.

She hurried to fetch her bonnet and gloves, impatient for the chance to speak to him and to discover his intention in coming to Meryton, and whether it would fulfill her dearest dreams.

Darcy seemed disinclined to say anything as they walked through Meryton, though. Elizabeth was conscious of curious eyes watching them. When they reached the outskirts of town, she could no longer stand the silence and uncertainty. "It has been a long time since I have seen you in Hertfordshire, Mr. Darcy. I did not know you maintained connections here."

"A few."

She felt oddly tongue-tied. Did his terseness indicate displeasure, or was he facing his own anxieties? "I hope Miss Darcy is well," she ventured.

"Quite well. And you? Are you pleased to be in Meryton once again? You must enjoy your walks in the countryside again."

"That is one of my pleasures." She need not tell him of the difficulty of living in her Aunt Philips's crowded home, and it did not matter now, anyway, not when he was beside her. Instead, she gave him an arch smile. "Jane told me that someone had invested in her husband's shop, but it did not occur to me it might be you. I had not realized you took such an interest in trade."

"It is nothing. I hoped you might worry less about your sister if her situation were more comfortable. I did not intend for you to know my part in it."

From his embarrassed look, she was sure he wished she had not discovered his secret. "I thank you."

"Please do not thank me. I did it to relieve my own mind."

She decided not to quibble, since he seemed determined to refuse credit. "It was a very selfish action on your part, then, sir. Is it my fate to never be permitted to thank you for anything?"

He laughed. "Miss Bennet, you are far too adroit at twisting my words."

His laughter lifted her spirits, but he did not seem to have anything further to say. She wished she had the right to say something to him, but it was a woman's role to wait, however little it suited her lively temperament. She played with the ribbon of her bonnet, glancing up to see his eyes on her in a manner that gave her a strangely warm feeling inside. She had to fight the impulse to draw closer to him. Instead, she turned her gaze to the sheep grazing in the field by the side of the road. What could she speak of now?

"That boy—is he a connection of yours?" She tried not to put undue stress on the words, which of course made it sound stilted, the exact thing she wished to avoid.

He tightened his lips. "No. He did me a service once, and I am returning the favour."

She felt embarrassed to have asked, since he clearly wished to avoid the subject. "For some reason he seemed a little familiar to me, but no doubt many young boys have that look."

His mouth quirked endearingly. "I first encountered Charlie on Gracechurch Street. That would no doubt account for it."

"On Gracechurch Street?" she exclaimed.

"Yes. One of his friends was the cook's boy at your uncle's house."

The letter that had appeared in her room, and Darcy's mysterious knowledge of her whereabouts. "*He* was your agent, then."

"He is a very enterprising lad."

"Does that mean he will be reporting back to you from Meryton?" She gave him a teasing look.

Darcy hesitated. "He cannot write."

"You did not answer my question, sir."

Darcy seemed to have developed an overwhelming interest in the carriage ruts on the road. Finally he said, "No, I did not."

This further evidence of his concern for her sent a thrill down her spine, but her dismay at the thought of having Darcy learn more of her menial activities outweighed the pleasure. "I do not require supervision, sir," she said tartly.

His cheeks flushed as he straightened, his haughty look back on his face. "I did not expect you would be in the shop, just near enough that he could see you occasionally. He will not spy on you. I wish reassurance as to your well-being, not knowledge of your private affairs." At her dubious look, he sighed and straightened his hat. "Eliz… Miss Bennet, can you not put yourself in my position? Imagine that someone you cared for was… facing challenges. Would you wish to spend months fretting over what she might be suffering, or would you seek a way to know if she needed assistance?"

Elizabeth's breath caught. "I am not in a position to accept your assistance."

"That could change." He seemed to be speaking to the leaves of the tree overhead.

She had to find the resolve to speak, though her pulse was pounding. "Could it truly? I cannot imagine that your family and friends would have approved of such an alliance, even before shame came on my family. Now it seems impossible. How could you countenance such a connection? My sister's disgrace makes me wholly unsuitable even to converse with your sister, much less to claim a relationship."

She did not know what reaction to expect, but it was certainly not that Mr. Darcy would freeze in place, his eyes closed, with an expression of such pain that she longed to comfort him. When he spoke, his voice was rough. "Pray do not speak so. Your family is as deserving as mine."

She touched his arm lightly, astonished at her own daring, but wishing only to ease his distress. "That is untrue. I appreciate your attempt to protect my sensibilities, but I can face the truth."

"I speak the truth. Miss Bennet, I need a moment to compose my thoughts, and greater privacy than an open roadway. Is there not a bench in the churchyard where we might rest a moment?"

Curious, and more than a little worried, Elizabeth led the way to the marble bench behind the church. Had he somehow known it was one of her favourite retreats, or was it but chance? The gnarled old oak she had once climbed as a young child shaded them from the sun and from peering eyes. The chill of the marble reached through her thin dress as she sat.

Mr. Darcy, despite his words, seemed disinclined to join her, and instead peered at an old gravestone. Her mind tried to race ahead of itself to discover his thoughts, as if bracing her against ill tidings.

At one moment he looked up, and she thought he was about to speak, but then he sighed heavily and turned to yet another gravestone. She had the distinct sensation he was oblivious to the words carved in it long before. Finally he began. "Please understand that this is difficult for me to speak of, and no less a situation than this could bring me to disclose it. I have a cousin, a young man who married several years ago. He recently adopted a child, who is generally considered to be a by-blow of mine. I have not discouraged the notion."

Her stomach clenched at the idea of him with another woman, though there must have been more than one. "Mr. Darcy, you need not tell me this."

He held up a hand to stop her. "I did not father him. I do not claim to be a saint, but that cannot be laid at my doorstep. The child is my nephew."

His nephew? But he had no brothers or sisters other than Miss Darcy, who was far too young for such an event. She could not imagine the shy young girl in such a position. She was still so young, no older than Lydia. But Lydia was in the same state. A horrified understanding dawned upon her. "*Miss Darcy*?"

He raised pained eyes to hers. "Two summers ago, when she was but fifteen, an old family friend came to see her and led her to believe herself in love with him. He took advantage of her innocence and then persuaded her to agree to an elopement to cover her shame. By God's grace I was fortunate enough to discover it before it occurred, but she was already—" He shook his head. "The man in question was George Wickham. His object was her dowry of thirty thousand pounds."

She had never imagined Mr. Wickham so vicious that he would risk ruining a young girl's life. "Poor girl," she said. "I had no idea."

"Apart from Colonel Fitzwilliam, you are the only one who knows the story. We arranged for Georgiana to retire to the country under an assumed name until the child was born. I came to Netherfield to avoid any questions about her whereabouts. There I met you. I fear I was not amiable company at the time."

No wonder he showed so little interest in the neighbourhood and its inhabitants. How little she had understood of him! She wished she could take back every saucy speech, every impertinence she had made to him then. "What a trial for all of you."

"Indeed, but no greater a trial than you face now. So you see, your family is no different from mine, except I had the resources to hide the unfortunate truth."

"But in Lydia's case, it was a foolish act in keeping with a lifetime of foolishness, not one mistake in judgment."

He swung to face her, unexpected anger in his mien. "Does that matter? Georgiana knew better. She had the finest care and education available. No matter the circumstances, she knew she should not allow him to touch her. She knew an elopement would disgrace the family. She knew it, and did it anyway, risking her future and mine and the Darcy family name. Her only excuse was her age, but even at fifteen, she should not have made such a choice." The tone of bitterness was unmistakable.

"It can be difficult for a young girl in love to make good decisions," Elizabeth said in an effort to offer comfort, still shocked at the magnitude of the secret he had disclosed.

"So you forgive your own sister for her faults?" His voice was sharp.

"I would, if she showed any sign of remorse and evidence of learning from her errors. But my sister would do the same again tomorrow, had she the opportunity. Would Miss Darcy do so?"

The lines of his face relaxed slightly. "No. She has been terrified of the slightest improper behaviour since then. She is just now beginning to regain her spirits."

She could see his anger was not completely passed. "And are you yourself not now contemplating an alliance that is ill-advised at best?

Darcy was silent for a moment and then he sat beside Elizabeth on the bench, his long legs resting to one side. He took her gloved hand in his. Elizabeth was too embarrassed to look up, but she felt all the power of his affection and the protection he wished to offer her. It was a moment before she realized that the pressure on her fingertips was because of his tugging on her glove. A fire seemed to kindle inside her at the realization that he planned to remove it. The smooth kidskin slipped away easily, but Darcy paused with her hand half revealed, as if asking her permission to continue.

When she made no protest, he made a slight sound of satisfaction and peeled the glove away. Elizabeth, dizzy with the sensation of exposure and his attentions, did not immediately realize the import of the harsh exhalation he made then, as she turned her averted eyes to gaze at him, she saw his pained look. With a sinking feeling, she realized the reason.

She had to fight the impulse to hide her chapped fingers; they seemed to have a will of their own and a desire to disappear. There was nothing to say. Her hands bore silent witness to the manual labours she had undertaken, and there was no disguising it. She would not allow herself to feel shame for doing what she must, so she raised her chin and looked off into the distance, as if his reaction did not trouble her.

"Elizabeth." His voice was little more than a hoarse whisper. "Let me take you back to London. I can speak with your uncle tomorrow."

She shook her head, tears stinging the corners of her eyes. "I cannot leave. I am needed here."

"Elizabeth, I cannot have you working in a shop!"

Elizabeth's lips tightened. "As it happens, it is not your decision, Mr. Darcy. I made the choice to work there, and I will continue to do so."

"I admire your courage and resolution, but surely you must realize—"

She overrode his words. "Surely *you* must realize that given a choice between knowing that my sister, who is close to her confinement and not well, must do the work, or doing it myself, I will do it."

"Mr. Browning can hire an assistant. I will speak to him about it."

"And leave what remains of my reputation in shambles?" she said. "I think not, sir. Besides, he would expect Jane to do the work, and she would do it. Or am I to suppose you would allow Miss Darcy to be in such a situation when you yourself could take on the burden and spare her?"

"Of course not." He struggled to regain control. "Please, Miss Bennet, I have no wish to quarrel with you, and although my ill-chosen words may rightly anger you, the sentiment behind them is well meant."

"Perhaps you should take that as your motto, sir."

"If it meant you understood that I wish nothing but the best for you, I would do so."

Embarrassed, Elizabeth made a half-hearted attempt to remove her hand from his in order to hide it once again in its glove, but she was not sorry when he resisted her attempt. She said, "Mr. Darcy, I seem to be missing something. Perhaps you should return it."

"Why?" His voice was low, far from his earlier anger. "You have had possession of my heart for these many months. Surely you can spare this lovely token for a few minutes."

"It is hardly lovely at present, sir."

Darcy's eyes darkened in a way that made Elizabeth forget to breathe. He raised her hand and tenderly brushed his lips along the back of one finger, then the next, until he had kissed each one, each touch seeming to reach deep inside her. "It is a hand that bears witness to love and an admirable devotion. It is full of beauty."

Elizabeth felt that she could no longer trust her heart not to jump out of her chest. She could not look away, and her fingers still felt the touch of his lips like a brand. When his gaze dropped to her mouth, the tension became almost unbearable.

A rustling behind them caused Darcy to drop her hand and move away abruptly. They sat in utter silence and stillness for a frightening moment. A small brown rabbit hopped across the path, pausing to stand on its hind legs and regard them quizzically, as if wondering what they were doing in his churchyard. Elizabeth's laughter sent him fleeing into the brush.

Darcy flexed his fingers. "A false alarm, but a proper reminder, I am sorry to say. Forgive my presumption, Miss Bennet."

"There is nothing to forgive. I think it unlikely that our small friend will gossip," Elizabeth teased, but she restored the glove to her hand. It was better this way; it would be too easy to allow further liberties, especially when they gave her such pleasure. "But we must return. Mr. Browning cannot spare me for long."

Darcy frowned darkly, but said, "As you wish."

She moved closer to him, wishing to see his smile again. "No doubt the presence of an apprentice will lighten the load for everyone."

"I can only hope so." He shifted slightly, but made no move to stand. "Will you promise to tell me if you are in need of assistance?"

"That is easier said than done," she said lightly. In truth, she was reluctant to make such a promise. There were too many possible circumstances of which she might wish him to remain in ignorance. "I have no means to contact you."

"The boy knows how to reach me and is discreet." Darcy's look begged for her understanding.

Elizabeth arched an eyebrow. "I am sure of it."

"Will you tell me, then?"

She knew the question went much further than the stated request. Suddenly struggling for breath, she said, "If you wish it, I will."

The tension between them became greater, like the air before a thunderstorm. "I wish it," he said, his voice almost a whisper. "That and much more. I hope you do not object."

She needed to break the spell of the moment. "I am not sorry to hear it," she said with a smile, "Though it mystifies me."

"Mystifies you? How so?"

"The same reason all of your relatives will be mystified. You could choose an heiress, a titled lady, a great society beauty, yet you are here in a country town with a woman of no prospects, no connections, and whose beauty you early withstood. I do not seek to devalue myself, but I do not begin to match your family's expectations. Is that not reason enough for mystification? Or perhaps you chose me with the express purpose of discomposing your family?"

"It is nothing of the sort. I cannot explain why I must be with you, except to say that the sun shines more brightly and the very air tastes sweeter where you are. By your side, I notice and rejoice in marvels of nature that are invisible to me otherwise. You make me wish to be a better man, and you remind me that there is still good in the human soul. When you laugh, I want to laugh as well. When you sing, it fills me with joy and a sense that all is right with the world. I cannot explain how it is that you have bewitched me, but bewitched I am."

Her throat became tight. "Perhaps it is nothing more than my impertinence."

He shook his head. "There are ladies of the *ton* who can make me laugh, but their humour is always at the expense of another. When you tease, there is no cruelty in it, only amusement. Your first thought, unlike theirs, is not for yourself. Perhaps society might think such a match ill-advised, but I do not. Your value is not in your situation, but in your soul."

Elizabeth could not but smile at him. "So the great Mr. Darcy has become an egalitarian? I cannot believe it."

"God help me, neither can I," he said fervently. "I do not know what I believe anymore. Do you know there are street children who have taken to sleeping in the mews of my house in London? The cooks feed them leftovers, and I pretend to know nothing about it. My family would tell me to evict them immediately, lest they trouble the horses, but they sleep by the horses to stay warm. Why should my horses deserve better treatment than children?"

She laughed. "You have fortunate horses indeed, to have such devoted children to watch over them at night."

He gave her a sidelong glance. "Yes, well, there is one less to watch over them now."

"The boy? You are hiring agents out of your mews?"

"Only the children. Not the horses."

Elizabeth burst out laughing at his droll look. His eyes darkened, and he raised his hand as if to touch her cheek, but paused when his fingertips were but a few inches away.

Elizabeth's skin tingled in anticipation, and she wished she did not have to stop him, but with a wry twist of his lips, he withdrew his hand and placed it by his side. She glanced down, biting her lip.

"Elizabeth, please consider what I have said. We both have much to think on, and I will not press you now, but you will be ever in my thoughts, and I hope you will not forget me."

She cocked her head to the side. "I do not think that is in the realm of possibility. You may rest easy."

"I will rest with dreams of a certain young lady, just as I always do." He took a deep breath as if trying to steady himself. "And I must return you to town now, before I begin to confuse dreams with reality."

She knew only that she did not wish to be parted from him so soon, even though it was ill-advised to stay. "You do not wish to make them reality?"

He swung to face her, his visage showing clearly how great was his temptation. "You cannot know how much I wish to make them reality, but not at the expense of your reputation."

Half relieved, half disappointed, she bit her lip once more, trying to hide her embarrassment at her forwardness and his refusal. She was about to come up with a teasing retort to lighten the moment when Darcy made a slight, half-strangled sound and moved so close to her that she could feel the warmth of his breath on her cheek. His hand was touching her cheek, and Elizabeth was consumed by a feeling new to her, a heady sense of anticipation and a deep desire for something more that she did not understand.

Time seemed to stop as he drew closer to her, his breathing ragged. She could not believe this was real; at any moment she would wake from this irresistible dream. Her eyes closed involuntarily as she felt the intimate warmth of his lips against hers. His restraint was so palpable it seemed as if the air trembled with it, yet she felt as if he were taking in the very essence of her, something no man had ever touched before. She was consumed by longing. How could so many sensations come from a mere touch of the lips? The exhilarating pleasure could not disguise her deep sense of rightness that this one particular man was kissing her.

He raised his lips from hers. His hands slipped down to her shoulders as he leaned his forehead against hers. "I cannot begin to tell you what you mean to me, Elizabeth. It is beyond my own understanding, far beyond anything I have thought myself capable of feeling. Do not keep me waiting too long, I beg of you." His voice was ragged, barely above a whisper.

She was still dizzy from his kiss. "As soon as I am free to return to London, you shall know of it."

He seemed to struggle to take a breath. "And you will not deny me?"

She had not thought it possible that her skin could burn more than it already did. How could she deny him? It would be against her every inclination. Every fiber of her longed to be with him, and for the sake of her family, she could not afford to turn him away. She hated herself for allowing such a thought to even enter her head, and it cooled the passion in her more than her own will ever could.

"Elizabeth?" he said anxiously. "I know I should not have said it, but—"

On irresistible impulse, she rose to her tiptoes and returned the kiss he had given her before, floating in the intoxication of his scent. "There is my answer, sir."

His look of heartfelt delight made it worth every bit of the risk she had taken. To feel so much joy from bringing joy to another was an unexpected gift. If only they did not have to part! Her world would feel empty once he was no longer by her side.

"I thank you." Darcy raised both her hands to his lips, propelled equally by the wish to protect her and to touch her just once more, but even then he knew he was fooling himself. A lifetime of touches would not be enough. Nothing could express the intense joy that Darcy felt or his profound relief that finally, finally all would be well.

Elizabeth had the opportunity to see Darcy once more before he left for London, after he emerged from a private meeting with Mr. Browning. At first he gave her bare acknowledgment, and she wondered with a moment of sheer terror if he had rethought the scandal she would bring with her. But then, when Mr. Browning's back was turned and there were no customers in the store, Mr. Darcy met her eyes with a warm smile, his silence telling her that his only concern was for her reputation.

The memory of that smile carried her through his departure. She tried to distract herself with her work, but her recollection of the sensation of his lips upon her fingers made her mind wander. Instead, she watched with amusement as Mr. Browning bustled about the shop as he showed Charlie where the merchandise was kept, his good mood evidence of satisfaction with his dealings with Mr. Darcy. She wondered how much more of an investment he had agreed to.

She did not have a moment alone with Charlie until the following day, but she did not miss how often his sharp eyes turned to her. She did not know whether she was more annoyed that he would be reporting her doings or pleased that Mr. Darcy had such a concern for her, but she did not intend to have her privacy invaded. "So, Charlie, I understand you are Mr. Darcy's eyes," she said tartly.

He gave her a cheeky grin. "That's right, miss."

"And what do you intend to report to him?"

"That'll be between me and Mr. Darcy, miss."

"So you follow his orders?"

"Mr. Darcy, he's a generous gentleman. I do what he says."

"So that is how the land lies! You will have no such good fortune from me, since I cannot outbid Mr. Darcy, but we can still make an agreement, you and I. After all, you would not wish *me* to report to him that you have been a lazy, disobedient apprentice."

Charlie cocked his head with what looked like admiration. "No, miss."

"We understand one another, then?"

The boy stuck out a dirty hand for her to shake.

Chapter 11

"Cousin Henry!" Georgiana exclaimed, rising to her feet. "I had not expected the honour of your company today. Welcome to Darcy House." She was still not accustomed to acting the part of the hostess, even for family. She surreptitiously wiped her hands on her skirt as she glanced around the sitting room. It was perfectly tidy, as always. There would be no cause for criticism there. The only problem was by her side. She was not supposed to sit with an upstairs maid as though they were the closest of friends, and it must be obvious they had been doing exactly that. Her brother did not mind what she did in the privacy of her own rooms, but he would not be pleased that the viscount had seen her in Mary's company.

As if reading her thoughts, Mary quickly retired to the corner farthest from the window, taking a seat in the shadows. With a piece of mending in her hand, she looked every inch the servant. Perhaps Henry might not have noticed.

"Georgiana, as lovely as ever, I see." He pressed his warm, moist lips to her cheek.

"I am sorry to say my brother is not here. I believe you can find him at his club." Georgiana in fact had no idea where her brother might be, but sending Henry off seemed preferable to an uncomfortable half hour listening to his stories, the ones that always made her feel as if she were being mocked in some indirect manner. She had cause enough to feel foolish on her own; she did not require help from her cousin.

"Then I will be happy with your charming company." Henry sat and stretched his legs in front of him as if planning a protracted stay.

An inspiration came to Georgiana. "I have just finished learning a new sonata by Mozart. Would you like to hear it? I am very proud of it." She put on her best pleading-child air. He could not tell stories while she was playing.

He laughed indulgently. "If you wish, poppet. But will you not offer me tea?"

She flushed. "Mary, will you bring some refreshments?"

"Yes, miss." Mary's voice could barely be heard, and she disappeared hastily on her errand. Henry's head swiveled as he watched her leave the room.

Oh, why had she brought his attention to Mary again? She would have to brazen it through and hope he forgot about it by their next meeting. "Mary is my new companion. I like her very much."

Henry raised a lazy eyebrow. "She is full young to be a suitable companion. Far too pretty, for that matter."

A few months earlier she would have been terrified and unable to speak. "Are companions required to be ill-favoured, then? Mary is young, yes, but Mrs. Annesley is available for those times when I require chaperonage."

"Rightly so. I cannot imagine that young thing could provide any protection."

Something about his tone made her nervous. "Shall I play now?" She did not await his answer before taking her place at the pianoforte. She made a show of flipping through her music and chose one of the longer sonatas, determined not to play it quickly, and flexed her fingers over the keyboard. The first notes were difficult; it was a challenging piece, and she always played stiffly at first when someone was listening. By the second movement, though, she escaped into the world of Mozart's music, her troublesome cousin left far behind.

When she reached the end, her fingers remained on the keyboard, as though loath to surrender their connection. She had a duty as hostess, though, so she reluctantly withdrew from the instrument.

Mary had returned in the meantime. A heavy silver tray of fruits and pastries sat on the table, and Mary was pouring tea for Henry. The porcelain cup clinked on the saucer, to Georgiana's surprise. Odd, Mary was not usually clumsy.

"Mary, are you well? You look ill," Georgiana said with concern.

"I am quite well, miss." Mary sounded subdued and withdrew to her back corner once more. Georgiana wondered if she had a headache, which would explain why she was so uncharacteristically quiet.

Henry gave a self-satisfied nod. "I knew she looked familiar. I saw her in Kent. Your *companion*, indeed, Georgiana."

"She *is* my companion, and my friend."

He examined the tray and selected a rich French pastry. "Is that what your brother calls her? I will have to speak with him."

As usual, she did not understand what amused him so. She would have to warn her brother that she had said Mary was her companion. He would not object, she was sure. "I am certain he will value your opinion," she said, trying to sound demure. Henry did not like women who asserted their beliefs.

He took a bite of the pastry and then put it aside, ignoring the crumbs that fell on the Aubusson carpet. "He is at White's, you say? Perhaps I will seek him there. I have some business to discuss with him."

Not ideal, since her brother would know nothing of their conversation, but at least it meant Henry would leave. "He would like that. I am sure he will be sorry to have missed you here."

"In that case, I will bid you adieu. Perhaps your *companion* can show me out."

Georgiana looked at Mary, who put aside her sewing with apparent reluctance. She was sorry to trouble Mary when she was not well, but there was no polite way to refuse Henry's request.

"Yes, my lord," Mary murmured. Georgiana breathed a sigh of relief as Henry followed her out. That had not gone so badly. Perhaps she was learning the knack of hostessing.

Darcy nodded to Simms as he handed the butler his hat. Finally he was home and out of the late afternoon rain, with his task successfully accomplished. Soon it would be safe to visit Elizabeth again. Not soon enough, but soon.

The butler cleared his throat. "Miss Darcy wishes to speak with you, if it please you, sir."

"Thank you, Simms." Darcy stripped off his gloves. "Tell her I will see her at supper. There is a matter I must attend to first."

"As you wish, sir." The butler's tone was deferential enough, but held a question in it.

"What is it?" Darcy asked irritably.

"I believe Miss Darcy is in low spirits. Very low, indeed."

What could have happened? She had seemed well when he left that morning. "Very well, Simms. I will see her now."

He found Georgiana in her rooms, pacing with great agitation, her eyes tearstained. She threw herself into his arms.

"Good God, what is the matter?" he exclaimed.

"Oh, Fitzwilliam! Mary has disappeared, and it is all my fault!"

"Disappeared? How could she disappear?"

Georgiana buried her head in his shoulder, the way she used to do when she was a child. "She was supposed to show Cousin Henry out, but she never returned."

"She left with him?" He could not credit such a thing.

"Simms says Henry was alone when his carriage came round, but that his hand was injured. He sent one of the servants for a bandage, but did not say why. There was nothing wrong with his hand when he left me. Poor Mary!"

"You think it had something to do with Mary?"

She wiped her face with a lace handkerchief that looked half soaked already. "It must have. I could see she did not want to go with him, but I was so glad he was leaving that I did not say anything. And no one has seen her since."

Darcy silently damned his cousin. "Then we must wait. Surely she will return when it grows dark."

Georgiana wrung her handkerchief. "That is why I am so worried! She has nowhere to go. She knows no one in London!"

There were always places an attractive young girl could go, but Darcy was not about to tell his sister that. "If she does not return by morning, I will send out men to look for her, but there is little else we can do at present."

Georgiana dissolved into sobs. In face of the pain he could do nothing to relieve, Darcy retreated to his rooms.

Supper was a somber meal. Georgiana seemed to be engaged in a constant struggle to hold back tears, and Darcy, cursing his inability to distract her with lighthearted conversation, glared at the maids in hopes that it would make them serve more quickly and give him an escape. The tense silence was finally broken when Simms appeared beside Darcy. "Yes?" Darcy said, more sharply than he had intended.

Simms glanced at Georgiana. "Mr. Darcy, Cook wishes to speak with you."

"Cook wishes to speak to me? What nonsense is this?"

Simms coughed. "Cook is in the kitchen, sir."

"Of course Cook is in the kitchen! Where else would she be?" He noticed the significant look Simms was giving him. Simms was not prone to false alarms. He threw his napkin on the table. "Very well, then."

He strode down the hallway to the kitchen at the back of the house. There, on a stool in front of the banked fire, sat Mary, wrapped in a blanket, her hair dripping. Cook was beside her, her arm around the girl's shoulder.

"There, there, Mary dear, 'twill be well; never fear."

He could barely hear Mary's response, since her voice was so broken by sobs. "I should have let him. Why did I not let him? Then I could have stayed here. It would just have been the once. Now there is only the streets, where I will have to let any man do it who will give me a shilling."

Darcy's lips tightened at the confirmation of his suspicions. Henry had gone too far this time. It might be his customary behaviour at home, but he had no business interfering with Darcy's staff. He cleared his throat. "Mary, my sister has been frantic with worry."

Her head whipped around to face him, her eyes wide. "I am so sorry, Mr. Darcy. So very, very sorry. I have been very wicked." A purple bruise covered her cheek.

Darcy raised an eyebrow. "Have you? I was under the impression, knowing my cousin, that the difficulty was that you were insufficiently wicked."

"Please do not send me away, sir. You may beat me, anything, but let me stay. I will do anything."

"I am not in the habit of beating my servants. Now tell me what happened."

Mary cast a terrified look at Cook, who nodded encouragingly. "I was showing his lordship to the door. He wanted… he wanted me to… he pulled up my skirts and put his hand over my mouth so I could not cry out, and—" She shrank away from him, silent sobs racking her body.

Darcy's stomach sank. "And what?"

"I bit him. I know I should not have, sir. I will never do it again, I promise, never!"

Despite the seriousness of the situation, he had to force back a smile. "Mary, listen carefully to me. If any man tries to force you while you are under my roof, you may bite him or hit him or kick him with my blessing. I expect you to do no less. Do I make myself clear?"

"But it was his lordship! And I hurt him!" She touched her bruised cheek gingerly. "He said you would beat me within an inch of my life and leave me on the streets."

"Apparently he does not know me as well as he thinks.

Do you think I would wish my sister to be accompanied by a girl who would allow men to do such a thing?"

"Yes, sir. I mean no, sir." She buried her face in her hands and sobbed.

Cook patted her shoulder. "There, now. Thank Mr. Darcy, then go find some dry clothes."

"Thank you, Mr. Darcy," Mary whispered and then bolted from the room, but not so quickly that Darcy could not see she was limping. Henry must have exacted his revenge.

Cook shook her head after the departing girl. "Poor child. 'Tis very good to her you were, Mr. Darcy, sir."

"Nonsense. Miss Darcy will be glad to hear she returned."

"'Twasn't so much that she came back, sir. One of my boys found her hiding in the mews. Soaking wet she was, and like to catch her death. I knew Mr. Simms was looking for her, so I brought her in."

"Well done." Again the mews. One of these days he would have to ascertain exactly who Charlie had brought to live there. "Please inform me if there are any further difficulties."

"Yes, Mr. Darcy." Cook bobbed a curtsey.

Darcy walked slowly back to the dining room, still furious, and considering all the things he might say to his cousin. He wondered if Henry would be surprised by his objections. After all, he had allowed Henry to believe he had done the same to Mary. Had he, by failing to confront his cousin and uncle at Rosings, laid the groundwork for this day's events? Was failing to object to his assumptions a form of tacit permission? The thought sickened him.

Georgiana barely looked up from her untouched plate when he entered. It reminded him that he needed to be strong for her.

"Good news," he said briskly. "Mary has returned safely."

His sister scrambled to her feet. "Where is she? I must go to her."

"You might wish to give her a few minutes first. She is soaked to the skin and should rest."

Georgiana looked momentarily confused. She glanced at her food, then at the door. "Did he hurt her?"

"Some bruises, nothing more." He did not need to add that she was fortunate it had not been worse.

"I will never forgive him. Never." Her vehemence was startling.

"I understand your sentiments completely, but Henry would not. The best thing we can do for Mary is to lead him to believe that she has disappeared utterly and that we know nothing of the matter. He is not above seeking revenge if he knows she is still here, and if I am not at home, there is nothing I can do to protect her. So our wisest course is to pretend nothing untoward has occurred."

She looked away. He could see that his answer had disappointed her. It disappointed him as well, but he recognized the necessity of it. Unless he was willing to follow Bingley's example and throw off all of society, he could not violate society's rules so far as to champion a servant girl over his cousin.

Chapter 12

Elizabeth was awakened by a pounding at the door of Mrs. Philips's house. She hurried to answer it, having a good idea what it might represent.

A disheveled Charlie stood on the other side. "Yer sister's taken to her bed."

Elizabeth pressed her hand against her chest. "Is she well?"

The boy shrugged. "Don't know. I just fetched the midwife. Mr. Browning said not to trouble you till morning."

No wonder the boy made such a valuable spy for Darcy. He knew when to disobey orders. She dressed quickly and hurried after him to Jane's bedside.

Jane's labour progressed slowly, as happened often with the first child, but she faced it with stoicism and her usual good humour. The day was broken only by the arrival of a letter from Mrs. Gardiner. Elizabeth opened it and began to read aloud, but paused when Jane whimpered softly. "Shall I wait?"

Jane clenched her jaw until the pain passed. "Please, keep reading."

Elizabeth smoothed the letter, squinting to make out the words in the dim light. "*I have good news regarding your sister. Lydia is to be married—*" Her voice rose in surprise on the last words.

"Married!" Jane exclaimed, propping herself up on her elbows. "How can that be?"

Elizabeth exchanged a look of wonder with her sister.

> *"To our great surprise, Lieutenant Ralston appeared on our doorstep yesterday with a bouquet of flowers in his hand and even more flowery words of apology to Lydia for his despicable behaviour, as he called it. He asked to speak to her privately, but under the circumstances, I could not agree to allow it, so in my presence he declared his violent love for her and his urgent wish that she accept his hand in marriage. He attributed his abandonment of her to the bad advice of friends. Lydia, of course, was all too ready to believe his sweet words and to ignore the past, though his easy manners troubled me somewhat. Still, he is prepared, if belatedly, to do the right thing, so I shall not complain. He has obtained a license and they will be married next week very quietly. Lydia would rather have a grand event, but given her condition, that is quite impossible. As for me, I am anxious for the event to occur as quickly as possible, before the young man changes his mind."*

"Oh, Lizzy, is it not marvelous? I knew he could not be so bad as everyone said!"

"I am relieved by the news," Elizabeth said slowly, "but somewhat dubious as to his motives. Why would he change his mind now, after all this time? He has not made any secret of his disavowal of her."

"Perhaps that was only play-acting. He must love her very much, to choose to marry her with no dowry or connections."

"You are far kinder than I. It makes no sense. He has never shown any regret for his behaviour. Why would he decide to marry her now? What does he stand to gain?" The memory of Mr. Darcy's face as she spoke of Lydia's disgrace flashed before Elizabeth. She carefully folded the letter and tucked it into her pocket. "Somehow I suspect money changed hands," she said slowly. "It is the only argument Lieutenant Ralston would understand."

"Do you think so? Our poor uncle! I hope he has not strained his finances unduly."

Elizabeth was almost relieved to see Jane's hands clutching the blanket as a new pain occurred. She did not want to discuss her suspicions about the source of the money, but it touched her heart to know that she was dear enough to Mr. Darcy to undertake such a mortification and expense. It could not be but for her sake.

Elizabeth remained at Jane's bedside through the night. In the morning the midwife, who had been dozing in snatches, announced that she doubted the babe would arrive before that afternoon, and that she planned to sleep while she could.

Jane's face fell at her words. Elizabeth said, "May I give her some more laudanum? She needs to rest, too."

The midwife shook her head. "Only a sip or two. Laudanum is both a blessing and a curse in childbed; it lessens the pain, but without the suffering, the labour may drag on."

After the midwife's advice, Jane would take only the barest taste of laudanum, and it calmed the pains but little. Elizabeth did her best to tend to Jane's needs, watching her increasing exhaustion with concern, and tried to provide entertainment by reading aloud and relaying all the village gossip.

"Tell me about Mr. Darcy," Jane said, her words slowed. "You never told me what he spoke to you about."

Elizabeth's heart was in her throat. Had Jane discovered her secret? She sighed with relief. Of course Jane knew that she had seen Mr. Darcy in the shop and walked with him and was but enquiring after an old acquaintance. "He is well, I believe. He has been in London with his sister."

"Oh, yes, he has a sister, that is right. The one Miss Bingley wanted her brother to marry."

How little Jane knew of what had truly come to pass! "I met Miss Darcy in London, walking in Hyde Park. She is a sweet girl, much younger than he is. Not at all what I had expected from Mr. Wickham's description of her. He called her proud, but she is nothing of the sort."

Jane's arms tensed. Elizabeth slipped the twisted rag between her sister's teeth and watched her bite down on it, tears leaking from the corners of her eyes. Poor Jane. How was she to keep her strength up if this continued much longer?

The least Elizabeth could do was to distract Jane a little. As Jane relaxed, Elizabeth wiped her forehead. "It was quite an encounter. Miss Darcy and her brother were passing by when Andrew fell into the Serpentine. Mr. Darcy was kind enough to fish him out, at the expense of his own clothes, I fear. They invited us to their townhouse so poor Andrew would not take a chill."

"You went to their house? What was it like?"

Seeing Jane's interest piqued, Elizabeth launched into a detailed description of the Darcy townhouse. She managed to make the tale last through two more contractions.

"It was kind of Mr. Darcy to take such pains. After all, it had been years since he had seen you, and even then, the acquaintance was slight."

"Did I not tell you I saw him again in Kent?" She imitated Mr. Collins's sycophantic tones. "He is the nephew of none other than Lady Catherine de Bourgh, who condescended to invite us to Rosings when he was visiting her." Her manner made Jane laugh weakly, so she continued, describing Colonel Fitzwilliam and the residents of Rosings in terms Mr. Collins might use.

Jane clutched Elizabeth's wrist hard enough to leave red marks, then, as she relaxed, said, "Why did you never tell me about him when you returned from Kent?"

"So much was happening with our father's illness, and then it slipped my mind." This was not the moment to admit that she had never mentioned it for fear of reminding Jane of Mr. Bingley's betrayal.

Jane leaned back against the bedstead, her eyes closed. "Mr. Bingley told me he saw you in London, as well."

"He did?" Elizabeth exclaimed. "Did he return to Netherfield, then? I never heard of it." Apparently Jane had been keeping her own counsel as well.

"No, he came here last summer, to see me. He wished to assure himself I was well."

Elizabeth swallowed an exclamation of surprise. She would never have expected such behaviour from Mr. Bingley. "And you spoke to him?"

"Yes. Do you know, he told me he had always loved me, and left only after being persuaded of my indifference towards him? Can you imagine? How could he have thought me indifferent?"

Elizabeth wondered more how Mr. Bingley had come to be having such a discussion with a married woman. "He should not have believed such a thing."

Jane's face tightened as a new pain began, one that seemed to last even longer that the others. At the end, she seemed to drift off into a half-sleep, hardly surprising, since she had not slept for two nights. Elizabeth kept silent to give her sister what rest she could, but it lasted only until the next pain began and Jane awoke with a scream of agony. As the pain passed, Elizabeth was surprised to see a slight smile on Jane's face.

"Do you know, Lizzy," Jane said, her eyes closed and her words slightly slurred, "I let him kiss me."

Elizabeth's astonishment knew no bounds, but she was not in a position to criticize, having allowed Mr. Darcy's kiss. "You did?"

"Yes, it was lovely." Jane's eyes opened, and she looked anxious. "I know you must disapprove, but I wanted, for one time in my life, to know what it meant to be kissed by the man I love. I have done my duty to my family. Was one kiss too much to ask?"

"No, indeed." Elizabeth stroked Jane's damp hand soothingly. "You need not fear; it will be our secret."

"You do not think me completely lacking in morals?"

"Of course not."

"I wanted you to know, before—" Jane's eyelids drifted down again.

Elizabeth's chest tightened, but she would not give way to tears that might worry Jane. "Nonsense. You are exhausted, Jane, nothing more. Once the babe is born, this will all be a fading memory, and we will laugh at it."

Jane turned her face away. "It does not matter. There is nothing for me here."

Elizabeth sought desperately for anything that might catch Jane's interest in living. "I have a confession of my own. Once I let Mr. Darcy kiss me."

Jane's eyes flew open. "Mr. Darcy? You didn't!"

She had to keep Jane alert. "I did. In London. For a time, he came to see me almost every day, when I walked in Moorsfield." Seeing Jane's interest, she continued to recount the tale of their walks, making it as amusing as possible, praying that there was no one outside the room who might overhear. "So after that day, I thought I would never see him again, and that I had spoilt all my chances, but then he found me in Hyde Park."

"And came to see you here. He must love you very much." Jane sounded wistful.

"Yes, well, that was before Lydia's disgrace," Elizabeth said briskly.

"It is a pity you told him of it, now that Lydia is to marry."

"I suspect it is the other way around. I told Mr. Darcy of her situation, and then Lieutenant Ralston proposed to her. I would be surprised if Mr. Darcy had no hand in it." She wondered how he had discovered the lieutenant's identity.

"He is a good man." Jane's breath caught as she struggled once more. When she could speak again, she said, "Wake Mrs. Stevenson. I need to push."

Elizabeth had rarely been so glad to hear anything in her life. She ran out of the room to fetch the midwife.

Mrs. Stevenson seemed pleased with Jane's progress, even as her agony increased with pushing. "'Tis normal, Miss Lizzy. It will take time, as she is so weakened already."

It seemed to go on forever, though afterwards, Elizabeth realized it could not have been more than an hour. During that timeless period, she could think of nothing but whispering encouragement to Jane, urging her not to give up. Once, between pains, Jane said, "Fear not, Lizzy. I plan to live to see you wed."

If it gave Jane reason to live, it was well worth having betrayed her secret love for Mr. Darcy. "I shall count on it." She wiped Jane's brow with a damp cloth.

"It is crowning!" Mrs. Stevenson exclaimed. "It will not be long now."

Indeed, Elizabeth could glimpse the top of a head covered with matted baby hair. The rest of the head took many pushes to emerge, but then the baby slipped out quickly into Mrs. Stevenson's waiting hands and duly began to howl. As the midwife tied off the cord, she said, "Miss Lizzy, run and tell Mr. Browning he has a lusty son."

A ghost of a smile curved Jane's exhausted lips.

Simms rapped lightly on the door of Darcy's study before opening it. "Mr. Bingley to see you, sir."

Darcy barely took a moment to replace his pen in its holder before striding across the room to greet his friend. "Bingley, what a happy surprise! I did not know you were back among us." He shook his hand firmly.

Bingley grinned broadly. "Not for long. I am only in town for business, some problems with our suppliers. But I decided that giving up old habits was no reason I must give up my old friends as well."

"Indeed not! I am glad to see you." Darcy crossed to the sideboard and filled two glasses with the brandy Bingley had always favoured. "Here, make yourself comfortable. You do still indulge, do you not?"

Bingley accepted the glass and held it in both hands. "I am not such a Puritan as that, old man. In Scarborough, one needs spirits to stay warm at night."

So Bingley still had not found a woman. Darcy had hoped that the distance and time would have allowed him to forget Jane Bennet. "How long will you be in London? Have you opened your townhouse again?"

"It is not worth the trouble. I plan to stay at the Clarendon." Bingley swirled the brandy and sniffed appreciatively.

"A hotel? Nonsense. You must stay here and tell me of all your adventures," Darcy said briskly. Bingley's presence would serve as a distraction from his worry over what might be happening in Meryton.

"Well, if you insist and it will be no imposition, I will accept your invitation." Bingley raised his glass to Darcy. "To old friends."

"To old friends," Darcy echoed. It was good to have Bingley back again.

THE NOTE FROM DERBY House was not a surprise. Darcy had been expecting a confrontation with Henry after the recent events and had made a point of remaining at home as much as possible. Georgiana should not have to face their cousin alone. A meeting at Derby House was better, in any case. This way Georgiana would not hear any details of their discussion. He read once more the note written in an elegant secretary's script. *The Right Honourable the Viscount Langley requests the honour of your presence at your earliest convenience*. There was no point in waiting, so after leaving Simms strict instructions that Georgiana was not to receive callers during his absence, Darcy proceeded to Grosvenor Square.

He had never liked Derby House. It was too ostentatious for his taste, dark and imposing. Today he was not in a humour to pay his surroundings any mind. At least his uncle was not at home; he did not need that conflict as well. He found Henry in the parlour, his feet up and his hand prominently bandaged, two servants tending to him.

"More wine, damn your eyes!" Henry made an attempt to cuff the manservant, who flinched away. "Now, I said! Do you not realize I am ill? Oh, Darcy, you are here. It took you long enough."

"I am sorry to hear you are unwell." Darcy's mouth twisted. Henry was always ready to play the invalid role at the least excuse.

"Unwell? Look at this?" Henry belligerently stuck out his hand, lifting off the bandage to reveal puncture marks between his thumb and forefinger. Apparently Mary had sharp teeth. His hand was red and swollen near the wounds, but the injury was certainly not such that Henry could not have gone about his everyday activities. Then again, given what Henry's daily activities were likely to include, perhaps Darcy should be thankful to see him staying at home where only his own servants would be the recipients of his ill temper.

"Look what your damned brat of a girl did to me." Henry eased his hand down as if the effort caused him enormous pain, something Darcy seriously doubted. "She deserves to be whipped within an inch of her life."

"For defending herself?" Darcy asked mildly.

"For disobedience, damn it. You need to take your servants in hand. That slut was taking advantage of Georgiana, who should not even be in the same room with her. Since you are so damned soft with your servants, I decided to teach her a lesson about keeping her place. Your father knew how to handle servants. I do not know why you let them run wild."

The sad thing was that Henry no doubt believed himself in the right. It was hopeless to try to convince him otherwise. "I would hardly say they run wild. I was aware of the time Mary spent with Georgiana, and I had no objection to it. In any case, the decision is mine to make."

"Why should you care what happens to the little vixen? Do not tell me you have come to care for her! No bedmate is worth that."

"Hardly, and she is not my bedmate." He had not meant to say it, but it was a relief to do so.

"At Rosings, you were not so fastidious. Do not put on your church manners for me."

The heat of anger coiled through Darcy's chest. "Not even then. I said it to safeguard the girl from you. I do not take pleasure in hurting young girls."

"Hurt her? She was lucky to have such an opportunity."

"So you believe! Have you ever considered whether those less fortunate than you might have sensibilities as well? Is your birthright a license to abuse others at will? If so, I hope you never encounter someone with power greater than your own, or you may learn why you are so resented and disliked." Darcy could hardly believe the words coming from his mouth.

"You forget yourself, Darcy." Henry bit his lip.

Darcy recalled Mary sobbing in the kitchen, her face bruised. "I would rather say that I have remembered myself. Do not interfere with my staff again."

His cousin surged to his feet. "Your servants are not the only ones who are above themselves. I see I must teach *you* a lesson you will not forget, cousin." He swayed slightly. "As soon as my hand is healed, you may be sure I will attend to it."

"That may have been effective when we were boys and I was half your size, but it will not work now." It had happened often enough. Henry had frequently bullied both Richard and the young Darcy. Now Darcy realized that his habit of giving way to Henry was nothing more than a childhood fear of an older boy.

Henry's lips pursed and his face grew red. "Perhaps we should use men's weapons, then."

Was his idle, indolent cousin actually challenging him? Darcy would have been tempted to laugh, had fury not controlled his being. Henry no doubt expected him to back down as he always had, but he had come too far for that. With a start, he realized that he would be all too happy to meet Henry at sword's point, and not only because he knew himself to be the better swordsman. He gave a stiff nod. "I will wait to hear from you."

His blood thrummed in his ears as he stalked out of Derby House, grabbing his hat and gloves unceremoniously from the butler. Once outside under the cloudy skies, he took a deep gulp of London air, tasting the ever-present soot. He strode across the square, past a crowd of noisy roisterers, with a heavy heart. There could be no good outcome from this.

Jane cradled the baby in her arm as he nursed. "Lizzy, I am quite recovered. You should return to London."

Elizabeth did not need to ask why Jane was so eager for her to depart. "You should not put so much stock in Mr. Darcy. I will leave in a few days, perhaps, if you are stronger."

Jane's brows drew together. "You doubt his constancy, after all this time?"

"I do not doubt his affections or wishes. I also do not doubt that his family will be violently opposed to any match between us. It is easy for him to love me privately, but making it public is another matter. He may decide the price is too high." It was not a subject she enjoyed contemplating.

"He knows your worth, Lizzy. No price is too high." Jane's eyes grew dreamy as she gazed down at her son.

Nothing could reach Jane when she was lost in loving contemplation of the infant. "If you say so." A racket of bells came from the shop. "I should go help." She placed a cloth over Jane's shoulder before passing through into the shop.

The cause of the noise was immediately clear. Lydia cried Elizabeth's name and flung herself into her sister's arms with a histrionic flair that would have better befitted the stages of Drury Lane than the streets of Meryton. Lieutenant Ralston followed her in a more sedate manner, his smirk winning him no favour in his new sister's eyes. Lydia fluttered her left hand prominently in front of Elizabeth. "I declare, when I went away I had no notion of being married when I came back, but it is a fine joke, is it not?" She spoke loudly, as if any of the customers could have missed her entrance.

"Odd, I would have thought you might have had at least a slight notion," said Elizabeth dryly. She could tell that the smiles directed at her visibly increasing sister were derogatory rather than admiring, but to Lydia it seemed to make no difference.

"Nonsense," Lydia declared. "You are jealous that I am a married woman and you are not. Mama says I was very clever."

"Cleverness of that sort has never been my goal, but you have my best wishes."

Lydia grabbed Lieutenant Ralston's hand. "Do I not have the handsomest husband?"

"I always admire a gentleman whose behaviour is as handsome as his face."

If Lydia noted the slight in Elizabeth's words, she gave no sign of it. "Dearest Ralston, that red ribbon would look so handsome on my new bonnet, would it not?"

"Very handsome, my dear, but we came here only to greet your sister. You must wait until another day to purchase your trinkets." It was clear Lydia's pouts had no effect on him. His lack of attentiveness to his new bride told Elizabeth that her suspicions had been correct; his motives for marrying Lydia had little to do with affection.

She wondered how much Mr. Darcy had paid him. It seemed unfair that Lieutenant Ralston had been able to see him when she herself could not. Did he know what interest Darcy had in the matter? She could not bring herself even to admit to the question of whether he knew anything of Darcy's mind concerning her.

There was only one way to find out. She seized her chance when Lydia was distracted by a friend who provided an audience for the no-doubt embellished story of her marriage. "Lieutenant Ralston," Elizabeth said, "we must become better acquainted now that we are brother and sister. All the knowledge I have of you is hearsay from mutual acquaintances."

He bowed graciously. "I hope their words were kind."

"Indeed, I believe they have given me an accurate portrayal. Do you know we share an acquaintance in London as well as many here in Meryton?" She gave him a pointed look.

Charlie materialized at her elbow wearing his most earnest look, the one that usually hid some form of mischief. "Miss Bennet, I think your sister is calling for you. I can help the lieutenant."

"What remarkable hearing you have, Charlie," she said with an amused flick of her eyebrow to show him she was not fooled. "I was just speaking to Lieutenant Ralston about our mutual acquaintance, Mr. Darcy."

The lieutenant took an involuntary step backwards, glancing around furtively. "I was unaware you were acquainted with that gentleman."

"A surprising coincidence, is it not?"

He bowed again, apparently at a loss for words.

Charlie reached past her for a pair of shoe roses, stepping between Elizabeth and Lieutenant Ralston. "Perhaps Mrs. Ralston might like these, sir. Very fashionable, they are."

Whatever the connection between the lieutenant and Mr. Darcy, Charlie was clearly part of it and determined to keep her in ignorance of it. The pieces of the puzzle came together at last: Mr. Darcy must have sent Charlie to Meryton to divine the culprit in Lydia's condition. She had not been able to tell him directly when he asked, so he had discovered it in his own way.

It was too entertaining an opportunity to miss. "Charlie has met Mr. Darcy as well, have you not?"

"Mr. Darcy? Yes, he's a very fine gentleman, Lieutenant. Very fine indeed." Charlie winked at Elizabeth, apparently not the least put out by the improvisation.

Lieutenant Ralston said, "I cannot argue with you. I had not realized he had so many *connections* to the Bennet family." His eyes raked down Elizabeth's form. It was not difficult to guess what relationship he thought she had with Mr. Darcy.

Elizabeth's cheeks grew hot, though she could not have said how much was embarrassment and how much was anger at his presumption. She did not wish to think closely about how many people might come to that same conclusion, given the evidence.

Charlie drew himself up to his full height, which was still below Lieutenant Ralston's chin. "Mr. Darcy is an honourable gentleman, and he wouldn't take it kindly if somebody implied otherwise," he said belligerently.

The lieutenant's hand fell to the hilt of his sword, but Charlie did not so much as flinch. It was amusing to see the young boy facing down the uniformed officer of His Majesty's militia. But Lieutenant Ralston would not dare draw the sword, and should it come to fisticuffs, Elizabeth would put her money on Charlie's cleverness over his opponent's brawn.

Still, she was relieved to hear Mr. Browning's heavy footfalls behind her, though he seemed oblivious to the conflict at hand. His proud attention was all on the swaddled infant in his arms. Elizabeth suspected that there was not a soul in Meryton who had not been subjected to one of Mr. Browning's presentations of his son in the last fortnight. One would think he was the first man in history to father a child.

"Lydia, you will want to meet your new nephew," he said, as if granting her a great privilege. "Is he not a handsome, lusty boy?"

Lydia looked up from the ribbons in her hand just long enough to give the baby a disinterested glance. "All babies look alike to me. Where did you get these hideous ribbons? They are no longer at all the fashion in London." She dropped them in an untidy heap on the table.

Mr. Browning's brow darkened. "Must I speak to you yet again about proper respect?"

"You cannot tell me what to do. You no longer have any authority over me, for I am a married woman now." Lydia wore a triumphant look.

Lieutenant Ralston placed a hand on Lydia's arm. "Now, now, my dear, I am sure you did not intend to give offense."

Lydia yanked her arm away, giving him a disbelieving look. "You need not take his side. You are an officer, and he is a mere shopkeeper."

"He is still your brother, my dear."

Lydia sniffed. "I need not acknowledge him. We all know Jane married him only for convenience."

The veins stood out on Mr. Browning's temple and his face grew red. "You need a lesson in respect, young lady, married woman or not!"

The baby began to howl in response to the angry voices. Elizabeth took him from his irate father and swayed soothingly from side to side. Mr. Browning half-dragged Lydia by the arm through the door between the shop and the house, despite her cries of protest. Lieutenant Ralston seemed disinclined to intervene.

As the baby's screams grew to a deafening level, Elizabeth decided that even the busy street would be a more peaceful environment than the shop. She slipped out the door and walked down the cobblestone street to the green, speaking softly to the infant. Finally, in the shade of a tree far enough away to drown out the raised voices of Mr. Browning and Lydia, he began to quiet. Elizabeth patted his back gently until he grew drowsy. She had no inclination to face Lieutenant Ralston, Lydia, or even Charlie again. He would not have forgotten the humiliating look the lieutenant had given her.

As if her thoughts had conjured him, Charlie appeared, dodging pedestrians as he ran towards her. His face was flushed and he panted out the words, "Miss Bennet! You must come immediately! Hurry!"

Darcy was not in the best of humours. His uncle's urgent summons had caused him to be wakened from a delightful dream of Elizabeth, just as her phantom fingers were trailing their way down his cheek and her lips waited for his kiss. He would have preferred to enjoy the conclusion to his dream, especially if it continued in such a promising manner, than once again to make his way to Derby House in the first morning light. No doubt Henry had told the earl of their disagreement, and Darcy did not imagine the upcoming interview would be anything but highly disagreeable. If only the bonds of family did not require that he treat his uncle with respect! His parents, however, had drilled into him at an early age the responsibility owed to his relations, especially the earl.

To his surprise, Darcy was shown immediately to Henry's private chambers. The room was dark and stifling, the heavy curtains drawn. Several men crowded around the bed. A rank smell assaulted Darcy's nostrils.

From his vantage point at the end of the bed, the earl turned to Darcy and beckoned. Darcy expected it to be another of Henry's performances. No doubt he had a mild cold and was playing it up as a deathbed scene. He caught sight of his cousin, his face red and beaded with sweat, his breathing rapid and laboured. This was no act; Henry was truly ill.

His uncle said, "He asked to see you. No idea why."

Darcy had no idea either. He took a step forward. "Henry?"

His cousin opened bleary eyes. "Darcy. You are here."

One of the other men, a doctor, judging by his tools, said, "Has he taken the laudanum?"

Henry's valet hovered nearby, a cup in his hand. "Most of it, sir."

"Good. Remove the bandages, though I doubt we will see any improvement, given his fever."

Henry moaned as the bandages were unwrapped gently. The doctor leaned forward, lamp in hand, examining the swollen fingers. Pus oozed over the surface, and with a shudder Darcy realized the cause of his cousin's illness.

"As I suspected, we have the beginnings of gangrene." With a frown, the doctor gestured to his assistant. "We need maggots here, to cleanse the necrotic flesh."

His assistant made a show of opening his bag and withdrawing a clay flask. Darcy watched with horrified fascination as he removed the stopper and shook out a handful of squirming maggots. With an odd delicacy, he spooned them into open sores on Henry's fingers and then wrapped the fingers again in a loose bandage. Henry cried out in pain at the movement, but made no protest. Darcy wondered how much of the proceedings he understood through the haze of laudanum.

The doctor turned to the earl. "My lord, that will aid the healing, if he somehow manages to survive the infection, but you can see those streaks up his arm where the poison is spreading. As I told you last night, it threatens his very life. My recommendation is unchanged. I urge immediate action."

"Bleed him again," the earl ordered. "I will not have him crippled."

"Bleeding will make no difference, my lord. The infection has travelled too far. His life is in jeopardy; his only chance is if we remove it."

"If that is the best you have to offer, begone!" The earl waved imperiously at the door, his ominous look sending the doctor scurrying away.

Darcy doubted his uncle would listen to reason from him any more than from the doctor, but even though he bore Henry no love, he could not stand by and watch him die unnecessarily. "Many men are missing limbs from the wars. Henry would hardly be unique."

"The future Earl of Derby is not *many men*. He must be greater than other men, not half a man."

"If the doctor is correct, he may not live to be Earl of Derby, unless they operate. Surely a son with one arm is superior to a dead son."

The earl gave his firstborn a long look, his face expressionless. "I have other sons. He was a fool to allow this to happen." He stalked out of the room without another word.

Darcy could hardly believe his ears and hoped that Henry's closed eyes meant he had mercifully not comprehended his father's words. Darcy wished he had not heard them, either. The valet was looking at him with a fearful expression, but there was no response he could give, no reassurance that all would be well. He crossed to the window to catch a breath of what passed in London for fresh air. If only Elizabeth were there, her presence and her lavender scent would help him forget the odor of putrefaction that permeated the sickroom.

"Darcy." The barely audible dry rasp did not sound like his cousin, but it was he.

Reluctantly Darcy approached the bed. "I am here."

"Send my man away."

Darcy looked over at Henry's valet and jerked his head towards the door. The man hastened to obey.

With the door closed behind him, Henry said, "Find the doctor. Tell him to do it."

"To amputate?"

"Yes."

"Are you certain?" It was the only sensible course, but it was unlike Henry to disobey his father, the holder of the purse strings.

"Do it." His head fell back on the pillow as if the effort to speak had exhausted him.

The earl would have no mercy if he discovered Darcy had called the doctors back. Should he do so, and Henry was so fortunate to recover, Henry would most likely deny ever making the request, which was why he had not wanted the valet to hear it. If Darcy did as he asked, the price would be the loss of his family. Despite his current quarrel with Henry, he could not picture a future without them.

It did not change the fact that he could not be party to his uncle's casual dismissal of Henry's life. It did not matter that he himself had wished Henry dead more than once. It was up to God, not to him.

"I will return with the doctor. You should drink more laudanum; you will need it." Darcy left the room before Henry could change his mind.

He was fortunate; the doctor had not yet departed the house, and Darcy was able to speak to him privately. The doctor seemed unsurprised by the request and sent his assistant for the surgeon. Darcy's spirit was curiously light as he returned to the sickroom. Elizabeth would be proud of the choice he had made.

"That is quite a tale!" Bingley said after Darcy reported an expurgated version of the day's events. "I hope he recovers."

"It is in God's hands." Personally, Darcy thought it unlikely. He would not soon forget the final scene at Henry's bedside, where he had assisted in holding his screaming cousin down while the surgeon did his bloody work. He had not wanted to put the duty on a servant who could then be punished by the earl.

"Does his lordship remain in ignorance?"

"I assume so, since I was permitted to leave without any difficulty. He must have discovered it by now. If he comes here, I strongly advise you to slip out through the kitchen." He was only half-joking.

"You may have to join me in Scarborough after all," Bingley said with a laugh. "We can be exiles together."

"I think Pemberley will do quite well for me, thank you." He was glad of the assurance that Bingley would remain his friend, though.

Georgiana sat up straighter. "Oh, please, may we go to Pemberley?"

"Not yet. I have matters I must attend to," Darcy said. He could not leave before Elizabeth returned to London. He prayed it would be soon, now that her younger sister was married and had returned to Meryton. She would no doubt remain there until her sister gave birth, but that could not be long, if it had not happened already. "We cannot leave now, in any case, with Henry's health in such jeopardy. But soon, I promise you." He could hardly wait until the day when he would finally bring Elizabeth home to Pemberley. The thought made him dizzy with joy.

Chapter 14

A POUNDING AT THE front door interrupted Bingley's enthusiastic description of his ventures in Scarborough. At this late hour, it could hardly be a caller. More likely it was ill tidings about Henry. Darcy hardly attended to the conversation as he waited for word. It was only a matter of minutes until Simms entered with a silver platter, which he proffered to Darcy.

"An express for you, sir."

It was unlikely to be Henry, then. No one would send an express the short distance from Derby House, when a footman could do as well. Expresses rarely bore good news. Darcy examined the letter, noting the direction that was written in an unfamiliar, though distinctly feminine, hand. He ran his finger through the opening and broke the seal with a snap. His breathing quickened as he read the first words.

Penned at the dictation of Charlie Hopper by E. Bennet.

Dear Mr. Darcy,

I am sorry to report that we are facing some difficulties here. My master has taken ill with apoplexy and cannot speak or walk. My mistress, who only recently was brought to bed of a son (a robust young man—EB) is still weak from her labours. Between tending to my master and the baby, we are able to open the shop only for a few hours each day (and that owing only to the fact that Charlie appears to have given up sleeping—EB), but we are sorely lacking for direction in management of the shop. As Mr. Browning has no male relations apart from the babe to inherit the shop, I am writing to ask your further instructions. Miss Bennet wishes me to assure you that we are all well, apart from Mr. Browning, whose recovery is deemed unlikely by the apothecary.

I hope you will excuse the liberty of sending this express, which was the suggestion of Miss Bennet.

The letter was signed in large, shaky letters marred with several blots, followed by a postscript in Elizabeth's hand.

I have been teaching Master Charlie his letters, that he may someday write his reports to you directly. After all, who shall spy upon the spy?

Darcy's hands itched for the reins of his fastest horse, though it was too late in the day to travel. It would not help Elizabeth if he broke his neck riding on a dark road. He had been waiting so long, and now he had an excuse, and Elizabeth wanted him to come. His exhilaration was tempered by concern at her situation, which must be dire for her to take such a step, but a fresh breeze had blown through the stale air as he read each of her arch asides, and it was as if the candles burned brighter. If only she were here beside him! He stretched the fingers of his hand, the fortunate fingers that had touched hers.

"Darcy, what is the matter?" Bingley's voice penetrated his reveries.

"What? A letter, nothing more." Darcy hurriedly folded the letter, placing it in his pocket where he could touch it any time he wished. Given Bingley's strong sentiments regarding Jane, it would be best not to explain too closely.

Bingley still looked concerned. "Something is wrong. You need not protect me from unfortunate news, you know."

The words seemed to burn at Darcy. He had done this before; kept knowledge of the Bennet family to himself to protect Bingley, but it had not accomplished his goal. Bingley had suffered for it, as had Elizabeth, Jane, and Darcy himself. Elizabeth would have been his long before, had Bingley married Jane Bennet. He had lied by omission to his friend and had himself reaped the harvest of his deception.

He would not make the same mistake again. This time he would allow Bingley to make his own decision, not that there could be a happy outcome, but Bingley deserved to know the truth.

How to tell him? Darcy fingered the letter in his pocket, as if it still held some essence of Elizabeth. What would she do? The answer came to him without hesitation. Elizabeth would tell him directly and allow him to draw his own judgment.

He took a deep, cleansing breath. "It is a letter from an old acquaintance of ours, Miss Bennet."

Bingley's sudden movement knocked his wineglass to the floor, and it shattered, a dark red stain spreading across the Aubusson carpet. Bingley stammered, "My apologies for my clumsiness. Did you say 'Miss Bennet?'"

"Miss *Elizabeth* Bennet. The letter concerns her family's situation, with which she requests my assistance." Darcy rang the bell. A maid hurried in to remove the fragments of broken crystal.

Bingley's face paled. "Miss Elizabeth? What has happened?" He looked ready to leap from his chair. His previous relaxation vanished as if it had never existed.

"Are you certain you wish to hear this?"

"Darcy, if you do not tell me this instant, I will take that letter from you by force!"

Darcy held up his hand. "No need of that. Her sister's husband, Mr. Browning, is seriously ill, and her sister is recovering from childbed."

If Bingley was pale before, now he looked ashen. "A child? She has a child? Good God, how much more must I suffer for my errors?" He sprang to his feet and then looked around the room as if uncertain what to do next. "Excuse me," he said stiffly and hurried to the door.

He stopped with his hand on the doorknob and turned slowly back, his look ominous. "Darcy, how do you come to be involved with this? Why, of all her acquaintance, would she write to you, asking for your help? What are you not telling me?"

Darcy, feeling all the disadvantage of the moment, said, "I hardly know where to begin. Miss Elizabeth and I renewed our acquaintance some months ago, but I assume the reason she wrote to me is because I am an investor in Mr. Browning's shop."

"You?" Bingley said with disbelief. "Why would you invest in his shop?"

"You were distressed over her circumstances. I found I was, as well. I thought to ease her situation financially by making the investment."

Bingley's eyes widened, and he struck his forehead. "Of course! Why did I not think of that? What a fool I am!"

"I doubt Mr. Browning would have been prepared to accept funds from his wife's former suitor," Darcy said dryly.

"I must go to Meryton. Immediately."

"Are you certain that is wise?"

"Of course it is not wise! What has wisdom to do with it? I must see her!"

"Bingley, she is still a married woman, no matter how ill her husband may be."

Bingley turned a haunted face in his direction. "Do you think I forget that for more than even a second? I, who could have prevented it, if I had only listened to my heart? Did you know that she always cared for me? You were wrong when you thought her indifferent to me. She even followed me to London after we left Netherfield, did you know that?"

Darcy's palms grew damp. "Yes, I did know," he said in a low voice.

"You knew?" Bingley cried in disbelief, but then his countenance cleared. "Of course you knew. I told you of it myself last year."

"I knew before that. Your sisters told me of her presence at the time." Darcy braced himself for Bingley's deserved wrath.

Bingley turned red as his hands tightened into fists. "You knew, and you chose not to inform me?"

"I am guilty of that. I thought at the time to protect you, but I know now that was an unspeakable presumption on my part, and a grave error."

Bingley moved abruptly, and for a moment Darcy thought he intended to strike him. He had never seen Bingley in a rage such as this. The last year had changed him.

"An unspeakable presumption? That does not begin to describe it. How could you? And even after all this, you are still trying to keep me from her," Bingley spat out.

Darcy shook his head. "Only for the sake of her reputation."

"I suppose you expect me to forgive you," Bingley said contemptuously.

"Not at all." Darcy felt his calm slipping and poured himself a much-needed glass of port. "It would make little difference if you did, as I will never forgive myself." It was the truth; he could never forget his role in causing Elizabeth to face such discomforts as her life afforded. He should bear the burden of it. Bingley's wrath was but a minor punishment in comparison.

"Why, then, are you telling me this?"

Darcy had been asking himself the same question. He raised his glass to his lips to buy himself some time, and a vision flashed before him of Elizabeth's face on that fateful day she struck him. "Because I am no longer the man I was then."

"What, pray tell, does that mean?"

"I have been a selfish being all my life." Darcy struggled to find the words to express himself. "As a child I was taught what was *right*, but I was not taught to correct my temper. I was given good principles, but left to follow them in pride and conceit. I was spoilt by my parents, who, though good themselves, allowed, encouraged, almost taught me to be selfish and overbearing; to care for none beyond my own family circle; to think meanly of all the rest of the world; to *wish* at least to think meanly of their sense and worth compared with my own. But recently I have come to understand a truth *you* knew innately, that a man's value lies not in his birth or in his connections, but in the life he chooses to lead. In my pride, I thought my judgment superior to everyone else's, merely because of an accident of birth. I did what I thought was right, but rarely considered the effects of my words and actions on those of lesser situation, as if their comfort and happiness mattered less than my own." It was a relief finally to say it.

Bingley said, "I cannot believe what I am hearing."

"Believe it." Darcy drained his glass, welcoming the burning heat in his throat.

Bingley stared at him for another minute, turned on his heel, and strode off without another word.

Suddenly exhausted, Darcy sank into a chair, wondering if Bingley intended to leave his house. He could not blame him if he did; how could he expect Bingley to remain under the roof of the man who had wronged him so cruelly? He dared not imagine what he would feel should he discover Elizabeth had borne another man's child. Even the notion filled him with a primitive rage. He tried to calm himself. Elizabeth was not in the same situation; she would return to London soon and then she would be his wife.

But the friendship that had so recently been rekindled would now break irreparably. Reaching back, Darcy massaged the back of his neck. His other hand, as if of its own accord, reached for Elizabeth's letter. He scanned the elegant script again, almost able to hear Elizabeth's voice. Only she could manage to tease in such circumstances. The thought soothed his troubled nerves.

She needed his assistance. Her act of faith in writing him must be answered in full. Certainly he must travel to Meryton at first light, but what to do then? Elizabeth and her sisters would require protection; Mr. Browning needed care that would be difficult to obtain without the income from the shop; and who would provide for Mrs. Bennet? Her sister would shelter her, but he suspected it was Mr. Browning's financial support that made her situation tolerable.

He would have to take action, but how could he protect Elizabeth's reputation while he did so? Perhaps he could work through her cousin, Mr. Collins. Almost as soon as the thought occurred, he discarded it. He could not trust Mr. Collins to keep his actions private, especially from his aunt. Likewise, it would look suspicious if Mr. Gardiner were suddenly possessed of a large sum of money, and given Darcy's history with that gentleman, he might well suspect Darcy's motives.

He drummed his fingers on his knee. There must be a solution, and he had to find it for Elizabeth's sake. He must help her and protect her at the same time.

With sudden decision, he crossed to the writing desk and uncapped the inkwell. The pen blotted the first word he wrote, but a sharp knife in the drawer served to mend the quill. There was no sound beyond the scratching of the pen on paper.

He scattered sand over the freshly penned notes and then blew lightly on them to dry the ink. Perhaps the words would run, but they would be legible enough to serve his purpose, and time was short. Quickly he wrote the direction.

Simms appeared as soon as he rang. No doubt Mr. Bingley's raised voice had caused the butler to stay near in case his services were needed.

"Simms, I will be going out directly. Please arrange for

these letters to be delivered immediately. They cannot wait until morning."

"Will you require the carriage, sir?"

"A mount will suffice."

"Yes, sir."

As Simms left, Darcy turned a critical eye on his own attire. Good enough for everyday, but perhaps not for an interview of this consequence. A change of boots and his newest coat were in order.

It was late when Darcy finally returned to Brook Street, both weary and exhilarated. He had completed his tasks. Mr. Gardiner had received him and agreed to his plans with only minor alterations, and he had given Darcy his blessing. Mrs. Gardiner had fussed over him and told him he should not be on the streets alone at this hour. A smile crept onto his lips. It was a far cry from when Mr. Gardiner had called on him to return his letter and told him he had no character. Elizabeth's aunt and uncle understood that people could change and redeem their past mistakes. Darcy hoped the other people in his life would believe the same thing.

Simms opened the door for him and took his hat and gloves. Darcy nodded his thanks and then paused. "Simms, it is nearly midnight. You should be abed."

The butler looked taken aback. "I always wait up for you, sir."

"You should not. You are already at my beck and call all

the day and will be up again at dawn. One of the footmen can admit me so you can rest." If Henry were to hear this conversation, he would be certain Darcy had lost his mind.

"I am perfectly able to perform all my duties, sir."

"I am well aware of it. There is no reason why the burdens cannot be shared. I insist upon it." Darcy ignored his puzzled look and strode down the hall, well content with his evening.

To his surprise, Bingley's voice called his name as he passed the sitting room door. Darcy changed direction to greet him. "Bingley! You are still here."

"Yes, unless you wish me to depart."

"Not at all. I had thought you might wish to leave." For some unknown reason, this night he felt free to speak whatever came to his mind, without judging each word in advance. "I am glad you did not."

"I have a favour to ask of you." Bingley rubbed his hands together.

"Anything within my power."

"Will you be travelling to Meryton soon?"

"Yes. I plan to leave at first light."

"Would you deliver a letter for me?"

Darcy hesitated. "To Jane?"

"Yes." Bingley took a few short paces across the room and then turned to face him again. "I know it is improper and a risk to her reputation, and you would be completely justified to refuse to do it."

A year ago he would have done just that, trusting himself

to know better than his friend. "I will take it if you wish, if you have thought the matter through and are certain it is the best course."

"You will?" Bingley lowered his voice. "And will you really give it to her?"

"Bingley, I made an error in not telling you when she was in London, but when I say I will do a thing, you may count on it."

"I did not mean to imply you would not keep your word, but I know you do not approve, and—"

"Whether I approve or disapprove is irrelevant. I have made too many mistakes in my own life to think I have the ability to counsel others on theirs."

"You truly *have* changed!"

Darcy only smiled in response. In truth, it was not that he had changed, but that his love for Elizabeth had changed him. And in a few short hours, he would be in her presence once again.

Chapter 15

Once Charlie had posted the letter to Darcy, Elizabeth fell into a fevered waiting. She expected Darcy would respond in one manner or another, but whether it would be in the manner she hoped and longed for was another question. If he had thought better of the idea of marriage—and she could not blame him if he had—he might, out of generosity and affection, still provide material support. It would give relief of a certain sort, but the idea that it was all that might be forthcoming brought tears to her eyes.

Despite her fatigue, she could hardly sleep that night for worrying about it. It would be days or even weeks before she would have her answer, and she did not know whether she more desired it or feared it.

She regretted her lack of rest when she woke to the sound of the baby's cry. The noise was quickly silenced, no doubt by his mother, but Elizabeth dragged herself out of bed. The sun was already up, and there was work to be done. Kitty would arrive later in the morning to sit with Mr. Browning, but special soft food must be prepared for him, as well as sustenance to keep up Jane's strength. It was hard to believe she was the same girl who had once lived at Longbourn with servants to care for her needs.

She looped her hair up in a simple style and splashed water from the ewer onto her face for a moment's refreshment before facing the heat of the kitchen. As she approached the back of the house, she heard the clanking of dishes. Beside the hearth, Charlie stirred a pot of porridge.

He did not hear her over the crackling of the fire until she said, "I have heard it recommended that people should sleep at least once every few days, Charlie."

He looked over his shoulder at her with a cheeky grin. "Then they haven't learned how to sleep standing up, like I do."

"A useful skill, I am sure, but not often practised."

"What would Mr. Darcy say, if he knew I was lettin' you do all this work?"

For a minute she had actually managed to forget Darcy, but her anxiety swelled again. "We shall know soon enough, I suppose."

He laid the spoon aside and poured a cup of coffee. Handing it to Elizabeth, he said, "When will he get that letter?"

"It should have reached him yesterday if he was in London, another day or two if he has gone to Pemberley. You did not need to make coffee, but I thank you."

"I thought you might need it. Sounded like you had a restless night." He returned to the porridge. "I still don't understand how you drink that stuff. It smells so wonderful, I thought it would be tasty, but it's horrible bitter."

"It is an acquired taste, much like working through the night." The banter eased her anxiety a little.

Warm fur bumped against her leg. She looked down to see the ginger cat, proudly holding a wriggling mouse in her mouth. She dropped it on the floor and waited expectantly for praise. Elizabeth laughed at the tableau, sending the mouse skittering away, with the cat in hot pursuit.

"Caught a rat yesterday, she did," Charlie said. "Half as big as she is."

Elizabeth wondered what Mr. Darcy would think if he knew Charlie was discussing rats with her. It made her wish fiercely for his presence. He was the only one she could tell of her worries. "If the porridge is ready, I will take some to Mr. Browning," she said.

"I can do that, miss," Charlie said. "You sit and have some breakfast."

She gave him a curious look. Charlie did not usually interfere with her work. She must look more tired than she thought. "I will have time for that later."

Charlie crossed his arms, his slight figure a parody of a worried adult. "You didn't eat nothing of your dinner yesterday." His eyes widened at something beyond her. She looked back over her shoulder to see what had caught his interest.

Darcy stood in the open doorway, his tall form casting a shadow through the room, his gaze fixed intently on her. Elizabeth's first thought was that he must have left London before first light to reach Meryton by this hour.

It was not until then that she admitted to herself how much she had feared he would not come. With an inarticulate sound, she ran the few steps to him. As his strong arms closed around her, joy welled up from deep within her, and she knew she would never in her life be happier than she was at that moment.

Darcy had spent the hours riding from London in planning precisely what to say when he finally saw Elizabeth. He did not wish to make any foolish mistakes as he had that day in Moorsfield, especially since the deed was already done in this case. He could not imagine why Elizabeth would object to his actions, but she confounded his expectations on a regular basis, so he prepared his arguments as carefully as a barrister going before the judge.

All his planned words, though, flew out of his mind the moment he saw Elizabeth's fine eyes light up at the sight of him, and then she was in his arms. How had that happened? All thought stopped and there was only sensation—the softness of her, her intoxicating scent of lavender combining with the kitchen smells of smoke and baking bread, the tiny curls that escaped from her plait and lay trembling against his shoulder, and the fragility of her frame, which brought out his deepest protective instincts. An indescribable lifting of his soul accompanied the sense that his heart might break through his chest wall.

Every inch of his body was alive—his arms, holding Elizabeth close, his body, drunk on the shape pressed against him, his hands, splayed across the rough fabric of her dress. Never again would he allow her to wear such a garment; she deserved the finest satins and silks, and yet he was able to delineate the bones of her stays through the linen, see her delicate features in repose against the lapels of his coat, her fine eyes closed, her dark lashes striking against the fairness of her skin. To think that he would soon have the ability to experience this miraculous sensation whenever he desired!

It was altogether too soon for Darcy's taste that Elizabeth drew away from him, leaving his arms aching because of the loss of her.

"I beg your pardon, sir," she said in a shaky voice, wiping her eyes.

"Elizabeth." Her name slipped from his mouth like a caress. "You need never ask pardon for that." It was as if he were bound to her by invisible ties that sought to bring them together, and he had to struggle not to give in to the almost overwhelming force.

Elizabeth must have felt something of the same, because she closed the short distance between them until he embraced her again. He could never tire of this sensation. He whispered against her hair, "My dearest, loveliest Elizabeth."

"Thank you for coming," she said, her voice muffled as she pressed her head against his shoulder. "I did not expect you so soon. I know you have many other concerns."

"None as important as you. Surely you knew I would come."

Her silence was more telling than any words could be.

"You should have known it. I have been longing for any excuse to come to Meryton, and I was grateful that you wrote to me."

A female voice spoke from behind him. "Lizzy!" Jane exclaimed.

They leapt apart. Elizabeth, her immediate mortification at being caught in such a compromising position slightly ameliorated by her recollection that Jane was already party to some of her shocking behaviour, tried to busy herself by taking the baby from her sister's arms. Jane looked haggard, as if she had slept little. Charlie seemed to have vanished.

"Mr. Darcy, I had not realized you were here. Perhaps we should adjourn to the sitting room. The heat will be less there."

Elizabeth glanced at Darcy surreptitiously as he followed Jane, but he did not show any of the embarrassment she had anticipated. Perhaps he was well trained not to betray such sensibilities.

"Mrs. Browning, it is a pleasure to see you again, though I wish the circumstances were happier," he said when they had traversed the few feet to the sitting room. "I was sorry to hear of your husband's illness."

Jane nodded in acknowledgment. "It is good of you to have come all this way."

"I will be happy to do anything in my power to offer you assistance."

"I thank you and will keep your offer in mind."

Darcy ploughed on. "I have already taken some action in this regard. My solicitor is even now en route to meet with your uncle, Mr. Philips. Mr. Gardiner advised me he would be of assistance in letting a suitable accommodation for Mrs. Bennet and your family. There is also the question of providing the care Mr. Browning will require, should his condition fail to improve."

Elizabeth glanced at Jane, who sat with her hands folded and her eyes on the floor. Clearly the response would be up to her. "That is very generous of you, sir, but I do not see how we could accept your offer, as it is one we could never hope to repay." She dared not look at Darcy.

"I do not expect repayment. It is perfectly appropriate for me to provide for my wife's family."

Her attention snapped to his eyes. His steady gaze held her like a warm embrace. He was not smiling, but his satisfaction was evident. He said, more gently, "The notice of our engagement is to appear in today's newspapers. That will stem any notions of impropriety."

Was it so simple? She could not complain of his choice, since he could have no doubt about her acceptance of his hand, but the audacity of his actions was surprising. She cocked her head to one side and said, "You seem to have taken everything in hand quite quickly, Mr. Darcy. Tell me, are we married already? I would so dislike missing the event."

Now he did smile, the open, free smile she remembered from their walks in Moorsfield. "Unfortunately the rector insisted that I must wait for your presence, but there is no time like the present, Miss Bennet. I imagine the curate here is awake."

There was a soft gasp, and Elizabeth patted Jane's hand. "Do not fret, dearest Jane. Mr. Darcy is but teasing."

Jane rose to her feet. "I am glad of that, but I am far more delighted that you have come to an understanding with my sister, Mr. Darcy. Allow me to be the first to welcome you to the family." Although Jane's smile was warm, Elizabeth thought she detected shadows in her eyes. How could it be otherwise? This was a reminder that Jane had been forced to forgo the privilege now granted Elizabeth: marrying the man she loved.

Darcy bowed. "I thank you." There was one more duty he wanted to discharge before she left. He turned to Elizabeth. "Though I am loath to part from you, I must request a private audience with your sister."

To his surprise, Elizabeth looked more relieved than concerned. "You hardly need my permission for that, sir. I will see you later, I hope?"

"You may depend upon it." He hated to part from her even for the few minutes it would take.

The light seemed to grow dimmer when Elizabeth closed the door behind her, leaving him alone with her sister in the small room. Jane's mouth was set in a thin line.

"Mr. Darcy, if your intentions towards my sister are less than honourable, you must know that no amount of generosity could purchase my cooperation with such a proposal."

Taken aback by her sharpness, Darcy said, "Everything I have said to her today is true. I intend to marry her, and the sooner, the better."

Jane seemed to relax at that and used her foot to start the cradle rocking again. "I am sorry if I offended you. I could think of no other matter you would wish to hide from Lizzy."

"I apologize for the confusion. The matter of which I wish to speak to you has nothing to do with Elizabeth, or even with me. I am merely the messenger. I was asked to deliver a letter to you, and I thought it best done in private." He drew out the letter from his pocket and held it out.

Jane eyed it hesitantly, as if it were a serpent. "Who is it from?"

Darcy fixed his gaze on the mantelpiece before replying. "Mr. Bingley." He waited until he felt the letter tugged from his grasp and then he went to the window, pretending a great interest in the alley outside. It would be unfair to observe her in such a private moment.

The seconds seemed to tick by interminably. How long would it take her to read it? It had not appeared to be a lengthy epistle, though he knew what a struggle it could be to make out Bingley's words. From the wavy outline of her form reflected in the uneven glass, she seemed still to be reading it.

He heard a sniffle and bit his lip hard. He had been afraid it would upset her. It had gone against his instincts to give it to her, but he could not break his word to Bingley. He willed her to finish reading it so he could go to Elizabeth.

The reflection moved abruptly, and he turned to see her carefully place the letter in the cold hearth and set a candle flame to the corner of it. He watched with her as the corners of the paper curled up and turned black. When the flames had devoured the letter and died down, she straightened, looking far older than the carefree, smiling girl who had danced with Bingley at the Meryton Assembly.

"If you wish, I can deliver a reply when I return to London. No one need be the wiser." It was the only thing he could offer in the face of her pain.

When she looked at him, her eyes were full of unshed tears. "There will be no reply. Nothing has changed. You may tell him that, if you choose."

He nodded gravely. "I will."

She leaned over the cradle, gently folding back the edge of the swaddling cloth in order to see the baby's face better. Her strong emotions were almost palpable.

"Can I get you anything for your present relief? A glass of wine?"

She touched the infant's hand, and the tiny fingers wrapped tightly around hers. She gave a polite smile and said,

"I thank you, no. I am perfectly well. I wonder where Lizzy has gone."

Darcy knew a dismissal when he heard it. He executed a formal bow. "I will seek her out." He left the room, but he knew he would not soon forget the emptiness of her countenance as she watched her child sleep.

He looked into the shop, but it was still shuttered and empty. He had never been farther into the private apartment than the sitting room. He followed the narrow hallway past a dining room. The odor of spices told him the final door was the kitchen.

The heat of the room struck him first, coming from the hearth where two pots hung. Elizabeth stood with her back to him, her finger tracing words in a well-worn notebook. She took two onions, chopped off the ends, peeled the brown skin, and then looked back to the book. The sight of her stopped Darcy in his tracks.

Would he always feel as if the room had shifted when he laid eyes on her? Even doing such a mundane task, one suited to a servant, her liveliness could not be diminished. The elegant sweep of her arm as she reached for a handful of cloves was better suited to a ballroom than a kitchen, but even so, he could not help running his eyes along the sweep of bare skin below her sleeves. She took his breath away, even when he could not see her face.

His fingers ached to touch her, but he relished the chance to watch her unobserved. He had not made any fixed plans for where he would go once his tasks in Meryton were accomplished, but at that moment he decided that nothing would make him leave Meryton until Elizabeth could go with him. If it meant staying at the inn for weeks, so be it. He could not bring himself to leave her, even for a day.

He watched, mesmerized, as Elizabeth raised her hand to her face, as if wiping something away. With a start, Darcy awoke to reality—that the woman he loved, who deserved only the best of everything, whose life should be free of cares, was doing the work of a servant. He had known it to be the case when he saw her chapped hands, but it was different to witness it.

One by one she pressed cloves into the onions and then added them to the large pot hanging over the hearth. She stirred the contents, then, when she looked up, she spotted him. Her cheeks were immediately covered with the deepest blush.

Even in her discomfort, she gave him a cheeky smile. "Unless you perchance have a pressing interest in a recipe for curry soup, you may be more comfortable in the sitting room."

"How could I be comfortable there when you are here?"

Elizabeth put a hand on her hip. "This is not such a bad place to be."

"Perhaps not, but I would not wish to see you so."

"Nor do I, though my reason may be different from yours. Cooking, you see, is not among my accomplishments, and I deeply regret that I will have to eat the product of my labours. It is not a fate I would wish on a friend."

Once again, she had effectively disarmed him with her wit, but it still pained him to see the perspiration on her brow. "Where is Charlie?"

"No doubt emptying the chamber pots or bathing Mr. Browning. He has already made breakfast, been to the butcher and the greengrocer, built up the fire, and put on water to heat. He cannot read well enough to make out the recipe, so I do this part." She stuck cloves into the onion. "Please do not say anything; I do what is needed."

"You will have assistance soon. One of my maids will be arriving this afternoon and will stay as long as she is needed."

"You have been busy indeed! Have you spoken to Jane about this?"

"Not yet, but I shall. I hope she will not object; in this case, it is a fortunate happenstance. The girl needs to leave London, and your sister needs assistance."

Elizabeth surreptitiously wiped her irritated eyes. "If she has to leave London, is she suitable for working here?"

"It is not that kind of situation. She made an enemy in London through no fault of her own, and she will be safer beyond his reach. She is a country girl."

"You take a great deal of interest in your servants' welfare."

"My cousin says I am too soft on them."

"Colonel Fitzwilliam, or Miss de Bourgh?" She found it hard to picture either of them making such a statement.

"The colonel's brother, in fact. You have been spared meeting him, for which I thank God." There was a new hardness in his voice.

Elizabeth glanced up at him as her fingers unwrapped the package from the butcher. A veal knuckle; Charlie had chosen Mr. Browning's favourite for the soup. She added it to the pot and rinsed her hands in the last dregs of washing water. She removed the apron, carefully not meeting Mr. Darcy's eyes. "I must go out for a short time, sir. If you will excuse me."

"Is there any way in which I can assist you?"

She stopped short at his words. Cocking her head to the side, she made a show of looking him up and down. "I fear you are somewhat overdressed to fetch water, sir."

He did not return her smile. "You should not be fetching water."

"I have been fetching water for weeks, and it seems to have done me no lasting harm." She bobbed a quick curtsey and made her escape before he could object again.

He was quicker than she and blocked her way into the alley. She made no resistance when he took the buckets from her; it would hardly do to tussle over them.

He said, "I will do it."

Her lips twitched at the ridiculous idea of his finely dressed figure pumping water. "The pump is on the village green. You cannot go there without being seen. It will create talk."

"I know where it is. I have watered my horse there. You must know I cannot stand by while you do this, but I would be grateful to have your company."

Elizabeth concurred, since she did not think she could stand to be parted from him in any case. Besides, she hoped her presence might distract him from the stares that were bound to follow him, so she maintained a lively conversation as they walked. She had not anticipated, however, the pleasure she obtained in watching his economical movements as he pumped water, the flexing of his arms displaying a power not often seen among members of the *ton*. She noted his inexperience with the process with some amusement, however. "If you fill the buckets to the rim, the water will slosh over the side when you carry them."

"I am fortunate to have such a knowledgeable teacher." Darcy tipped the bucket, allowing a small portion of the water to spill out.

"Hardly fortunate! The greater part of the population is very well versed in this particular skill. You, I fear, are in the minority."

"Ah, but my teacher teaches my heart as well."

"I have never heard of anyone carrying water with their heart. It must be a very advanced skill."

Her teasing warmed him and made him wish they were alone. Although the townspeople were giving them wide berth, the clatter of hoof beats and cart wheels on the cobblestones reminded him that they were on High Street. The words he wished to say would have to wait. Instead, he hefted the buckets. While the weight did not strain him, it angered him to think that Elizabeth had been bearing such a burden, but even a demeaning chore such as this was a pleasure when Elizabeth's eyes were sparkling at him.

Elizabeth led Darcy back through the garden to the kitchen door. It stood open, allowing the heat to escape. Inside, Charlie was vigourously scrubbing the table. When he spotted Darcy carrying the buckets of water, his eyes widened. "I can take those, sir," he said, dropping the rag and hastening to relieve Darcy of his burden. He set the buckets in the far corner.

A wail pierced the air from the direction of the sitting room. Charlie said, "He's been at it again, Miss Bennet. I offered to take him, but she said no."

Elizabeth shook her head in disapproval and glanced apologetically at Darcy. "I wish I could offer you a more pleasant visit, sir, but I fear my sister requires my assistance. She should rest."

"You need not entertain me," Darcy said gravely. In truth, he needed no entertainment; being in Elizabeth's company was all he desired. He followed her into the hallway.

A few feet from the sitting room, she laid a hand on his arm. He stopped instantly. She tipped her head to the side, and with a mischievous look, she touched her fingertips to his lips. A shock of desire shook him at the unexpected, but more than welcome, touch. He could not resist catching her hand and pressing first one kiss, then another, into the curve of her palm. Elizabeth's sudden, sharp inhalation, along with the colour filling her cheeks, told him that she was not indifferent to his actions. If only he could take her into his arms! But for now, this new intimacy was enough. He closed his eyes as he touched his lips to her flesh once more.

"My dearest, loveliest Elizabeth," he said unsteadily. But anything further he might have said was drowned out by wails.

"I thank you for the compliment, but the other man in my life is calling for my attention, and he is less patient than you." In a swirl of skirts, she vanished into the sitting room, only to reappear a moment later with her nephew in her arms. The baby's cries would not be silenced, though, until she took him into the garden.

Darcy watched in fascination as she spoke quiet nonsense in the baby's ear, walking to and fro while rocking him against her shoulder. The baby's hand found its way out of the swaddling clothes, and it waved about for a moment before the tiny fingers anchored themselves firmly in Elizabeth's hair, pulling a curl out of its careful arrangement.

Behind him, the garden gate creaked open. He turned to see a woman accompanied by a servant carrying a covered basket. It was a moment before he could place her identity. It had been more than two years since he last saw her at Rosings.

"Lizzy, I brought you—" Mrs. Collins's words trailed off abruptly when she spotted Darcy. "Mr. Darcy! What brings you to Meryton?"

So Elizabeth had not taken her friend into her confidence. "Mrs. Collins, it is a pleasure to see you again. I hope your family is well."

"Very well, thank you. I hope Lady Catherine and Miss de Bourgh are in the best of health."

"I have not heard otherwise." Darcy stepped closer to Elizabeth. After all the time he had spent longing for her, it seemed that there was always someone wanting to take her attention from him.

"I am glad to hear it." She took the basket from the maid. "Annie, go ask Mrs. Browning what she would like you to do today." Once the maid had left, Charlotte gestured to the basket. "Lizzy, shall I leave these things in the kitchen?"

"Thank you, Charlotte." Elizabeth followed her friend into the kitchen, and Darcy trailed behind.

Mrs. Collins removed the checkered cloth from the basket and unloaded it. "Muffins, a raised giblet pie, a mutton shank, some biscuits, and a roasted partridge."

"You see that Charlotte takes pity on my lack of skill in the kitchen," Elizabeth said.

Mrs. Collins darted a curious glance in his direction. "I have a cook, and you do not. Is Mr. Browning any better today?"

"Much the same. He takes sips of broth." Elizabeth gestured towards the pot over the fire.

"Does his agitation continue?"

"I do not think that will change. Mr. Browning is not well suited to being helpless."

Mrs. Collins folded the cloth and replaced it in the basket. "And you, Mr. Darcy? Are you visiting or passing through town?"

"I plan to remain in Meryton until Elizabeth is free to return to London. I assume there will be a room at the inn."

Mrs. Collins turned a shocked gaze on him, and he realized he should not have used Elizabeth's Christian name before their engagement was announced. "I see," she said dubiously.

"Miss Bennet has just done me the great honour of agreeing to be my wife."

Her look of surprise was replaced with one of utter astonishment. "She has? You are? Oh, Lizzy, I am so happy for you!" She embraced her friend, baby and all, and did not have enough words to describe her pleasure. "In that case, if you will give me the baby, I will take over here."

"You need not do that," Elizabeth said.

"A girl becomes engaged to be married only once. Now you go off with Mr. Darcy and enjoy yourself for a bit, away from invalids and babies."

Elizabeth laughed. "I know there is no arguing with you when you have that look in your eye, so if it is agreeable to Mr. Darcy, I will accept your offer."

Darcy bowed. "It is very agreeable. I thank you, Mrs. Collins." The idea of being alone with Elizabeth was beyond agreeable. He silently blessed Mrs. Collins.

While Elizabeth ran inside to fetch her bonnet and gloves, Mrs. Collins turned to Darcy and spoke confidingly. "I hope you will marry soon. It would be a pity if your wedding were delayed because of mourning for Mr. Browning. He may not be long for this world."

Darcy nodded slowly at the sensible advice. "Time is of the essence, then."

"Exactly."

"Your point is well taken. I am in your debt, Mrs. Collins."

"If you take Lizzy away from here and treat her as well as she deserves, I will be the debtor."

The infant began to fuss. Mrs. Collins hurried off with him, leaving Darcy to consider how fortunate Elizabeth was in her friends.

Chapter 16

A WOMAN'S LOUD VOICE echoed in from the entrance hall. "Why, thank you, Simms, and a very good evening to you as well. Now, where are they?"

Georgiana sagged with relief as her Aunt Augusta strode into the parlour. Georgiana had never been so glad to see anyone in her life. She had not expected rescue, since it was long after the hour when anyone might be expected to call, but Aunt Augusta had always been eccentric at best. She offered up her cheek for her aunt's brisk kiss and was about to offer her a seat, but Aunt Augusta had already taken one.

The older woman stripped off her gloves, tossed them on a side table, and turned to Lord Derby. "And Joseph, it is a *pleasure*, as *always*, to see you again. Now, what is this I hear about you browbeating my niece?"

Georgiana's mouth dropped. How had Aunt Augusta known what was going on? Or was she simply guessing it from the look on their faces? She would not put it past her aunt to read minds.

"This is no business of yours, Augusta," the earl snapped. "I am waiting for Darcy."

"Poor boy," Aunt Augusta said. "And you know how much I *adore* making your business my own. Now, Georgiana, what is your uncle fussing about this time?"

Georgiana glanced over at her uncle, who looked ready to explode. Would it be worse to answer the question or not to?

Aunt Augusta shook her head in disgust. "How many times must I tell you not to let men intimidate you? Speak up, girl!"

It was easy for her aunt to say. She did not have to worry about what Lord Derby would do to her. She cared nothing for fashion, reputation, or connections, which was a good thing, as she had little of any of them left after her first legendary run-in with Lord Derby years before Georgiana had been born. "He is concerned about my brother's engagement," she offered weakly.

The earl slapped his hand on the table. "There is no engagement! Sheer nonsense. I will not let that boy be trapped by a country nobody."

"Oh, this is about Miss Bennet!" Aunt Augusta could not have sounded more delighted. "Splendid girl, that one. Clever, lovely, and strong minded enough to keep that stubborn boy in check. What more could you want?"

Georgiana was stunned. How had Aunt Augusta come to be acquainted with Miss Bennet? Her brother had said nothing about any connection between them.

Lord Derby snorted. "If *you* approve, then I know she is completely unsuitable to be a member of the family."

"Why, Joseph, I am surprised at you! You did not always feel that way about my judgments." She shook her head in mock disappointment.

"We *all* make mistakes," the earl snarled. "Did you put him up to this? Was it your idea?"

"What, you don't think the boy has the mettle to get into trouble on his own? How little you know him!" Augusta was clearly having a wonderful time baiting him. Georgiana only hoped it did not come to blows.

He ignored her. "Georgiana, for the last time, where is your brother?" he asked in a threatening voice.

Georgiana raised her shoulders helplessly. "I do not know."

Simms cleared his throat from the doorway. "Begging your pardon, my lord, I took the liberty of asking the stable boys if they knew where the master was travelling. He apparently said something about going to Brighton to visit a lady."

"About time!" Lord Derby stamped out of the room, and a moment later the front door slammed.

Augusta laughed heartily. "Brighton, Simms?"

Simms bowed. "The boy might have said Meryton, but my hearing is not what it once was. It sounded like Brighton."

"I commend your imagination, but never mind that. Georgiana, did he hurt you?"

"No, but he frightened me," she said in a small voice.

Simms said, "He threatened to beat her if she did not reveal Mr. Darcy's whereabouts. That was when I sent for you, madam."

"And quite right you were to do so. Now I need some refreshment. Dealing with Joseph always gives me such an appetite," she said with satisfaction.

As Simms disappeared, Georgiana said, "I had not realized you knew Miss Bennet."

"Never heard of her before I saw the announcement in today's newspaper. That was quite a surprise, I must say."

"But you said she was clever and strong minded!"

"Yes, well, I know your brother, and he does not care for weak-willed or mercenary women. It was a safe guess. Besides, I knew how much it would annoy Lord Derby. *He* is quite the opposite, which is why it was so amusing years ago when he decided I would make him a suitable bride. Ha! He thought my father would force me into it, as if he could ever make me do anything I did not want to." She chuckled. "Now, do you have any idea where this Meryton actually is?"

"It is a small town in Hertfordshire where Miss Bennet is living."

Augusta tapped her lips thoughtfully. "Well, since it seems I am so fond of Miss Bennet, I believe I should pay her a visit myself, and it would only be natural for you to come with me."

Georgiana smiled. "Indeed, Aunt Augusta."

Darcy scowled at the paper in front of him. It was nearly a quarter hour since he began the letter to Bingley, and he still had not progressed beyond the salutation. Despite his own happiness over reuniting with Elizabeth, he could not deny that almost everything he had to tell Bingley was likely to upset his friend. He had promised Bingley an honest and thorough account of the situation, though, and he did not intend to provide anything less.

It was bad enough that he was usurping Elizabeth's place in her former home. Propriety had demanded that Mrs. Collins invite him to stay at Longbourn during his time in Meryton, and that same propriety required him to accept the invitation, even though it meant spending time in the company of the intolerable Mr. Collins. Darcy sighed and stared again at the blank paper awaiting his pen.

I arrived in Meryton this morning.

Weak. Bingley did not need to be told the obvious.

The situation is much as we anticipated. Mrs. Browning's health appears good, although she tires easily and requires assistance from her family and friends in managing her household. Mr. Browning is an invalid, though his condition does not appear to be worsening. The Bennet family's financial reversals continue to create difficulty.

For family reasons, Miss Bennet and I have resolved

to marry sooner rather than later. Although I do not plan to announce it publicly until after the fact, our intention is to be united in matrimony in a fortnight.

His hand trembled as he wrote those last words, and joy shot through him at the thought. It could not be too soon for him. The memory of Elizabeth's sweet body pressed against his was but a taste of the happiness that awaited him. He had no such glad tidings for Bingley, though. With a sigh he dipped the pen into the inkwell and shook off the excess ink from the tip.

I plan to settle an income on Mrs. Bennet and her unmarried daughters. The papers to lease a small house in the village are already being prepared. It is my intent to speak to Mr. Browning tomorrow about plans for his future care and that of his family. He was quite agitated when I saw him today, and I judged it better to wait until he was calmer. I will inform you of the outcome of those discussions, if they can be called such, when I know more.

He could avoid the worst no longer. He wished there were some way of softening the blow.

I completed the task you set before me at the earliest opportunity this morning. I am instructed to tell you that nothing has changed. No further response appears to be forthcoming.

I plan to return to London following my nuptials and can give you further details at that time, if you wish.

He signed his name with relief and then re-read the entire missive, wondering whether Bingley would still be willing to receive him. He could not blame him if he did not.

Darcy shook his head, not wishing to contemplate it. Perhaps a walk in the fresh air would clear the somber reflections from his mind. He could go to the churchyard and remember every moment he had spent there with Elizabeth. The thought occurred to him that Charlie might still be awake, and he resolved to walk past the Browning residence in hopes of spotting a light. There were still many questions to which he desired answers, and there had been no opportunity to speak to Charlie alone. It would also be an excuse to be near Elizabeth, to be breathing the same air she breathed, even if he could not see her at this hour.

He had no wish to encounter Mr. Collins again that evening, so he found his way out of Longbourn through the dark kitchen, barely illuminated by the glow of banked coal in the hearth. It was double the size of the Brownings' kitchen. He had never given a thought to kitchens before. He wondered how many people worked in the kitchens at Pemberley. It seemed that there was a great deal of labour involved in making a simple soup, much less the wide range of dishes presented before him each day.

The night was cool and full of the sound of crickets. The

crescent moon shed just enough light for him to follow the flagstone path that led to the tree-lined drive. The tension began to leave his shoulders as he passed the small wilderness by the gate. How many times had Elizabeth trodden this ground? It was part of her, and she was part of him.

His thoughts were interrupted by the clattering of hoof beats. A single horseman, with a lantern hanging off his saddle, rounded the corner at a trot. Darcy stepped quickly out of the way, knowing how difficult it was to make out figures in the shadows. Indeed, the rider did not see him until he was upon him, then he reined in and wheeled his horse.

The man said, "Is this Longbourn?"

"Yes, right through there." Darcy pointed towards the house.

"Is there a Mr. Darcy there? I have an express from London. A boy in Meryton said he was here."

A cold chill wound around Darcy's heart and squeezed. What could have gone wrong? "I am Darcy." He held out his hand.

The rider rummaged in his saddlebag, then pulled out a letter. "Here it is, sir."

Darcy paid him, asked him to wait, and then hurried back to the house, ignoring the startled cry and protestations of Mr. Collins. He turned up the lamp so he could make out the words of the letter. It was from his Aunt Augusta.

My dear Fitzwilliam,

You have been missing all the excitement. When I

went to Darcy House today, I found Lord Derby looking much like Vesuvius about to erupt, badgering your sister in an attempt to force her to tell him your whereabouts. I am proud to say she did not give in. However, I was concerned enough for her safety to take custody of her until such a time as you return, as I think it unlikely your uncle will trouble me at home. He will, no doubt, spread his vitriol about me elsewhere. Such a pity—I doubt I shall be invited to Almack's this season.

Darcy snorted. His Aunt Augusta would likely prefer an invitation to Newgate Prison to an evening at Almack's.

Postscript: Lord Derby, who is currently on a wild goose chase to Brighton, dismissed several of your servants and had them thrown from the house. Needless to say, I invited them back and gave each a shilling for their trouble. I daresay they more than earned it.

Darcy cursed under his breath. He should have foreseen this. He had been too caught up in his concern for Elizabeth to consider the uproar that would follow his announcement. The scene must have been ugly indeed, for Aunt Augusta to step in. His lips tightened. His uncle would be hearing from him later on that score. At least Georgiana would be in safe, if highly eccentric, hands; his father's sister would not tolerate any nonsense from Lord Derby. The last he had heard, his aunt had threatened to set her hounds on the earl if he ever showed his face at her home. Perhaps he should set a similar rule at Pemberley.

His uncle's wrath at his engagement was not unexpected, except in its timing. Darcy did not wish to expose Elizabeth to it; although nothing the earl would say could change *Darcy's* mind, it was possible that his uncle's threats might intimidate Elizabeth into refusing him. That idea was not to be tolerated.

"Is all well, Mr. Darcy?" Mrs. Collins's concerned voice penetrated his consciousness.

He re-folded the letter decisively. "Quite well, madam, but I believe a change of arrangements may be necessary. Do you think we could impose upon the parson to perform the wedding sooner than planned?"

Mr. Collins bobbed out of his chair, rubbing his hands. "My dear Mr. Darcy, surely you could not plan to wed without first informing Lady Catherine. Her ladyship, despite her great condescension, might take severe offense to such an action."

"I will inform my aunt as I see appropriate. Now, Mrs. Collins, what do you think?"

She nodded almost imperceptibly. "I am sure he can be persuaded, sir. Would you like me to see to it?"

"Thank you; that would be most convenient." Having to bribe the parson was the least of his concerns.

The following morning, Darcy presented himself at the Browning residence at the earliest moment that could be considered decent. Even then, he had been waiting impatiently for more than an hour. Word must have spread through the town of his presence, since he was subject to many frank stares of curiosity from the townspeople.

He managed to steal a few moments of blessed privacy with Elizabeth in the hallway before Jane descended the stairs and told him that her husband was ready to receive him. It took an effort of will to tear himself away from Elizabeth's bright eyes.

Jane ushered him into the sickroom, indicating a chair at Mr. Browning's bedside. Mr. Browning shifted restlessly, his mouth drooping to one side and a wordless pleading look in his eyes, much like Darcy's father had appeared in his last days. For a moment Darcy could not speak. He collected himself, thoughts of a future with Elizabeth replacing his recollections.

He cleared his throat. Jane had assured him that her husband had no difficulty understanding what was said to him, but how could Darcy be certain? "Mr. Browning, I would like to have a word with you, in my role as Miss Bennet's intended husband, to apprise you of the plans I have made. We intend to marry within the next few days, after which she and I will depart for London and then Derbyshire. I am arranging to let a house here for Mrs. Bennet and will settle a small income on her. Kitty will also live there, and there is room for you and your wife as well, should you so choose."

Mr. Browning's hand picked at the bedclothes. He made an obvious effort to lift his head, moving his lips as if he could force words out of them. Darcy wished he could understand the silent effort.

Instead, he continued. "There is another option as well. Miss Bennet, being quite attached to your wife and unhappy to leave her at such a time, joins me in inviting you and your family to live at Pemberley. It would mean leaving your friends in Meryton, but I can promise you pleasant surroundings and the best of care. Your son would be raised alongside my own future children and educated as befits a gentleman."

Mr. Browning's good hand stirred, and he raised it a few inches before allowing it to drop once more, but this time Darcy suspected he understood what the man wished to know. "I will make it my business in any case to assure your son's future, whatever he may choose. He will be my nephew and will have the opportunities congruent with that."

Mr. Browning searched Darcy's eyes as if looking for some sort of answer there and then let his head tip to the side. For the first time, the fingers of his good hand stopped their constant dance of motion.

Darcy rose. "I presume you will wish some time to consider your option. I will return tomorrow." He did not know how they would manage to communicate then, but Jane appeared to have some method of gauging her husband's mind. He bowed crisply, feeling all the incongruity of such behaviour in a sickroom, and was astonished when Mr. Browning grabbed his wrist, his dry, paper-like skin warm and flaccid.

"Would you like something further?" It was a foolish

question to ask, since he could not expect a response, but Darcy did not know what else to say. His attentiveness seemed to be enough to calm Mr. Browning, though the beseeching look returned to his rheumy eyes.

Speaking of his family's future had calmed him before. Perhaps it would work again. "You have my word that both you and your wife will be well provided for. Your wife told me that you had intended to ask me to stand as godfather to your son, and I assured her I would be honoured to do so. He will be under my protection always, and he will be a gentleman."

The hand on his wrist relaxed, and one side of Mr. Browning's mouth turned up in an attempt at a smile. He lay back and closed his eyes, looking more at peace than he had on Darcy's entrance.

Darcy stepped out of the room quietly so as not to disturb him. Jane was waiting just outside the door, and he quietly said, "He seems calmer now."

"Whatever you said must have reassured him."

"I told him I would care for his son and raise him as a gentleman."

She nodded her understanding. "That would be it. He has long wished for children and had such hopes for our son. It is good of you to offer your protection in his stead."

"His paternal affection is commendable." Darcy could imagine the fear of leaving one's child unprotected in a world where fatherless children wandered the streets of London in rags. A voice echoed in his head saying coldly, *I have other sons*. Mr. Browning was a mere shopkeeper of no great distinction, a country tradesman Lord Derby would scorn, yet Darcy could not imagine he would ever say such a thing.

Why did placating Lord Derby have such importance for him? The radical thought almost threw Darcy off balance. He had been raised to honour family and duty above all else, but he was no longer a child, and his uncle was not someone he could respect in anything except for his birth. What was the value of keeping such a tie? London society would frown on him if he quarreled with his uncle. Darcy might have wealth enough to buy acceptance, but his uncle was titled, an incontrovertible advantage. But would that be such a loss? His marriage to Elizabeth would be grounds for scandal in any case. Did he wish to expose his own future children to the cesspit of London society?

The realization hit him with startling clarity. He did not need Lord Derby, Lady Catherine, or the *ton*. He had Pemberley, Georgiana, and Elizabeth, and that was all he needed. He was the most fortunate of men. Why look beyond them for a recognition that, in the end, meant nothing?

It was time to make some changes in his life.

Chapter 17

THE NEW MAIDSERVANT TURNED out to be a strikingly pretty girl named Mary. She curtsied gracefully to Elizabeth when Darcy introduced her and was clearly already acquainted with Charlie. It took only a few minutes for Elizabeth to realize that Mary shared Charlie's tendency to follow Darcy with her eyes, as if attuned to his every movement, but what looked like charming loyalty when seen in Charlie was oddly unnerving in a girl with a woman's shape. Elizabeth tried to quell her anxiety. After all, Mary might watch Mr. Darcy, but Mr. Darcy's eyes were all for Elizabeth. Still, it was a disturbing thought that Mary must know more of the everyday details of Mr. Darcy's life, his likes and dislikes, how he behaved when different moods took him, than she herself could begin to grasp.

But as soon as Charlie led Mary off to show her the space in the attic room that was to be hers, Elizabeth's fears were eased as Darcy immediately took both her hands in his and pressed them to his heart. She experienced the usual delicious shiver of anticipation at his touch, and his devoted look melted any doubts that remained.

He seemed equally caught up in her; his eyes darkened as his breathing became more rapid. He shook his head a little, as if waking himself from a dream, and said, "I am glad Mary is here, as now there will be no need for you to attend to household tasks. You will find her hardworking and sensible."

"Another paragon? I am only just accustomed to Charlie, who always manages to know my next action even before I do. I am certain that within the hour he will have instructed your girl in everything that needs to be done, settled her sleeping arrangements, unpacked her belongings, restocked the entire store, and taken a quick jaunt to France to put poison in Bonaparte's soup. He is a most efficient young man."

"I am glad he has been of assistance."

"Mr. Browning was… is quite fond of him. He often had Charlie help customers, because he said Charlie could sell salt water to sailors and get a good price for it."

"Somehow that does not surprise me." He cleared his throat. "My sister is very fond of Mary."

His remark seemed to carry some sort of significance, but Elizabeth was puzzled by its meaning. "I hope Miss Darcy will not miss her presence, then."

He shifted his weight slightly. "I imagine she may, but it is better for Mary to be here." His tone did not leave any room for questions. "I am due to meet with Mr. Philips shortly, so I must leave you. May I return once our business is completed?"

"Of course. I would like that." It was embarrassing to realize she would miss him even for such a short separation.

"Then nothing will keep me away." He kissed her hand, his lips lingering longer than strictly necessary.

Elizabeth gathered a hamper of dirty linens. Between the infant and the invalid, there was a never-ending supply of washing. She brushed a loose strand of hair from her face with the back of her hand and picked up the hamper to take to the washtub outside.

She did not make it past the kitchen. Mary and Charlie left off their whispering at her entrance. Mary handed Charlie a knife and then took the basket of wash from Elizabeth. "You're not to do this. Mr. Darcy says."

Elizabeth raised an eyebrow. "Mr. Darcy says? And what of what *I* say?"

The two exchanged puzzled glances, as if she were speaking Chinese. Charlie told Mary, "The washtub is in the garden."

She nodded, made as much of a curtsey as she could manage holding the large hamper, then carried it through the open door.

Elizabeth folded her arms and, amused, glared at Charlie. "So Mr. Darcy makes the rules in my sister's house?"

He flashed a grin. "No, miss, you do. Exceptin' when Mr. Darcy disagrees with your rules. Once you're Mrs. Darcy, you can make the rules for *him*."

"I see." She gazed outside. Mary's hair glinted golden in the sunlight as her lithe figure poured water into the washtub. What was Mr. Darcy's interest in her, and why had he kept it from Elizabeth?

"She don't warm his bed, if that's what you're thinking." Charlie's voice floated into her reverie.

Elizabeth straightened abruptly. "That is hardly an appropriate topic of conversation."

"She thought she was supposed to at first, but he said no. Now she's Miss Darcy's maid. He don't mistreat the staff the way some gents do."

"I am relieved to hear it," Elizabeth said dryly. "Pray, how much does Mr. Darcy pay you to sing his praises?"

Charlie's crooked teeth showed in a grin. "Not a thing. Why should he? You'd have to be mad not to go with him. But he's a decent man, and I won't say that of many."

"What will you do once your work here is done?"

"Dunno. I'll go back to London, I figure."

"Mr. Darcy does not have plans for you already? How uncharacteristic of him."

Charlie shrugged. "I'm not in service to him. He pays me to do things from time to time, that's all."

"Will you miss Meryton when you leave?"

"Maybe. It's too quiet here. Streets should be noisy. I'll miss the meals and the warm kitchen, though."

"The meals have hardly been something to remember."

He gave her a disbelieving look. "I've had breakfast and dinner every day since I came here. That's something to remember."

Colonel Fitzwilliam did not believe in neglecting family responsibilities, even when they were as onerous as visiting his brother's sickbed. Still, he fortified himself with a generous glass of port before braving the inevitable litany of complaints. Henry had always been a difficult patient, and losing an arm was unlikely to improve his temperament or his sensibilities.

It was a pleasant surprise to discover that the drapes were no longer drawn. He had always thought that Henry's bedroom at Derby House looked more like an overdecorated prison cell than a pleasant space, with all natural light shut away. Henry sat by the window, gazing out at the small garden, an invalid's blanket over his legs.

It was hard not to look at the stump of his arm, swathed in yellowing bandages. The colonel had seen plenty of men who lacked a limb, but it was different in Henry. His older brother was supposed to be hale and whole.

He covered his dismay with a jovial manner. "Good to see you sitting up, Henry. I was beginning to believe you intended to spend the entire year in bed."

Henry turned a pallid face towards him for a moment and then looked out the window again, even as he spoke. "There are matters I must attend to."

"Certainly nothing urgent, I hope. You have been quite ill."

"I am much recovered."

This was most unlike Henry. Richard sent a questioning look towards the valet, who pointed to a small, stoppered bottle. Laudanum, no doubt, which would account for Henry's unusual demeanour.

Richard joined his brother by the window, peering out to see what had captivated Henry's interest, but he could see nothing unusual beyond a footman heading towards the stable. "It must be pleasant to enjoy the view."

Henry gave him a suspicious glance. "I am waiting."

"Until you are stronger? Very sensible."

"No, no. I am waiting for a sign."

"A sign of what?"

Henry lowered his voice. "I do not know, but the messenger said there would be a sign, and I would know it."

He must have had the entire bottle of laudanum, given how insensible his replies were. Richard made another attempt. "What messenger? Did someone write to you?"

Henry looked impatient. "No, the messenger who chased the devil away."

Long years of practise in disguising his feelings kept Richard's face unperturbed by the concern he felt. "The devil?"

"The devil wanted me to die unshriven, so that I would

burn in hell," Henry said, as if sharing a confidence. "But the messenger said my fever was a warning, a taste of what awaited me if I continued to follow the devil's path."

"I see." Richard studied his brother's face carefully. He could see no telltale flush of fever, but this seemed to go beyond laudanum dreams. Hopefully it would resolve in a few days, and if so, the less said now, the better. "You would perhaps do better not to mention the messenger to our father. He might not understand."

Henry nodded at the sage advice. "Yes, you are right. His eyes have not yet been opened."

Richard decided he would definitely have a word with Henry's valet about watering the laudanum.

A carriage clattered down High Street towards Darcy. He saw the movement out of the corner of his eye, but the familiarity of it reassured him. It took a moment before he realized that his carriage should be in London, not Meryton. He thought that whatever it might portend, it was going to delay his reunion with Elizabeth. He had not seen her since the previous evening, which, in his view, was far too long.

He reached the door of the Browning house just in time to see a footman handing his Aunt Augusta out of the carriage, followed by Georgiana. He advanced towards them. "This is an unexpected pleasure, Aunt," he said dryly. "*Very* unexpected."

"There you are, Fitzwilliam," Aunt Augusta said. "Will

you not invite us in? I am in desperate need of a strong cup of tea."

Darcy looked around, certain that Charlie would be nearby and observing. Indeed, he was just beyond the door. "Charlie, please inform Mrs. Browning that my family is paying us a surprise visit."

Charlie hurried inside, while Darcy asked after their travels and Georgiana's health, hoping to give Elizabeth and Jane a few minutes to prepare for their unexpected guests. The boy returned quickly, his face flushed with exertion, and said, "Mr. Browning requires his wife's presence, but Miss Bennet has ordered tea and will join you in the sitting room in a few minutes, if you please, sir."

Darcy sincerely hoped Elizabeth was not in the kitchen preparing the tea herself as he ushered the two women into the small parlour. He wondered if Georgiana had ever been inside a house such as this, small and practical, with few luxuries and little decoration. He had not spoken to her of Elizabeth's financial status; it would be a surprise for her. Aunt Augusta was less of a concern. He doubted anything could surprise her, and she was always at home in unconventional circumstances. A little too much at home, his parents would have said. It was fortunate that Elizabeth had already made the acquaintance of his maternal aunt, Lady Catherine; she would not be shocked to discover he had some eccentric connections. He rather wished than believed that Aunt Augusta would be on her best behaviour.

Elizabeth did what she could to bring her hair into some sort of order, but there was nothing that could disguise her well-worn everyday dress and slippers. If this aunt of Mr. Darcy's proved to be anything like Lady Catherine de Bourgh, it could prove a highly unpleasant experience. There was nothing to be done for it, though; his family would accept her, or they would not, and she could do little to influence the outcome. There was no point in delaying, so she took a deep breath and entered the sitting room.

"Elizabeth, may I present my father's sister, Lady Seaton." As Darcy made the introductions, his aunt's eyes assessed her. Lady Seaton herself made little concession to fashion, though her clothes were well made and of fine material.

"So you are the mysterious young lady who has been causing such an uproar. Since you are to be part of the family, you might as well call me Aunt Augusta. It is traditional to say it with a certain degree of exasperation."

"Aunt Augusta!" Darcy said. "This is hardly the time."

She pointed at him. "You see, Fitzwilliam is providing a fine example. He has the tone almost perfect. A few more years of practise, and he will sound exactly like his father."

Elizabeth made a slight curtsey. "You will have to forgive me, madam. It is beyond my thespian abilities to seem exasperated with someone I have just met. You will have to do something to exasperate me first."

The older woman let out a bark of laughter. "I see you will do very well. By the by, Fitzwilliam, I told his lordship that I was already acquainted with Miss Bennet."

Darcy's eyes held a slight look of a hunted animal. "I am sure you must have had a reason," he said with resignation.

"I said it to annoy him, of course. There are so few pleasures of life to enjoy at my age; one must seize the opportunities as they come." She looked distinctly pleased with herself.

"And you are so very skilled at annoying him," Darcy said. "I wonder that you did not marry him all those years ago so that you would have the pleasure of tormenting him all his life."

"He is far too ill-tempered for my taste, not to mention that I cannot abide a man who sulks. Besides, it was much more enjoyable to see his face when I told him I had accepted Lord Seaton, who had none of the prospects, fortune, or youth he had. He could not understand why I would prefer an old man to him." Almost as an afterthought, she turned to Elizabeth. "But, Miss Bennet, if you insist upon marrying a young, healthy man, you could do far worse than our Fitzwilliam."

Elizabeth's lips trembled in holding back a smile. "Why, thank you. I believe he will do admirably, despite not being in his dotage."

Aunt Augusta gave a hearty laugh. "Well said, but still, old men make the best husbands; the older, the better. My goal was to become a widow as soon as possible. As a maiden

I belonged to my father; as a wife I would belong to my husband. Only as a widow can a woman belong to herself. Lord Derby was a poor prospect in that regard. I daresay I could have chased him into an early grave, but it seemed more trouble than it was worth, when there was an adequate supply of elderly gentlemen happy to marry a well-dowered young girl."

Elizabeth gave Darcy an arch look and then said, "I do not doubt it, but as I am not well-dowered, perhaps it is fortunate that I am not averse to entering into a marriage with a younger gentleman."

"If he gives you any trouble, tell me, and I will make him wish he were older." Aunt Augusta's smile took any sting from the words.

"I thank you, but I hope I will be able to rely on my own methods of persuasion."

Aunt Augusta snorted. "No doubt. You will be good for him."

Darcy said, "Do not worry on Elizabeth's account. She is quite able to defend herself, believe me." He rubbed his hand over his cheek ruefully.

Elizabeth flushed, remembering all too well how she had defended herself that day in Moorsfield. She could hardly believe he would refer to it publicly. "I doubt that will ever be necessary, now that we have both grown in understanding of each other."

Aunt Augusta looked from Elizabeth to Darcy and back again. "Did you really?" she asked with fascination.

Elizabeth was far too embarrassed to speak, but Darcy took pity on her. "She did indeed, and quite forcefully, I might add, so you need not spend a moment worrying about her."

"Did you deserve it?"

The response consisted of an affirmative from Darcy and a definite no from Elizabeth, leading to an outbreak of mirth from Aunt Augusta.

Georgiana, apparently just realizing the topic of the conversation, clapped her hand over her mouth.

Elizabeth said firmly, "Although I did not understand it at the time, Mr. Darcy is the best man of my acquaintance, Lady Seaton."

Darcy's features softened as he smiled at her, a private look.

"I told you to call me Aunt Augusta."

Elizabeth pursed her lips a moment, and then, with a creditable imitation of Darcy's earlier exasperation, said, "Yes, *Aunt Augusta.*"

Chapter 18

The dank smell of mold and stale air greeted Elizabeth as she entered the shuttered sitting room of the cottage. Darcy stopped in the doorway and said, "It requires cleaning, naturally, but do you think it will it suit your mother? It is not Longbourn, I know."

"It is a great improvement over her present situation." Elizabeth pulled the heavy curtain, releasing a small cloud of dust that made her cough. The window latch resisted her best efforts until Darcy reached around her and gave it a firm twist. With a loud creak, the latch came free, and Elizabeth pushed open the window, highly aware of the proximity of Darcy's body to hers in the deserted room. It was so rare for them to be alone together, though tomorrow that would change forever. She leaned her face out the window, and a playful breeze made the curls beside her face dance. "There," she said briskly. "Now we can see the room more clearly."

Darcy smiled down at her ruefully, as if understanding her need for distraction. "And anyone who passes by can see us."

"Indeed," Elizabeth said, looking up into his eyes. "I believe it will suit admirably."

His fingers fleetingly touched the back of her hand. "More than admirably." His tone told her he was not speaking of the house. "The agent says it can be ready within the week."

"I must thank you again for your generosity to my family."

He took her hand in his. "Tomorrow they will be mine as well, just as my family will be yours. You have already won over Georgiana and my aunt."

"Your Aunt Augusta was most amiable, though not precisely what I expected," Elizabeth said with a teasing smile.

"She is not what anyone expects. Fortunately for her, she cares little for society manners and has an independent income, so she need not rely on anyone."

"Ah, yes, the advantages of marrying an old man." She pursed her lips in imitation of Lady Seaton.

Darcy shrugged. "She has never mentioned that before, but I am hardly surprised. I do not remember Lord Seaton; he died when I was still quite young, and we rarely saw Aunt Augusta during those years. She and my mother were not on the best of terms, but since my mother's death, she has been a regular visitor to Pemberley. Even so, my father avoided mentioning her outside the family."

"What had she done, to be so disregarded? It sounds as if she made a good marriage."

"I do not know the details, because it was not spoken of in my family. It has something to do with my uncle, Lord Derby, who wished to marry her. She refused, against her father's wishes, although my father apparently supported her decision. She was sent away to repent of her disobedient ways, but returned unrepentant and engaged to Lord Seaton."

"And, apparently, she still carries a grudge against Lord Derby." Elizabeth pulled aside a dusty cloth to expose a plain wooden table. Not Longbourn indeed, but it would do.

"She is hardly alone in that. He cares only for himself and for what can bring advantage to the family. I have always managed to be civil to him, but of late, even I have come to realize that he is not a man I can respect." Darcy shook his head. "I am not in his good graces these days. It is a matter we should discuss, as it will have an influence on you as well."

"How will it influence me?"

Darcy frowned. "Although my sister and Aunt Augusta are quite pleased to make your acquaintance, I think it more than likely that Lord Derby, as well as Lady Catherine, will refuse to recognize our marriage. I am sorry to bear such tidings."

To his surprise, Elizabeth laughed merrily, and then her countenance took on a more sober mien. "I am sorry only to the extent to which it causes you pain, sir. I have never been under the impression that they *would* accept me, so it is no loss to me."

"Many fashionable members of the *ton* will not risk offending my uncle by associating with us." Darcy looked out the window as if distracted.

Elizabeth paled. "Are you attempting to tell me that you have had second thoughts about our engagement?"

"No! Not at all." He gathered her hands in his, gripping them for emphasis. "*No*. I have no second thoughts, none at all. None."

Elizabeth's lips twitched. "I am relieved by the sentiment, and no further repetition is necessary, but if it is true, I do not understand your intent in warning me so seriously of the many disadvantages to you of this match. I am well aware of them, and I regret them more than you can imagine."

"You do not understand. Please do not think I blame you in any way. I merely wished for you to understand that marrying me might not bring you all the advantages you have the right to expect. There is no disadvantage to me." He paused, searching for words. "I do not wish to associate with those members of my family. I am heartily ashamed of them. My opinion of the *ton* is no better. I would be quite content to live my life with you at Pemberley and never attend another society ball or soiree. In fact, I prefer it so. I hope I will not be a disappointment to you in this way."

Elizabeth smiled. "It seems to me that as your wife I will have such extraordinary sources of happiness that I will not repine. The loss of the opportunity to experience Lady Catherine's great condescension in attempting to direct my every action may, it is true, be seen as a disadvantage, but upon the whole, I believe myself capable of determining the placement of shelves in a closet without reference to her vast compendium of knowledge."

"Such extraordinary sources of happiness." He did not even realize he was speaking aloud, but her words brought him such a cascade of joy that he could not help savouring them in his mouth as he gazed into her laughing eyes. How easily Elizabeth could chase his worries away!

"It is true, but I shall say no more on that subject, lest your vanity and pride grow overweening."

He shook his head. "No fear of that. By you I have been properly humbled, and I am a better man for it."

"I am the one who has been humbled, not you."

"Your circumstances may be humbler, but your understanding has always been superior to mine. I have learned so much from you, my dearest, loveliest Elizabeth." His breath caught in his throat, and he desired nothing so much in the world but to take her soft form in his arms and drink deep from her lips. He could see her eyes growing dark and soft, making his heart pound with anticipation.

She broke away from his gaze, shattering the intensity of the moment, instead looking out the window into the lane. In a voice laced with amusement, she said, "Yes, Charlie?"

Darcy silently damned the boy for interrupting and turned to give him a level look. To his surprise, it seemed to cow the usually fearless boy.

"Sorry, Mr. Darcy, but I thought Miss Bennet should know that there's a gentleman what's come calling on Mrs.

Browning, and she were upset by it, crying, and she told him to go away, but he's still there."

"A gentleman?" Elizabeth jumped to her feet. "Did he give a name?"

"I saw his card. Big-something, I think it said."

Darcy's hands clenched. "Bingley."

"Could be that, sir."

Elizabeth rubbed her hands on her skirt and glanced at Darcy apologetically. "I must go to her. You were right to tell me, Charlie." She was halfway to the door before Darcy realized her intent and strode after her.

Bingley would have received his letter the previous day, and already he was in Meryton. This did not bode well, but Darcy could understand neither why Elizabeth was so distressed by the news nor why her fascinating lips, instead of being curved with humour, were in a tight line. "Elizabeth," he said, "What is the matter?"

"I cannot believe she has done this!" She spoke under her breath.

"What has she done?" Darcy was bewildered.

"Summoned Mr. Bingley. I know that she—" Elizabeth broke off abruptly and walked even faster.

"I think it more likely that he arrived of his own volition," Darcy said. It had been difficult enough to keep Bingley in London when he left.

"His timing is remarkable, then. Why would he come now, of all times, if she had not sent for him?"

"That is perhaps my fault. Bingley was with me when I received your letter. He was quite distressed; he has never forgotten your sister."

"*That* is not news." The taut lines of her face were a radical change from her earlier smiles.

"You are distressed."

"To say the least." Elizabeth slowed her pace and then said in a calmer voice, "I am sorry. It is not your fault, and I should not punish you with my ill temper."

Darcy reviewed in his mind the letter he had sent Bingley. He did not think there was anything in it to provoke this sudden action, but had he missed something? "Perhaps it is my fault. I delivered a letter from Bingley to your sister." He waited to see anger flash in her eyes. Was a little peace to enjoy their brief engagement too much to ask? After tomorrow he could be alone with her whenever he wished, but he wanted it to be with joy.

To his relief, instead of anger, she seemed more at peace, and she took the arm he offered, leaning on it a bit. "You did not know the circumstances. Last autumn, he met illicitly with Jane."

"I knew he had spoken with her, but I assumed it was in public." Good God, what had Bingley been thinking? If they had been discovered, the Bennets would have been disgraced and in the hedgerows.

"I should not have told you. Jane would not have wished it."

He placed his hand over hers. "You may rely on my discretion. It is my dearest hope that you will be willing to confide anything in me, and this is something I need to know, if I am to protect your family."

She gave him a tentative smile. "You are too good, sir." They reached the Browning abode, and Elizabeth led him into the house through the garden, not the front door, and stopped just before the sitting room. Darcy stood as close behind her as he dared, letting her soothing scent of lavender drift over him. She cared for him. What more could he want in life?

Bingley's voice sounded clearly, and when Darcy leaned forward over Elizabeth's shoulder, he saw Bingley on his knees beside Jane. "I beg of you, come away with me. I cannot bear this." His words made Darcy's joy slip away.

Jane turned her face away, tears running down her cheeks. "I cannot. I cannot."

"There is nothing to keep you here any longer. You can do nothing for *that man* now. You do not love him. He cannot live long."

Jane hunted for a handkerchief, slowly dried her tears, and then looked at Bingley, with almost preternatural calm. "Even if I do not love him, I can do my best to make him comfortable. I can prepare his favourite foods. I can read to him and tell him all the news of the village. I can sit by his bedside where he can rest his eyes on me. He likes to do that. He is a real person, not merely an impediment."

"But what can he offer you?"

"He can offer me nothing now, but when I had nothing, he helped me. He supported my family. He was good to me in my time of need. I will not abandon him in his."

Bingley's face was ashen. "I cannot blame you. It is my fault you were in such a situation. You had nothing because I was a fool. How could I expect you to forgive me for deserting you to this fate?"

Jane rested her hand lightly on his arm and their gazes locked. "It was not meant to be. I wish it could be different. For all of us."

"Someday you will be free. I will wait for you, I swear it."

"Do not say such things. I must ask you to leave." Jane's hand remained on his arm.

Elizabeth decided it was the time to interrupt. "Mr. Bingley, please do not distress my sister any further."

At the sound of her voice, Jane pulled her hand away as if it had been burnt. Bingley leapt to his feet, his face flushed. "I do not wish to distress her. It is my greatest desire to make her happy."

Jane chose that moment to burst into tears. Elizabeth put her arms around her sister, directing a glare at Bingley. Her look moved Darcy into action. He took Bingley by the elbow. "Come, man. I must have a word with you."

"Not now, Darcy!" Bingley tried to pull away.

"Yes, now!" He half-dragged Bingley out of the room and through the shop, ignoring the looks they received from two young women passing by. He did not release him until they were well back in the alley, out of sight of the street. "How dare you? You claim to care for her, but you were willing to risk great harm to her to meet her in secret last autumn, and now you are prepared to do it again. I cannot believe it!"

"Darcy, it is not what you think!"

"How can it not be what I think? You left London in disgust at society's lack of morals, immediately after seducing a married woman and risking her reputation, her security, and that of her family."

Bingley winced. "It was not like that. I *love* her. Neither of us meant it to go so far, but neither of us could say goodbye. You do not understand what it is like, having the woman you love in front of you and knowing she will never be yours."

Darcy knew only too well, and the thought made his stomach churn. "So now that her baby is born and her husband is too ill to object to your presence, you are here to take advantage of her vulnerability once again."

Bingley blanched. "I had no idea about the baby or her husband's illness until you told me in London, I swear it. I would never take advantage of Jane."

"Then why are you here, if not to take advantage of her?"

Bingley opened his mouth, then closed it again and shrugged helplessly. "I have no explanation. I could not bear not knowing. I wished only to see her, to talk to her. On my honour, that is all."

"And to ask her to go away with you."

"I did not intend that, by all I hold holy! I could not stop myself. You have seen her circumstances, her misery, her fatigue. How could I leave her here?"

How could Darcy criticize him, when he had faced the same dilemma not so long before? He was the fortunate one; he could marry the woman he loved. He shifted restlessly from one foot to the other, wishing he were not in the close confines of the alley and could pace to his heart's content. "You must leave here, Bingley. I will take responsibility for Jane's circumstances. I have already taken steps to increase her comfort and that of her family. Your presence can do nothing but endanger her. I hope no one here has recognized you."

"I—" Bingley cleared his throat. "Mrs. Long greeted me when I arrived." He turned a beseeching look on Darcy, as if asking for forgiveness.

Darcy swore under his breath. "So it will be all over Meryton by tomorrow." Tomorrow, when he wanted to think of nothing but his wedding. Perhaps that was the solution. "We will have to minimize the damage. We can tell people you are here to stand up with me tomorrow. You will have to spend the night here."

"Will Jane be at the wedding?"

"Naturally, but I expect you to keep your distance. You owe her that much."

"I would do anything for her."

"Then do not jeopardize her reputation any further!"

Bingley nodded slowly. "You have my word."

Chapter 19

Elizabeth was glad to escape upstairs to make her final preparations. Jane helped her change into a stylish dress borrowed from Charlotte. The hem dragged on the floor a bit, since Charlotte was the taller of the two, but otherwise Elizabeth could make no complaint. She was glad she would not have to walk up the aisle to Mr. Darcy in a dress that showed the wear of two seasons.

Mary laid out the curling irons in the hearth and then began to brush out Elizabeth's curly tresses. It had been a long time since anyone had done Elizabeth's hair for her, and it was an odd sensation, taking her back to her days at Longbourn, where there was always a sister or the maid to help. The brush became caught in a tangle, and Mary tugged to free it. Elizabeth gritted her teeth against the sharp pain but said nothing.

Mary must have sensed her reaction, though, since she said, "I'm so sorry, miss. I have never worked on such curly hair before. It's beautiful." She began carefully teasing the snarled hair apart.

"It can be troublesome," Elizabeth agreed. "Miss Darcy's hair must be easier to manage."

"Easy to comb, but hard to get it to hold a curl. Her lady's maid is the only one who can do it satisfactorily. I've watched a few times."

"Have you worked for the Darcys long?"

"Not me. Just a few months is all." Mary separated Elizabeth's hair into four strands and began to weave them together in a complicated pattern.

"I hear that Miss Darcy is very fond of you."

"Aye, she's a sweet lady, without a doubt. She likes having someone near her own age around, and I make her laugh. She didn't laugh much when I first met her. Too much time with old people, I figure."

"Old like Mr. Darcy?"

Mary laughed. "Oh, he's not so old as all that. Quiet, that's all. He's a good man, but I suppose you know that. I owe my position to him."

How could she possibly feel jealous of a servant girl an hour before her own wedding? But it seemed odd that someone other than the housekeeper would be choosing maids, and Mr. Darcy had a mysterious interest in Mary. "Mr. Darcy hired you?"

"Aye, I met him in Kent when he was visiting his aunt, Lady Catherine de Bourgh. I was supposed to go in service to Lord Derby, but Mr. Darcy decided to take me instead. Very lucky I was, I'd say. Lord Derby, he's a bad-tempered one." Mary frowned at her handiwork and redid one section of hair.

More mysterious all the time! Elizabeth wondered if Mr. Darcy would explain Mary's provenance to her if she asked directly. "Is he why you had to leave London?" Elizabeth tilted her head to one side to allow Mary to comb the tendrils of hair that drifted across her cheek.

Mary seemed completely unembarrassed by this question. "His son, actually." She squatted by the hearth and tested a curling iron, sprinkling a few drops of water on it and making it hiss satisfyingly.

Elizabeth held very still when Mary held it next to her face and wound a strand of hair tightly around it. She could feel the heat coming off the iron rod, and the pungent smell of hot hair tickled her nostrils.

Mary withdrew the iron and examined the tight curl left behind. "Aye, your hair does take a curl beautifully." She turned her attention to the other side. While the curl was settling, she said in an odd, low voice. "Mr. Darcy, he's a very good man."

The tone of her voice made Elizabeth feel oddly protective of her, and, even not knowing the circumstances, proud of her beloved.

The girl stepped back to admire her handiwork. "Oh, you do look lovely, Miss Bennet! Mr. Darcy won't have eyes for anyone else. Not that he ever does, of course." She set the iron curling rod on the metal rack to cool.

A squeal of children's voices from below told Elizabeth that the Gardiners must have arrived. She thanked Mary for her assistance and hurried down to meet the new arrivals.

It was an unlikely congregation, Elizabeth thought as she walked towards the altar on her uncle's arm. Miss Darcy and Lady Seaton sat erect in all their finery; her mother and sisters in carefully turned out and mended frocks from several seasons prior; Mr. Bingley looking as if he had slept in his topcoat and breeches; and Mary and Charlie, their faces scrubbed clean, sitting with the townspeople. Mrs. Bennet was already dabbing her eyes with her favourite handkerchief, but Elizabeth knew her primary sentiment at this occasion must have been relief.

Elizabeth shared the feeling, though her reasons were different. Through these last few days of happiness, she had been unable to put aside a fear that for some reason this wedding would never come to pass, that Mr. Darcy's family or friends would stop it, or that he would realize the great disadvantages of the match to him and call it off himself. She had been hardly able to sleep the previous night for wondering if she would wake up to discover it was all a dream and that she must go back to working in Mr. Browning's shop without hope for the future. But here she was, standing beside Mr. Darcy at the altar, the recipient of his loving gaze. His was not a temperament that overflowed with mirth, but the power of his happiness at this occasion could not be doubted.

She herself felt such lightness of being that she could barely attend to Mr. Roberts's droning voice as he spoke the familiar words, "...ordained for the mutual society, help, and comfort, that the one ought to have of the other, both in prosperity and adversity..."

"Enough!" A deep, angry voice sounding from the back of the church made her jump, pressing her hand to her heart. "I demand that you stop this farce."

A well-dressed older gentleman strode towards them. Beside her, she could hear Darcy draw a sharp breath through his teeth. Elizabeth took an involuntary step backwards at the sight of the newcomer's rage-suffused face. Behind him stood a younger man, the sleeve of his black coat pinned to his side.

Darcy took a protective stance in front of her, standing between her and the stranger. Without looking at her, he said coldly, "Miss Bennet, allow me to present my uncle, the Earl of Derby. Lord Derby, I must ask you to join the others in the pews while Miss Bennet becomes Mrs. Darcy."

"I will not permit it!" Lord Derby snarled. "Darcy, come outside with me. I will not allow this nonsense to proceed."

Darcy's lips tightened and he turned towards the parson. "That decision is mine. Please continue, Mr. Roberts."

The parson glanced nervously from one man to the other. "Thirdly, it was ordained—" he said hesitantly.

"No! You there—curate—if you perform this ceremony, you will live to regret it!"

"Sir," Mr. Roberts addressed Darcy quietly, "perhaps we should discuss this in private."

Darcy's countenance became sterner than Elizabeth had ever seen it. "I will be happy to discuss it after the ceremony is concluded and not a moment before."

Lord Derby sidled up to his nephew. "Darcy, listen to me. This is a grave error. Think of your responsibility to Georgiana, your responsibility to your parents, and to the Darcy family name."

"Do not pretend you are interested in anything beyond the Fitzwilliam family name and fortunes, Uncle. I am sorry if you perceive this alliance as a disadvantage, but I do not, and you will not change my mind," Darcy snapped.

Lord Derby's mouth twisted with fury. "Did you not do enough damage to this family already, when your slut attacked Henry?"

At his side, Elizabeth blanched. Darcy put a reassuring hand on her arm as months of anger bubbled up in him, stoked by the injury his uncle was attempting to perpetuate upon Elizabeth. Elizabeth. He would not let his uncle harm her, even if it meant bringing the conflict to the fore in these public circumstances. "My *maid* did nothing but defend herself when Henry assaulted *her*."

Lord Derby gave a hiss of dismissal. "How dare you defend her! She is nothing. She should have been honoured by his attentions."

A cold rage settled in Darcy's bones, setting free words he had previously decided he would never speak. "As her mother was honoured by *your* attentions, nine months before her birth. Do you think Mary should have been honoured by her *brother's* attentions?"

A dead silence descended. Georgiana clutched Aunt Augusta's arm. Henry sank into a pew, all colour gone from his countenance.

Finally Lord Derby spoke, his voice full of venom. "This is nothing but a foolish rumour."

"Perhaps you would like to believe so. I sent an agent to enquire into the matter." Darcy snapped his fingers, and Charlie appeared by his side. "Charlie, what did Mary's mother tell you?"

Charlie drew himself up to his full height and spoke, not in his usual manner, but in a remarkable imitation of Darcy's own accent. "She identified Mary's father as Lady Catherine de Bourgh's brother, the Viscount Langley."

Darcy said, "As we all know, the then-Viscount Langley succeeded soon after to his father's title of Earl of Derby, but that intelligence only confirmed the matter. She has enough of the Fitzwilliam looks that I suspected her parentage long before that."

The earl's face contorted with disbelieving rage. "Before or after you lay with her?" He did not spare a glance for either Charlie or Mary.

Mr. Roberts stepped forward, holding his hands out. "Gentlemen, please. We are in God's house, and there are ladies present." He might as well have kept his silence, for all the attention anyone paid.

Darcy raised his chin. "I never touched her."

"You lie! You told us that day, and quite well pleased with yourself you were!"

"I said she had pleased me. I did not tell you *how* she had pleased me, which was by leaving my presence immediately at my request. You are my mother's brother, so I will allow this one insult to pass, but should you ever accuse me of lying again, I will respond as a gentleman must."

"Why, you… you are no better than your—" Lord Derby's words were cut off when Aunt Augusta, in a most unladylike manner, pushed herself between the two gentlemen like an avenging Amazon.

"That is enough, Joseph," she snapped icily, with no trace of her usual amiable eccentricity. "It is time for you to sit down. Now." Her eyes shot out warnings.

"I will not." He crossed his arms and glared at her.

"If you do not take the *gentleman's* part and allow this ceremony to proceed, you will have cause to regret it. You and your precious family name will never be the same."

If Darcy had stood any farther from his uncle, he would not have heard his next words. "You would not dare."

"You have always underestimated me, Joseph." Their eyes continued to wage war until, to Darcy's complete and utter surprise, Lord Derby harrumphed and stalked to sit beside his son.

Aunt Augusta's fierce scowl melted into a beatific smile. She patted Darcy's arm and said, "Please forgive my untimely interruption on such a solemn occasion. I pray you to continue."

The parson, his eyes still darting from side to side, clumsily re-opened his prayer book and flipped through the pages with trembling fingers. As he searched, Elizabeth whispered with amusement to Darcy, "And I feared *my* family might create a scene!"

Her words allowed his rage to dissipate into the air, and as his vision cleared, he saw her framed in the morning light shining through the stained glass. He drew even closer to her, and with his whole heart he said, "*You* are my family."

Her sparkling dark eyes met his, and he could see the love shining in them. Soon they would be bound through all eternity. He was indeed the most fortunate of men.

Mr. Roberts cleared his throat. "I believe we were considering the causes for which matrimony was ordained. First, it was ordained for the procreation of children, to be brought up in the fear and nurture of the Lord, and to the praise of his holy name. Secondly, it was ordained for a remedy against sin, and to avoid fornication; that such persons as have not the gift of continency might marry and keep themselves undefiled members of Christ's body. Thirdly, it was ordained for the mutual society, help, and comfort, that the one ought to have of the other, both in prosperity and adversity. Into which holy estate these two persons present come now to be joined.

Therefore if any man can shew any just cause why they may not lawfully be joined together, let him now speak or else hereafter forever hold his peace."

Mr. Roberts allowed a brief, tense silence to fill the church, and then, with a look of great relief, he proceeded with the rest of the ceremony, which passed with blessed normalcy. Still, Darcy did not relax his guard until the parson had pronounced them man and wife. He had never before realized how beautiful those words could be.

Elizabeth's eyes sparkled as he took her arm to walk back down the aisle. He placed his hand over hers, rejoicing in the knowledge that it was his right to do so. Even his uncle's grim face as they walked past could not lower Darcy's spirits, but he noticed that the earl was sitting alone. Darcy quickly scanned the church for his cousin.

Henry stood in the shadows at the back of the nave. His face was drawn, and Darcy could see he had lost weight. His clothes were unusually sober, more suited to a funeral than a wedding. Darcy nodded at him as they passed, but Henry's gaze seemed fixed on the altar, and he was not certain his cousin had noticed him at all. Or perhaps Henry had chosen not to notice him; Darcy doubted that his earlier statements had found favour with his cousin.

He was at the church door, and his attention was drawn back to Elizabeth and the warmth of her hand resting on his arm. His wife. He could scarcely credit it. Not even his family could interfere with his joy and relief. He released

Elizabeth's hand only long enough to sign his name in the register and to enjoy watching her sign her name as Elizabeth Darcy. At last.

Mary managed to kneel and stand at the appropriate moments during the wedding, though she wished nothing more than to crawl under the pew and hide there until everyone was far away. She knew they must all be staring at her, at the scandalous natural daughter of the earl. Even the wedding service could not compete with the scandal, as the low murmurs around her attested. She could certainly not bring herself to look at anyone, not even Mr. Darcy and Miss Bennet, and certainly not at *that man*. The earl. She could not apply the epithet of father to him.

Since she had been a child, she had looked into the face of every gentleman who had visited Rosings, hoping to see a trace of resemblance, but her imaginings always included a pleasant gentleman, not one like the earl. Of late, she had begun to wonder if it might have been Mr. Darcy's father, which would explain the favour she had been shown, both by him and by Miss Darcy. It would have made for a far happier discovery than this had been. She did not want *that man* to be her father. It was wrong of her to think ill of a peer of the realm, but how could she forget her first impression of him, that horrible day at Rosings? She had never been inside the great manor, which looked to her eyes like a palace until his servant, the one who bought her from her stepfather, brought her to his lordship for his approval. He had inspected her as if she were a brood mare before dismissing her with a laugh and instructions to please Mr. Darcy. And *that man* was her father. She repressed a shudder.

The events of that day had not been unexpected, apart from Mr. Darcy's unusual behaviour. She had always known that poor girls' lives could not be called their own and that she would be at the mercy of any great gentleman who looked her way, but she shrank from the memory, as she had not at the time. These few months in Mr. Darcy's household had been the first time in her life she could recall feeling safe.

Charlie elbowed her, reminding her of where they were, just in time to allow her to join the rest of the congregation in a response. A few rows ahead of her she saw Miss Darcy's fashionable figure. Had Miss Darcy known the truth of her parentage? Was that the explanation for the extraordinary kindness she had shown? No, Mary could not imagine Miss Darcy keeping such a secret. She simply had a kind and generous heart.

Before she knew what had happened, the service was over, and Mr. Darcy and Miss Bennet—no, Mrs. Darcy now—were at the church door. There was a tug at Mary's sleeve.

"Hssst!" Charlie said. "Follow me." He pushed past a few villagers to exit the pew at the side. Mary murmured apologies in his wake. He grabbed her hand and wove past an old woman, heading towards the front of the church.

Mary could not imagine what could be so urgent, but for the moment, she was happy to resign the responsibility for making decisions, so she trailed behind him until they reached the gated pew where Miss Darcy sat with her aunt. She gasped at his audacity as he opened the gate and walked right into the private pew.

Lady Seaton turned a surprised look on them. "Who are you?"

"I do errands for Mr. Darcy, and this here is Mary."

"Ah, yes, Joseph's get. What can I do for you?"

Charlie flashed his engaging grin. "Nothin'. Since himself is afraid of you, I figured the best place to be was next to you, begging your pardon, madam."

"Indeed? A sensible lad, I take it."

Mary finally raised her eyes to Miss Darcy's face. She was pale, but appeared to be watching her sympathetically. Mary ventured a wan smile.

Lady Seaton rose to her feet. "Well, if I am to be your protector, I will do it properly. Come along." She held the aisle gate open as Miss Darcy exited the pew. Mary, uncertain, hung back.

"Come, child, enough of that!" Lady Seaton placed a gloved finger under Mary's chin and pushed upward. "Chin up. You have no reason for shame, and you must not let his lordship see that he intimidates you. Now walk beside me."

"Beside you, my lady?" Mary was horrified. "I cannot!"

"Rules of etiquette are made to be broken, and I cannot keep my eye on you if you are behind my back. Now come!"

Mary could not think but to obey such a command, but as soon as they were halfway down the aisle, she spotted the earl to one side, watching their progress, his lip curled. She shrank back a little.

Lady Seaton urged her forward. "Now, Mary," she said, her voice loud and carrying, "tell me, are you fond of hounds?"

"Hounds, my lady?" Mary was completely confused.

"Yes, hounds. Fine creatures. I have four of them in London. Thor, Odin, Frigg, and Frejya. You would like them."

"Yes, my lady," and then they were out the church door, and away from *that man*.

The one-armed man approached the parson. "May I have a word?"

In truth, Mr. Roberts wanted nothing more than to retreat to his parsonage for a well-deserved glass of port, but he was a conscientious clergyman. "Yes, my son?"

"I have had a sign from God, but I do not know what it means."

"A sign? Are you certain?"

"Most certain. I have seen visions that have told me to watch for a sign, and today I received it. I have sinned most grievously."

Mr. Roberts frowned. It was often difficult to tell the difference between a holy man and a madman, but if he had to guess, he would say that it was the latter who stood before him. Still, it was better to be safe and make certain of his judgment. "You are not from this parish. What is your name?"

The man swayed. "I am Henry Fitzwilliam, Viscount Langley. It was I who sought carnal knowledge of a young woman, not knowing she was my sister."

Thank God he had not given way to impulse and ordered the man away! "My lord, perhaps we might discuss this in greater privacy. My parsonage is just across the road."

Viscount Langley nodded abruptly and then looked up at the stained glass window above the altar. His eyes grew momentarily wider before he slid unconscious to the ground.

Chapter 20

Lady Seaton whisked Georgiana and Mary into a small carriage and gave the driver orders to make for Longbourn. At first, Mary did not dare protest. After all, she could walk back to Meryton from the Collins's house as easily as she could from the church. But when they reached Longbourn and Lady Seaton declined to allow her to leave, Mary could no longer hide her agitation. "Truly I must return to Mr. Browning's house. I am needed there."

"I am certain they can make do without you for a few hours."

"Mr. Darcy will be angry if I do not return." Mary could think of few worse outcomes.

"I will tell Fitzwilliam that it is entirely my fault. He will be certain to believe *that*. Now, let us go in."

Mary glanced at Georgiana, who nodded encouragingly, then followed the two women into Longbourn. She did not understand what had possessed Georgiana's aunt since the wedding ceremony, but she was clearly not brooking any disobedience. It must have to do with *that man*.

She curtsied automatically to Mrs. Collins, wondering if she was to assist her with the wedding breakfast. With the hustle and bustle surrounding her, it seemed that another set of hands could be useful.

Lady Seaton said briskly, "Now, Mrs. Collins, my nephew tells me you are a sensible sort of woman. I hope you will be able to help me."

"How may I be of assistance, Lady Seaton?" Charlotte barely paused in her directions to the servants setting out dishes.

"I am in need of a dress suitable for a respectable young lady, one who should not appear today in her current clothing."

Charlotte's brow furrowed and then cleared as she noticed Mary by Lady Seaton's side. She looked her over as if assessing her and nodded. "There is a dress belonging to my sister upstairs that I believe would suit. Would you care to see it?"

"That would be lovely."

Mary followed Lady Seaton and Miss Darcy upstairs and into a bedroom. Mrs. Collins removed a frock of sprigged muslin from a closet and held it up, saying, "Is this appropriate?" Mary could not see why Miss Darcy would wish to change from her current lovely blue dress into one not half as elegant, but it was not her job to question.

Lady Seaton cast a practised look at the dress, then at Mary. "That will do very well. Mary?"

Embarrassed that she had forgotten her duties, Mary hurried to take the dress from Mrs. Collins. As she had been trained, she gently shook it out to reduce wrinkles and set it out on the bed, smoothing the sleeves. She stepped back to allow the women to consider it while Mrs. Collins excused herself from the room.

"No, Mary," Lady Seaton said. "It is for you to wear."

Mary looked at her in astonishment. Miss Darcy had said that her aunt was eccentric, but this exceeded all expectation. "It is far too fine for the likes of me, madam."

"Nonsense. You are the daughter of an earl."

Georgiana said, "Oh, yes, do try it, Mary. I cannot wait to see you in it."

"But—"

"No buts," said Lady Seaton briskly. "Put it on."

Would Mr. Darcy be more angered by her presumption if she wore it, or if she refused his aunt's direct command? If Miss Darcy agreed with her, it could not be so bad. Reluctantly she loosened the ties that held her servant's dress closed and removed it, standing in her thin, worn shift. Her practised maid's fingers had no difficulties with the more elaborate closings of the new dress, but once she slipped it over her head, she realized she would need assistance with the buttons on the back.

To her great embarrassment, Miss Darcy stepped forward and began to fasten the buttons. Mary was certain the world must come to an end. Miss Darcy had always been most generous and amiable with her and tolerated much impertinence, but to do a servant's work for her benefit? She was immensely relieved when Miss Darcy finished and stepped back to admire her handiwork.

"Oh, Mary, you look lovely!" Miss Darcy exclaimed.

Mary looked down at herself. The fabric was finer than anything she had ever worn before, and more amazing than that, there was lace, real lace, on the sleeves, right next to her own skin.

"It fits well enough," Lady Seaton declared. "But that cap must go, of course. Georgiana, will you find someone to deal with her hair?"

Georgiana hurried out with an excited smile, leaving Mary alone with Lady Seaton.

Mary had to try one last time. "Lady Seaton, this is most improper. I cannot possibly appear in public like this."

To her surprise, Lady Seaton looked sympathetic. "I know it is difficult, Mary, but now that your parentage is open knowledge, we cannot leave you hiding as a maid. When the earl sees you at the wedding breakfast, it must be perfectly clear that you are under our protection and not subject to his whims. In a case like this, appearance is everything. Did you truly attack his pig of a son?"

"I bit him," Mary whispered. "I did not mean to injure him."

"Bit him, did you? Good for you. If he ever comes near you again, I suggest you bite harder, though I suppose even Henry will draw the line at incest, now that he is aware of the situation."

Mary's thoughts tumbled in disarray. She could not bring herself to think of Viscount Langley as her brother. She might as well claim the moon as her plaything. It struck her then that she was, after all, related to Miss Darcy, albeit as a cousin, not a sister. The idea made her smile. Even though she would have to go back to being a servant once the charade was over, she would always have that knowledge.

The simple wedding breakfast at Longbourn ran smoothly under the efficient eye of Mrs. Collins. Darcy would as soon have forgone the entire event, but it was an important moment for Elizabeth, an opportunity for last farewells, and he would not deprive her of it. He was on edge for the first half hour, watching the door each time it opened to admit a new guest. Fortunately, Lord Derby and Henry did not make an appearance, thus avoiding a scene unpleasant to them all. He wondered, though, at the absence of Georgiana and Aunt Augusta. Although Darcy could trust his aunt to keep Georgiana safe, their tardiness likely meant Georgiana was distressed by his earlier revelations. It was not how he would have chosen to inform her about Mary's parentage, but it was done, and done for the best.

Bingley stood ramrod stiff by the tea service, his eyes following Jane's every movement, but paying no other attentions to her. Darcy hoped the behaviour would continue after their departure. Jane had more than enough worries without

Bingley adding to them, and the lines around her eyes showed her strain.

Darcy and Elizabeth circulated around the room, engaging each person in turn. Mrs. Bennet's delight could not be contained, and almost disguised Lydia's sulkiness. He managed to respond politely when Sir William Lucas congratulated him on carrying away the finest jewel of the county, a sentiment he had mentioned to Darcy on at least three previous occasions. Mr. and Mrs. Gardiner were all that was warm and amiable as Elizabeth expressed her wish that they should all come to Pemberley for Christmas.

Finally Aunt Augusta appeared with Georgiana by her side. Darcy searched his sister's countenance for traces of tears, but to all appearances, she was in good spirits. She looked almost lively as she conversed with another young lady, while Aunt Augusta appeared smugly satisfied as she made her way to the tea table. Darcy's feeling of relief was interrupted by Elizabeth's hand tightening on his arm. When he glanced down at her, she seemed to be watching Georgiana with a surprised and amused expression.

Elizabeth leaned closer to Darcy and said quietly, "I assume this must be your aunt's influence."

Puzzled, Darcy followed her eyes, but he could see nothing out of the usual about Georgiana, except her unexpected sociability with the unknown young woman. Finally it struck him. Her companion was Mary, dressed and coiffed as suited a young lady on such an occasion, instead of in her usual drab maid's attire.

"Not a word." Aunt Augusta's cheerful voice penetrated his thoughts. "Best to take it gracefully, Fitzwilliam."

"Aunt Augusta," he said warningly.

She beamed. "So much like your father. I do hope marriage will mellow you."

Elizabeth made a strangled sound that might have started its life as a laugh. "*Dear* Aunt Augusta, this has been a very exciting day in many regards, and I am certain that another surprise must be quite irresistible, but I must beg you to have mercy on Mr. Darcy, lest he be quite overcome."

"Of course, my dear. I would not dream of troubling him, today of all days!"

Darcy wished, not for the first time, that his family were less inclined towards eccentricity. He noticed Charlie standing at his elbow, still wearing his church clothes, his very proper look spoilt by his disheveled hair. Darcy raised an eyebrow.

"Mr. Darcy, sir, I wondered if I might have a word." His quick breathing suggested he had been running.

Tired, Darcy wondered what could possibly be wrong now and wished he could believe that Charlie was mistaken in believing something needed his attention more than his wedding breakfast. Unfortunately, Charlie had a history of being preternaturally correct about things. He excused himself to Elizabeth and tried to weave his way through the crowd of guests without responding to their greetings. Once he was safely in the hall, he turned a dark look on Charlie. "This had best be important."

"It's the viscount. He were talking to the parson after the wedding, and then he collapsed. He's at the parsonage, and his lordship says he's taking him back to London now, but the apothecary says he mustn't be moved. Hope that's important enough, sir."

Darcy cursed under his breath. His family had already caused quite enough problems today. What business of his was it whether Henry was healthy or not, or what his uncle wished? He glanced longingly back in Elizabeth's direction. "Very well. Please inform Miss… Mrs. Darcy of these events, and tell her I will return shortly." He strode off towards the parsonage, barely stopping to put on his hat. The sooner he dealt with the matter, the sooner he could return.

Mr. Roberts seemed almost pathetically glad to see him. "I do not know what happened, Mr. Darcy. The viscount came up to me after the service and asked me for my counsel. I did not realize he had been so ill." He led Darcy to a small sitting room where Henry reclined on a fainting couch, a faded blue coverlet draped across his body, his face pale. His eyes flickered open as Darcy approached him.

Darcy drew up a chair and sat beside him, wishing that at least it could have been the cousin he liked and respected. "I hear you are unwell," he said brusquely.

Henry turned his head to the side. "My strength is still less than I would have hoped, but it is no matter. It is in God's hands."

It was going to take some time for Darcy to accustom himself to religious expressions from his wastrel cousin. "I am sorry for it. I understand there may be some difficulty regarding your return to town?"

"I do not plan to return at present. The apothecary was of the opinion that I should rest for a fortnight first. My father had different plans and was as insistent as ever, but not quite ready to have me carried against my will to the coach, so he left with many imprecations and dire threats."

Darcy had been dragged from his wedding breakfast for no reason. He tightened his lips. "It seems you have settled matters yourself."

Henry grasped his wrist. "Darcy, I must warn you. My father is very angry with you."

"That is not news, and I cannot say my opinion of him is any better."

"He tore the page out of the church register. He means to have your marriage annulled. I thought to warn you."

Was Henry actually thinking of someone else for once? It was an even greater surprise than his newfound devotion to religion. "I thank you for your concern, but he will not succeed without my cooperation, and he will never have that. As long as I say she is my wife, the register is unnecessary."

"He plans to wait until you tire of her first."

"He will be waiting forever, then. My wife and I are married until death do us part."

"Good." Henry coughed into his handkerchief. "I am sorry to have brought trouble upon you on your wedding day."

Religion, thoughtfulness, and now an apology! Soon Henry would be turning water into wine. "Thank you for the warning. It is helpful to know his plans. But now I must return to my wife." It could not be soon enough for Darcy.

"That girl—is it true, what you said? Or was that purely for my father's benefit?"

"That she is your half sister? It is true. I had not intended to make it public knowledge."

"It was God's will that you did. It is the sign I have been awaiting, and now I know what I must do. My path is clear." Henry closed his eyes as if exhausted. "Please give my best wishes to Mrs. Darcy." His voice trailed off.

Darcy suspected the man was only half conscious. "I shall do that." Darcy slipped out of the room to discuss Henry's care with the parson.

Darcy's spirits were heavy as he strode past the arched iron gates at the entrance to Longbourn. There was nothing to be done for it; his responsibilities were clear. He needed to arrange for a place for Henry to recuperate, perhaps in Mrs. Bennet's new house, and then there was the matter of keeping Henry and Mary as far apart as possible for the duration of his stay in Meryton. All this would have to be settled before he and Elizabeth could leave to begin their life together. Until then, they would have to remain in Meryton. With luck, it would be a matter of only a day or two until arrangements could be made. Two days did not mean forever, but it felt interminable when he had expected to enjoy Elizabeth's sole attention in a matter of hours.

He did not make it to the front door. A figure rose from a bench beside the house, revealing itself to be Mr. Gardiner. Inwardly, Darcy cursed the additional delay, but counseled himself to be patient with Elizabeth's uncle.

"Mr. Darcy, one expects a bridegroom to be joyous, yet that does not seem to be true in this case," Mr. Gardiner said mildly. "One might even say you appear displeased."

"It is nothing of importance," Darcy said automatically.

"A trouble shared is a trouble halved. And although I gave my niece into your keeping earlier today, I am certain you will understand that I remain concerned for her well-being." His quiet words were steely, making Darcy remember their first meeting, when the furious Mr. Gardiner had come to return his letter.

He could understand the concern; if it were Georgiana's bridegroom who disappeared during the wedding breakfast, he would want an explanation. In a clipped voice, he informed Mr. Gardiner of Henry's circumstances. "While he will recover, he must remain here to regain his strength. I will need to make arrangements for his care, and I cannot leave Mary or Charlie here where he can find them. But if I send them away, new servants must be found for Jane. None of this will be difficult, only time consuming, and I had hoped to leave with Elizabeth today, which no longer appears feasible.

I am sure you will understand why I am impatient for that, hence my current lack of spirits."

Mr. Gardiner pursed his lips. "Perhaps I may be of assistance. If you will entrust me with it, I will make certain that your cousin has whatever care he needs, and Jane as well. Charlie and Mary can return to London with me. I doubt your relations will look for them on Gracechurch Street, and there is always enough employment for a few extra hands."

"I cannot ask that of you."

"You did not ask it; I offered. It is your wedding day."

It went against the grain to have another take on his responsibilities, but the chance to escape with Elizabeth was beyond tempting. Since Darcy's father had died, there had been no one to watch out for his interests. Servants took care of many matters, but they could not care for him as a parent would.

Darcy nodded slowly. "I thank you. If it will not discommode you, I would appreciate your assistance in these matters." He felt as if he were handing off a long-carried burden.

"Now go back to your lovely bride, son, and do not give these matters another thought." Mr. Gardiner clapped him on the arm.

Darcy smiled. "I assure you, there is nothing I would rather do."

Inside Longbourn, Elizabeth darted a glance at the window, then back to Charlotte, who laughed. "You cannot fool me, Eliza. I am certain he will return soon, and he must have had a good reason to leave. I have never seen a man so enamoured."

Elizabeth only smiled. Charlie had given her a good idea of what had drawn Darcy away from their wedding breakfast, and she had great faith in her new husband's ability to deal with his troublesome relations, with the possible exception of Lady Seaton. The subject of her thoughts was nearby, handing a cup of tea to Mary, who looked astonished and uncomfortable at being given the extravagantly expensive beverage to drink instead of serving it herself.

At that moment her new husband entered the room, and Elizabeth lost interest in anything apart from him. She could not believe there had ever been a time when she did not love him, when her heart did not give a little jump the moment she saw him. She hardly attended to his words as he apologized to her for his absence.

Elizabeth said, "I am glad all is well. I believe I have spoken with everyone here, so we may make our escape whenever you wish."

Darcy's eyes lit up. "I will be more than happy to do so immediately, but one more task remains. If you will join me?" With Elizabeth by his side, Darcy made his way to his aunt. Nothing could interfere with his joy now.

Aunt Augusta rubbed her hands together at his approach. "Ah, Fitzwilliam! And Mrs. Darcy. We meet again. I did not have an opportunity to tell you earlier what a lovely wedding it was. Family, friends, who could ask for anything more?"

Elizabeth made a sound, perhaps a muffled laugh, and said, "It was certainly a memorable occasion. I have never attended a wedding quite like it."

Aunt Augusta beamed at her. "You will be a fine addition to the family. Fitzwilliam is in great need of more teasing."

Darcy cleared his throat. Elizabeth hardly needed encouragement in that regard. He turned to Mary. "We will be departing shortly. Mary, I have made arrangements for you to return to London with Mr. Gardiner. You will remain as a member of his household until such a time as I send for you."

Mary bobbed a servant's curtsey, incongruous in her ladylike dress. "Yes, sir."

Aunt Augusta stepped forward. "Actually, Fitzwilliam, I have a favour to ask of you. I have been seized by a sudden urge to travel to—Georgiana, where was it I wished to travel?"

"Travel?" Georgiana looked confused. "Oh, yes, travel. Was it perhaps Bath?"

"Ah, yes, Bath. My rheumatism, you know, Fitzwilliam. I really must go there, but I despise travelling alone. I hope you will permit Georgiana to accompany me."

He endeavoured to give her a stern look. "I do not recall ever hearing that you suffered from rheumatism." Given the rather reckless manner in which she rode with her hounds, he found the idea highly improbable.

"One never knows, and I feel as though it might be coming on," Aunt Augusta said briskly, not the least troubled by his words. "You would not have me neglect my health, I hope."

Georgiana looked at him pleadingly. This was clearly not a struggle worth fighting. After all, Aunt Augusta would keep Georgiana safe from his uncle, which was the important matter. "Very well. If Georgiana has no objection to accompanying you, you have my permission."

"Of course Mary must accompany us, as well." Aunt Augusta's familiar self-satisfied expression did not waver.

"Of course," he said drily, not fooled for a moment as to her intentions. "I hope the waters at Bath prove efficacious in treating your—Georgiana, what illness did Aunt Augusta mention?"

"Rheumatism," Georgiana whispered, her cheeks scarlet.

Aunt Augusta laughed and nodded at Elizabeth. "You see, my dear, what a fine influence you have. One might almost think he has a sense of humour."

"Only a man with an excellent sense of humour would choose to marry me," Elizabeth said with a knowing smile.

Chapter 21

Bingley could not decide if the wedding breakfast was pleasure, torture, or equal parts of both. At least he could watch Jane, and since they were at Longbourn, he could pretend that she had never married and was waiting for his addresses. But Jane had never worn a cap in those days, and now she did. He could not forget her husband when she wore a married woman's cap. Two years earlier he would have been at her side, speaking to her, but he had promised Darcy he would keep his distance.

Jane looked in his direction, and their gazes met. Her cornflower-blue eyes held his like a lifeline, but he kept his word and did not move. Jane did move, though. She glided across the crowded floor as if nothing could stand between them, until she was by his side.

Bingley looked nervously for Darcy, but he was already in the hallway with Elizabeth, preparing for their departure.

Surely Darcy could not expect him to ignore Jane when she approached him. He would make polite conversation, but nothing more. There were too many ears nearby for anything private, even if he were tempted.

"Mr. Bingley, I am glad you could return to Meryton for my sister's wedding. I hope your journey back to town is pleasant."

He bowed, fighting the urge to take her hand. "Thank you. I will be returning to Scarborough, where I now reside. I was in London for some business, which fortunately happened to coincide with today's happy event. London is not to my taste these days."

Jane's charming brows knitted slightly, but she did not enquire further. "I must go as soon as the bride and groom depart. I did not wish to spoil their special day, so I have not told them that Mr. Browning is doing quite poorly today. We cannot rouse him, and he has taken no food or drink for more than a day. I am sure you will understand that I cannot stay away long, although it means missing some of the festivities." Her voice sounded as calm as ever, but she was wringing her hands.

Bingley did not wish to speak of Mr. Browning, but courtesy obligated him to respond. "I hope you will find Mr. Browning improved on your return."

"I thank you, but I think it unlikely. He is failing rapidly."

Failing rapidly? Why was she telling him this? Bingley's heart leapt at the possibilities. "What do you plan to do?"

Jane looked down. "My sister has invited me to live at Pemberley, along with my son."

Pemberley. He could go to Pemberley whenever he chose, and no one would think it unusual. "I am a frequent visitor at Pemberley. You will find it most comfortable, I am sure."

"Perhaps I will see you there someday."

There was a flurry of activity in the hall, and Mrs. Collins called out, "They are ready to depart!" The guests began to press towards the door to join in waving off the newlyweds. Jane took advantage of the hubbub to leave his side. Bingley looked after her, committing her features to memory.

Across the room, Mary said to Lady Seaton, "Mrs. Browning is leaving, and I must go with her."

Lady Seaton frowned. "I am sure she will have adequate assistance without you."

Mary gulped. "I will not be leaving for London immediately, so my place is by her side, until Mr. Darcy says otherwise."

"If Mr. Darcy told you to jump off a bridge, would you do that as well?"

Mary paused to consider what the best answer would be and decided on honesty. "He would not ask me to do that."

Lady Seaton barked a laugh. "True enough. Very well, girl, you may go. We will speak more in the morning."

Georgiana said, "But I thought—"

To Mary's relief, Lady Seaton shook her head. "Leave it be, Georgiana."

Mary bobbed a curtsey and hurried off to Mrs. Browning before Lady Seaton could change her mind.

Georgiana climbed into the broad window seat of her room at Longbourn, pulling her knees up and wrapping her arms around them as she looked out over the moonlit gardens. She missed the embrace of the hills of Pemberley. She always felt safer when the peaks rose around her with their granite boulders that looked like toys left behind by long-vanished giants. Hertfordshire was too flat.

An upholstery button stabbed her leg, and she shifted to avoid it, her nightshift rustling with the movement. It was not loud enough to disguise the click of the opening door behind her, but she did not look back to see what servant it might be.

"What, brooding, my chick?" The unexpected sound of Aunt Augusta's strong voice made her jump.

Georgiana considered denying it, but she knew better than to think Aunt Augusta would accept a polite reassurance that all was well. "It has been a long day."

"Yet you look troubled. That is not from the long day. Perhaps you would do better to speak your mind."

Georgiana doubted that, but the words rushed from her anyway. "I thought Mary was coming to Bath with us. Why did you let her go back?"

"She will indeed go to Bath with us, but for tonight, it is best to allow her to return to Mrs. Browning's home. It is what the girl wished. Think of all the shocks she had today and how out of place she must have felt. Her familiar routine offers comfort, even if it means working as a servant."

"So she will remain a servant, then?" Georgiana could not hide her disappointment.

"I have no idea what your brother may have planned for her, though I have a few ideas of my own. I doubt your uncle will make any difficulties."

"He will do nothing for her. He does not care what happens to her."

"I agree. No doubt he has dozens of illegitimate children scattered hither and yon and never gives them a second thought. What is one more or less to him?"

"He brought them into the world. He should provide for them, not leave them unprotected and suffering."

"I cannot argue the point, but Lord Derby is not known for doing things simply because he should." Aunt Augusta shook her head disapprovingly. "Mary is fortunate that your brother took her in."

"Fortunate now, but she has told me about her childhood, and how other children tormented her for being born out of wedlock." Georgiana's voice quavered as she remembered Mary's stories. She had kept asking her to repeat them, as if to punish herself. "It was his fault." She buried her head in her knees to hide her tears.

"What is the matter, dear? Surely you are not surprised by his behaviour."

"It is not him. It is me. I am no better than he is."

"*That* is perhaps the most ridiculous statement I have ever heard, and I have heard some quite ridiculous ones."

"It is true! You do not know."

Aunt Augusta's eyes narrowed. "What do I not know, Georgiana?"

"I cannot tell you." Her chest ached. Her brother would be furious with her for saying this much.

She felt movement as Aunt Augusta settled herself on the window seat beside her. "My dear, everyone makes mistakes. Some of us regret the harm done by our mistakes. Some do not care who suffers from their errors. *That* is the difference between you and Lord Derby."

Georgiana stilled. "You know?"

"You are not the first woman to have faced such a dilemma. It is far more common than you might think. There can be no good outcome to such a situation; we can only try to protect those we love as best we can. It is an error to bring up young girls in complete innocence of the ways of men."

Georgiana struggled with the novel idea. Would she have been more able to resist George's blandishments had she been more worldly? She could not imagine it; she had known she should not let any gentleman touch her, but each time, George said it was all right, that he loved her and would never harm her. Three lies. She wondered if she would ever forgive herself. "I should have known better. I am a Darcy."

"If it is any comfort, you are not the first Darcy this has happened to. I found myself in the same situation when I was a girl, and the world did not come to an end. I married well and went on with my life."

"You?" In her shock, Georgiana forgot to hide her face and stared at her aunt.

"Yes, even I." Her aunt's voice was unusually gentle.

"But how… I am sorry, I did not mean—"

Aunt Augusta stood up briskly. "Sometimes one has no choice in the matter but to make the best of it."

"How did you make the best of it?"

"I made certain my son would be raised as a gentleman and would never know want. He has grown into a fine, upstanding young man, despite his unfortunate beginnings. I am sure you have taken the same precautions."

"Fitzwilliam says the baby is well cared for and will be raised by a respectable family. He will not tell me anything more."

"Your brother is a man of his word, and I cannot imagine he would leave a child unprotected, but it is unkind to leave you in ignorance."

Georgiana shook her head. "He means only to be kind and to protect me. He hopes I will forget."

"Foolish boy. As if any woman could forget a child she has borne! Would it relieve you to know more?"

"I… yes. I wish I could see him, to know he is well. Every time I see a baby, I wonder if he might be the one. I cannot bear it." Georgiana's voice caught.

"I can understand that, though I did not face it myself. I knew where my child was and could watch him from a distance. I will speak to your brother."

"No! You must not! He will be furious at me."

"No, he will not. He knows I can be trusted with a secret, and I think he will understand why you need to know more."

The gloom of the previous year closed in on Georgiana, leaving her barely able to breathe, and then, for the first time, she felt a ray of hope that it might someday lift. "That would please me."

Aunt Augusta tapped her finger against her lips. "That gives me an idea. Yes, I think a slight change of plans may be in order."

Darkness was falling as Darcy and Elizabeth finally reached London. At first the familiar road had passed by quickly in Darcy's curricle, drawn by matched greys who seemed to delight in speed, but one had gone lame en route, necessitating a stop at a posting inn to acquire a replacement. Darcy would not permit the greys to be separated, and the new horses were substantially slower. As the carriage approached the outskirts of the city, Darcy stopped again to light the lanterns and hang them from the front of the curricle. He did not wish to risk another delay.

Apart from the necessary business, the couple spoke but little on their journey, though if one were to count meaningful looks and stolen caresses, their conversation was continual. Elizabeth's emotions were in constant tumult between joy, anxiety, and an odd worry that somehow it would all prove to be a dream. It was indeed the most familiar route to her, she realized as they neared Cheapside. "Are we to stop at my uncle's house, then?" she asked.

"No." Darcy said no more, so Elizabeth waited curiously until she recognized their goal. The expanse of Moorsfield, a riot of green hedges and tall summer wildflowers, opened before them, and Darcy skilfully steered the curricle onto the cart path through its midst before halting the horses near the copse where they had met so often. He said nothing, the reins loose in his hands, his eyes fixed ahead.

Elizabeth laid her hand against his, reminding herself that they were married and she need not worry about such an action. "Is anything amiss?" she asked.

Darcy shook his head slowly and then shifted to look at her. "I was recalling all the times I had to leave you here, and how I ached to bring you home with me, how empty my life felt when we were apart, and I had no hope of seeing you until the next morning. Our short hour together was such a delight, but it highlighted how much I missed you the remainder of the time. But I could not stay away, even when I tried."

Elizabeth's eyes misted. "I had no notion you felt it so strongly. I knew you enjoyed my company, but I did not let myself contemplate that it might be anything more, though I missed you terribly that time you disappeared for thirty days."

"You counted?"

"I could not help it."

His brow furrowed for a moment. "Elizabeth, when I returned after that journey to Kent, that day when we misunderstood each other so painfully—did you think of me as anything more than a friend at that point?"

Elizabeth laughed. "It will no doubt feed your vanity and pride, but I wished for something more. I thought it impossible, though. I was too low to be your wife and too proud to be anything less."

"I am sorry, beyond sorry, to have been so unclear in my intentions that day. I paid painfully for it."

"You must have thought me quite mad!"

"No, although I did not know how to understand your refusal at first. I thought it might be some attempt to punish me for my misdeeds." He rubbed his hand along his cheek absently.

"I am still mortified that I went so far as to strike you."

"That, madam, was the least of my concerns. I knew I deserved it for attempting to kiss you."

"If it was the least of your concerns, I must not have tried hard enough."

Darcy laughed. "You have no need to try harder, and I hope I will never give you cause to do so again."

"Well, sir, I am sorry to begin our lives together with a threat, but I believe I will be forced to strike you again if—"

"If what?"

Mischief danced in her fine eyes. "If you do *not* kiss me."

He took a deep breath to still his suddenly pounding heart. "You intend to strike me if I do *not* kiss you?"

"I shall be sorely tempted, I fear."

"Here, in the middle of Moorsfield?"

"That did not stop you last time, sir, but if you insist, I will permit you to take me home before you kiss me, but my threat stands."

He laughed. "Take you home—I like the sound of that. And although I cannot fear you, I will, on this occasion, accede to your demands." He took advantage of the darkness to lean towards her, gently brushing his lips against hers.

She shivered as the heat of it raced through her. It was not enough. She wanted to forget the sorrow of Moorsfield and think only of him. He drew a deep breath at her look, and his eyes darkened as he drew her close and kissed her again, his warm lips clinging to hers as though near desperate.

All too soon, he drew away and straightened his shoulders. "Elizabeth?"

"Yes?"

"On this particular subject, you may feel free to threaten me at any point."

"You do not, then, dislike the exercise?"

He leaned closer until his lips touched her ear, pressing a feathery kiss against the lobe. He whispered, "Elizabeth, with my body I thee worship. On that you may depend."

Chapter 22

Colonel Fitzwilliam shook the snow from his coat before handing it to the hovering footman. "Is Darcy at home?"

"Yes, sir. You are expected?" The man sounded unexpectedly dubious. Usually the servants at Pemberley were better trained.

"This is a surprise visit."

The man cast a glance out the window, clearly wondering at the sanity of anyone who took on a long ride in the midst of a snowstorm, even if it was starting to lighten. "Perhaps you would like to wait in the parlour while I inform Mr. Darcy you are here."

"Very well." He strode down the hall, expecting the parlour to be empty. Instead, he was met by three snarling dogs and took an automatic step backwards.

"Frejya! Frigg!" A girl's melodic voice spoke sternly. "Odin, I will thank you to sit, sir!" Instantly two of the dogs draped themselves by the feet of a lovely girl with blond hair, while the largest of the three sat erect by her side, his teeth still slightly bared as he eyed the colonel.

Richard extended a hand to the dog to sniff. The hound's hackles slowly went down, and the colonel reached back to scratch the canine's ears with a practised hand. The dog preened with pleasure. "Odin, you old softie." The colonel laughed. "All bark and no bite."

"He would bite you soon enough if I told him to, young man!"

He turned to see Darcy's aunt regarding him with satisfaction. He bowed. "I have no doubt of it, Lady Seaton. I am sure he is well trained to the scent of Fitzwilliam blood," he said dryly.

Lady Seaton smirked. "They have learned to subdue that particular instinct of late."

He bowed once more. "On behalf of my entire family, I thank you. But I do not believe I have met this charming young lady whom your lapdogs are so eager to protect."

"Lapdogs, ha! Colonel, allow me to introduce Miss Mary Seaton, my newly adopted daughter. Mary, this is Colonel Richard Fitzwilliam, your… well, one of your not-so-distant relations. But do not worry; he takes after his mother."

Mary rose to her feet. She curtsied gracefully and glanced at Lady Seaton, who gave her a slight nod of encouragement.

Richard tilted his head to one side. "A relation?"

"A very close one, in fact," Lady Seaton said with definite smugness.

His puzzled look gave way to surprise, and then he threw back his head and laughed until tears came to his eyes. When he finally could keep something remotely resembling a sober mien, he said, "Ah, Lady Seaton, I hope to have the pleasure of being in a distant country when my father hears this news."

"Odd, I am looking forward to seeing his face myself," Lady Seaton said, snapping her fingers. One of the hounds padded to her side.

Richard chuckled. "I am sure. Have you thought of training a few extra dogs for the occasion? A little additional protection might not go amiss." He bowed again to Mary. "I beg your pardon, Miss Seaton. Pray forgive my unseemly mirth."

"You are forgiven, Colonel," Mary said in a quiet voice.

Lady Seaton said, "Chin up, girl. How many times must I tell you? Look them in the eyes. And do not fret, Mary, this particular Fitzwilliam whelp does not bite, unlike his sire."

The girl obediently, if timidly, raised china-blue eyes to him, and he smiled encouragingly. "Indeed, I am quite a tame hound. But how shall we categorize our new acquaintance? Perhaps since you are now my cousin's cousin, you could call me Cousin Richard."

Miss Seaton looked rather as if she thought it would be a hanging offense to do anything of the sort, but she said, "As you wish."

Lady Seaton said, "Just a warning, colonel. Mary does bite."

Miss Seaton turned pale and looked away at Lady Seaton's word.

Richard took pity on the girl and said gently, "So I have heard, but I believe it is only in the very best of causes."

It was at this point that Darcy came upon them. "Welcome to Pemberley, cousin. What brings you out today? The fine weather, perhaps?" he said.

Richard looked down ruefully at his soaked boots. "I am here for congratulations."

"Bingley will be glad of it. He should be down soon, though he may need to re-tie his cravat a dozen times first," Darcy said dryly.

"Bingley is here?" Richard asked. "I had not realized."

"But you said you wanted to congratulate him. Or perhaps you meant to offer your belated congratulations to Mrs. Darcy and me."

"No, although I am happy to offer those as well. I was asking for *your* congratulations."

"For what?" Half of Darcy's attention was on the hallway, where he hoped Elizabeth would soon appear.

"I am engaged to be married."

It was the last thing Darcy had expected, and it finally drew his full attention to his cousin. "*You* are engaged? Who is the lady unfortunate enough to have fallen for your charms?"

Richard's grin broadened. "Lady Mary Howard. It will be in the papers next week."

"Lady Mary?" Darcy's voice rose in disbelief. "I know she is fond of you, and I do not doubt your sterling qualities, but how will you win her father's consent? He would have considered me marginally suitable for his daughter, and you are a second son."

Richard's face grew sober. "Then you have not heard?"

For a shocked moment, Darcy thought that Henry's illness must have ended his life, but then he realized Richard would be in black if that were the case, and certainly not sounding so cheerful. "Heard what? We receive little news here."

"My father has changed his will. My future is brighter than I ever dreamed, although I am sorry to say it is at my brother's expense."

"He disinherited Henry?" Darcy heard a gasp from Mary's direction. "I knew he was angry, but I never thought he would go so far."

Richard shrugged. "It could not be helped, or, as Henry put it, it was God's will. His mind is rather addled, in my opinion. He has not been the same since his illness."

"Still, worse men have remained as their father's heir."

"Yes, but *they* did not tell my father that they were determined to go into the church. Henry has declared his intention of taking orders."

"Henry? A *clergyman*? Wickham would be better suited to the role!"

"I could hardly believe it myself, but he would not be moved from it, even when Father threatened to disinherit him. Henry said the riches of the world mattered nothing to him. He seems to have taken over your role as the family

Puritan with a vengeance. We are all sinners, by Henry's new standards."

"He must indeed be addled. Either that or possessed," Darcy said, half to himself.

"And, to make matters worse, in love, but I imagine you are well aware of *that*."

Elizabeth appeared in the doorway, a vision of loveliness in one of the new dresses he had ordered for her, her cheeks flushed and her eyes bright. She seemed to bring sunlight with her, even when there was nothing but snow and grey skies outside. The soft look she gave him made him wish he could take her in his arms. He had to tear his attention away from her. "Elizabeth, do you recall my cousin, Colonel Fitzwilliam?"

"Of course. We met at Rosings Park. You are welcome to Pemberley, colonel." She held out her hand to Richard, who bowed over it.

"You are most gracious. I hope that you will call me Richard, especially since I have sold my commission."

"Indeed?" Elizabeth said. "I hope that means we will have the pleasure of your company more often in the future."

Darcy struggled not to feel annoyed that his wife's attention was turned to any man but him. After all, he had not seen her for hours! "So, who is the lady who has captivated Henry's black heart?" he said gruffly.

Richard shifted from one foot to the other, glancing sideways at Elizabeth. "I thought you would have heard."

"I would not have asked if I had known," Darcy said.

"It is Mrs. Darcy's sister, Katherine."

"Kitty?" Elizabeth said in astonishment.

"Never!" Darcy said firmly. "I will not permit it."

Richard chuckled. "Best of luck to you, my friend! Henry is posturing like a distraught Romeo deprived of his Juliet. He speaks only of Miss Bennet's innocence, purity, and nobility of character. He claims she is an angel sent by God to rescue him during the darkest night of his soul. Apparently she nursed him during his convalescence at your mother-in-law's house in Hertfordshire. He swears he will not be parted from her. That was the final straw for Father. He ordered Henry out of his sight and called for his solicitor."

"So Henry is cast out completely?"

"Father would have liked that, but the title and the original Derby estate—that old ruin in the North—are crown grants, so they must go to the eldest son. Everything else goes to me. All the land the family has acquired in the last three hundred years, the new estate, and more importantly—to Lady Mary's father, that is—everything in the Derby coffers. I do not delight in my brother's misfortune, but I cannot but rejoice that now I can marry the woman I despaired of."

"It seems you have much to celebrate," Elizabeth said warmly. "It is a day of celebration here already. May I hope you will remain through the festivities?"

Richard bowed. "It would be my pleasure, Mrs. Darcy, although I do not know what festivities you refer to."

Elizabeth glanced at Darcy. "Why, the wedding. My eldest sister is to marry today. We will be leaving for the church as soon as the weather permits."

Bingley swooped into the room, fiddling with his cuffs. "There you are, Darcy. Do you think it is time? I do not wish to keep anyone waiting. Oh, pardon me, Colonel Fitzwilliam. I did not see you."

Elizabeth hid a smile at the idea that anyone could be more impatient for the event than Mr. Bingley. The colonel gave her an enquiring look, and she said, "Mr. Bingley will soon be my brother."

"This is indeed a day of surprises!" Richard shook Bingley's hand heartily and offered his congratulations.

A half hour later, the snow had stopped enough to make the short journey to the church feasible. Darcy took a fur-lined cloak from the footman and wrapped it tenderly around Elizabeth's shoulder, pausing to appreciate her scent of lavender. He followed her through the open door to the sleigh with its battered red trim. He had given orders for the new sleigh to be used for the bride and groom.

A few lazy flakes of snow drifted down onto Elizabeth's hood. He knew from her mischievous glance that if she had been alone with him, she would have tried to catch a snowflake on her tongue. Elizabeth seemed endlessly delighted by the deep snows of Derbyshire.

Colonel Fitzwilliam and Georgiana were already ensconced in the sleigh's facing seat. Darcy silently thanked his sister for taking the unaccustomed seat so that he could be beside Elizabeth. He handed his wife in, settled himself on the cushion beside her, and spread a thick blanket across their laps. The hot bricks at his feet added welcome warmth, but not as much as the knowledge that Elizabeth was by his side.

The driver clucked to the horses and snapped his whip. One of the greys tossed his head, his harness jingling, but set off obediently beside his mate, first at a walk and then a trot as they cleared the vicinity of the house. Snow puffed up around the rapidly moving hooves.

"It seems a small party for a wedding," Colonel Fitzwilliam said. "Is this one of Bingley's sudden whims?"

Darcy shook his head. "It is a very private affair, because Jane has been a widow but four months, and Bingley did not wish to wait a full year to wed. Under the circumstances, it seemed best to proceed quietly."

Colonel Fitzwilliam whistled. "Four months? That is quick, even for Bingley!"

Darcy glanced at Elizabeth. "Their attachment is long-standing. It is only the wedding that is quick."

Elizabeth said with a smile, "Quick, small weddings seem to be quite the fashion in my family of late."

"So I hear. I was sorry to miss your wedding, though I gather my family was over-represented as it was. Someday I hope you will tell me the entire story. I have heard only bits and pieces, and I imagine some of the highlights were left out of the telling."

Darcy laughed. "That may be for the best. It was a most unusual wedding. Unforgettable, one might say."

"One would hope our wedding would be unforgettable even if nothing untoward had occurred," Elizabeth said tartly. "But it is true, today's ceremony risks seeming dull by comparison, but then again, Jane has always been more proper and sedate than I."

Darcy leaned close to her and whispered in her ear, "You are perfection itself, my love." Once again he found himself caught by her fine eyes, and he had no desire to look away.

Colonel Fitzwilliam cleared his throat. "Speaking of proper and sedate, I had not realized your aunt had taken a new member into her family. Dare I ask how that came to pass? Was it your idea?"

Darcy shook his head. "Hardly. Aunt Augusta took Georgiana to Bath after our wedding, with Mary along as a servant. They arrived here a fortnight ago with Mary transformed into a proper young lady and her adopted daughter. No doubt she imagined it would annoy your father more than anything else in her power. We have given out here that Mary is a distant connection on the Fitzwilliam side."

"I am glad to call her my cousin," Georgiana declared with a hint of defiance.

"I do not object. It seems to make our aunt happy, and that is the most important thing," Darcy said. "In any case, we will see more of Mary, as Aunt Augusta has announced her intention to visit us often. She says she needs to make certain that Georgiana and I do not revert to our old humourless ways, but I believe it is more that she does not wish to miss any opportunity to remind me that my wife is too good for me. Not, of course, that I have any doubt of this myself."

"Darcy, if I had any doubts that this was a love match, you have long since put them to rest."

The sleigh pulled up in front of the church. The path to the door had been cleared of snow, but the flagstones were already covered by a light dusting of new flakes.

Inside, the curate was waiting at the altar, white-haired and bent with age. He had held that role since Darcy could remember. All those years he had sat with his parents in the family pew, trying to subdue the restlessness natural to a young child, always trying to behave as a Darcy should.

How different it was now! His parents would have disapproved of all aspects of this assembly. Aunt Augusta, who had been married in this same church, had not been welcome at Pemberley during his mother's lifetime. He could imagine his father's fury if he had known that the earl's illegitimate daughter was also sitting in the family pew. They would never have permitted Darcy to marry Elizabeth; they would have disapproved even of his friendship with Bingley, because of his family in trade. Georgiana and Colonel Fitzwilliam were the only people present who would have been acceptable to his parents' pride.

Elizabeth squeezed his hand, reminding him of his duty. As the only adult male connected to the Bennets, he was to give Jane to Bingley. Could he have ever foreseen such an occurrence when he first advised Bingley to avoid Jane? Now he was instrumental in bringing his friend happiness. It was true cause for pride. He kissed Elizabeth on the cheek—one bit of joy!—and went to take his place.

Epilogue

After their wedding, Mr. and Mrs. Bingley relocated to an estate in a neighbouring county, and Jane and Elizabeth, in addition to every other source of happiness, were within thirty miles of each other. Although Mr. Bingley treated young Edward Browning in the very same manner as the children Jane eventually bore him, Darcy remained an active presence in the life of his godson and, as promised, made certain the boy had a gentleman's education, and eventually set him up in a legal practise in London. It was a surprise to no one when several years later, the industrious and well-connected young man became a respected judge.

Charlie remained in London, where he proved an invaluable apprentice to Mr. Gardiner. He continued to hunger for knowledge from any source, and Miss Margaret Gardiner was delighted to find someone willing to listen for hours to her discourses on history. Soon he was reading history books himself, in order to present his own arguments to her. After several years of hard work and saving his wages, Charlie presented Mr. Gardiner with a difficult choice: to agree to marry his eldest daughter to a young man of no pedigree whatsoever or to lose an employee who had increased the profits of his business substantially and was well on his way to partnership. Mr. Gardiner agreed and then sent the new couple to Manchester, where Charlie would act as his buying agent at the mills, and the couple took advantage of the proximity to Pemberley to become frequent visitors. Thus it came to pass that when Mr. Charles Hopper finally travelled to Pemberley, it was as a member of the family, with his new bride on his arm. Mr. and Mrs. Darcy scarcely recognized the stylishly dressed young man as the urchin they had known in years past, but sometimes when no one was looking, Charlie flashed a knowing grin at the master and mistress of Pemberley.

Some years later, the living at Kympton came open. Darcy, knowing that Elizabeth would enjoy having her younger sister nearby, offered it to his cousin Henry, who had indeed taken orders, hoping that Henry's religious meanderings would not prove too tiresome. Lord Derby unexpectedly took the gesture as an olive branch, since it put his reprobate son far from any contact with fashionable society, and he resumed contact with Darcy as if there had never been any disagreement. With much gentle persuasion from Elizabeth,

Darcy agreed to resume occasional contact with his uncle, though the gentleman remained as overbearing and difficult as ever. Darcy's chief concern was to avoid the possibility of any overlap between the earl's visits to Pemberley and those of Lady Seaton, who took a continuing proprietary interest in her nephew's family. The parishioners of Kympton did not immediately accommodate Henry's hellfire and brimstone preaching, but still enjoyed the notoriety of having an impoverished aristocrat as their minister. In later years they were known to note that life had become much simpler for fathers of attractive young girls, since all the young men of Kympton were firmly convinced that carnal knowledge of a woman without benefit of marriage would lead directly to loss of their limbs.

Mr. and Mrs. Darcy made an annual trip to Meryton each Easter to visit Mrs. Bennet, who, to Elizabeth's relief, preferred to remain in Hertfordshire, where she could with delighted pride talk to all her acquaintance about Mrs. Darcy, Mrs. Bingley, and the future Countess of Derby. Afterwards, the Darcys would continue to London to allow Mr. Darcy to inspect the Foundlings Home he had established in a poverty-stricken part of London, which on occasion he fondly referred to as "The Mews." The scandal of their marriage died down over time, but the Darcys rarely took part in London society, leading some to name them unfashionable and others as infernally proud. The couple and later their children, however, preferred the society of the Gardiners to the excitement of

Almack's and White's and instead enjoyed annual tours of Moorsfield and Hyde Park, which excited gratitude in their hearts for the good fortune that had brought them together to celebrate a love and understanding that only increased with the years.

Acknowledgments

This book would never have been completed without the help and support of many people. My thanks to the readers who encouraged me by asking for one more Pride and Prejudice Variation, and to those who read it as a work in progress. They can claim responsibility for certain twists of the plot, though I must apologize that I couldn't figure out a way to bring bloodthirsty sharks into the same vicinity as the Earl of Derby and his eldest son. Inspiration credit goes to my medical friends who asked so nicely for just a *little* medical scene and then laughed when I wrote one that incorporated treatments still in use today (yes, even the maggots).

I must also thank my extraordinary editor, Deb Werksman, for her belief in my work, as well as my agent, Lauren Abramo, for her patience in explaining the workings of the book world to a very ignorant pupil. Danielle Jackson of Sourcebooks walked me through the publicity minefields.

My colleagues at work deserve credit for coping with the shock that not only did I write books, but ones with love scenes (and yes, I promise to write only emotionally and physically healthy love scenes!). Bonnie Conway gets the Sherlock

Holmes award for figuring out about my secret writing life, and Nancy Bullian and Judy ("And they're really HOT sex scenes, too!") Johnson kept my "other" work life running smoothly while providing support and encouragement.

Last, but never least, I want to thank my beloved husband, David, for undertaking the cooking, laundry, and lots of other things so that I'd have the time and energy to write; my daughter, Rebecca, for inspiring different characters through her dedication to marching to her own drummer (or should that be lute?); and my son, Brian, for making sure all the cats got enough grooming and attention while Mom was writing, and occasionally cleaning his room.

About the Author

Abigail Reynolds is a lifelong Jane Austen enthusiast and a physician. In addition to writing, she has a part-time private practice and enjoys spending time with her family. Originally from upstate New York, she studied Russian, theater, and marine biology before deciding to attend medical school. She began writing *Pride and Prejudice* Variations in 2001 to spend more time with her favorite Jane Austen characters. Encouragement from fellow Austen fans persuaded her to continue asking "What if…?", which led to four other *Pride and Prejudice* Variations and her contemporary novel, *The Man Who Loved Pride and Prejudice*. She is currently at work on a sequel to *Mr. Darcy's Obsession*, as well as the companion novels to *The Man Who Loved Pride and Prejudice*. She lives in Wisconsin with her husband, two teenage children, and a menagerie of pets.

Mr. Fitzwilliam Darcy:
THE LAST MAN IN THE WORLD

A *Pride and Prejudice* Variation

ABIGAIL REYNOLDS

What if Elizabeth had accepted Mr. Darcy the first time he asked?

In Jane Austen's *Pride and Prejudice*, Elizabeth Bennet tells the proud Mr. Fitzwilliam Darcy that she wouldn't marry him if he were the last man in the world. But what if circumstances conspired to make her accept Darcy the first time he proposes? In this installment of Abigail Reynolds' acclaimed *Pride and Prejudice* Variations, Elizabeth agrees to marry Darcy against her better judgment, setting off a chain of events that nearly brings disaster to them both. Ultimately, Darcy and Elizabeth will have to work together on their tumultuous and passionate journey to make a success of their ill-timed marriage.

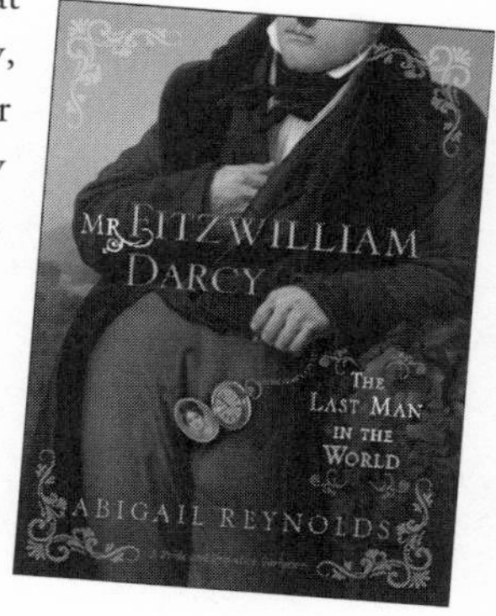

What readers are saying:

"A highly original story, immensely satisfying."

"Anyone who loves the story of Darcy and Elizabeth will love this variation."

"I was hooked from page one."

"A refreshing new look at what might have happened if..."

"Another good book to curl up with... I never wanted to put it down..."

978-1-4022-2947-3
$14.99 US/$18.99 CAN/£7.99 UK

Mr. and Mrs. Fitzwilliam Darcy: Two Shall Become One

Sharon Lathan

"Highly entertaining... I felt fully immersed in the time period. Well done!" —*Romance Reader at Heart*

A fascinating portrait of a timeless, consuming love

It's Darcy and Elizabeth's wedding day, and the journey is just beginning as Jane Austen's beloved *Pride and Prejudice* characters embark on the greatest adventure of all: marriage and a life together filled with surprising passion, tender self-discovery, and the simple joys of every day.

As their love story unfolds in this most romantic of Jane Austen sequels, Darcy and Elizabeth each reveal to the other how their relationship blossomed from misunderstanding to perfect understanding and harmony, and a marriage filled with romance, sensuality, and the beauty of a deep, abiding love.

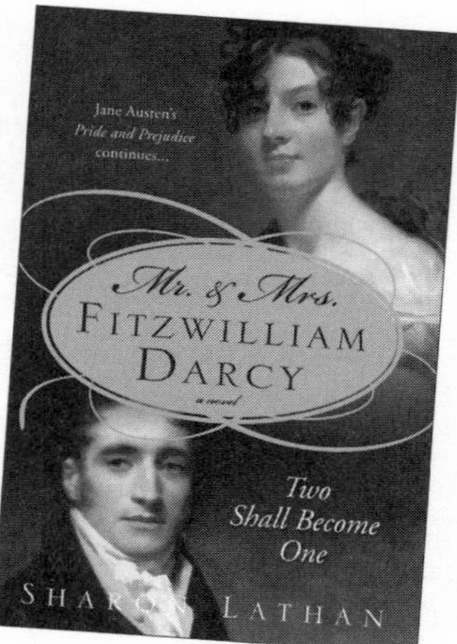

What readers are saying:

"This journey is truly amazing."

"What a wonderful beginning to this truly beautiful marriage."

"Could not stop reading."

"So beautifully written...making me feel as though I was in the room with Lizzy and Darcy...and sharing in all of the touching moments between."

978-1-4022-1523-0 • $14.99 US/ $15.99 CAN/ £7.99 UK

Loving Mr. Darcy: Journeys Beyond Pemberley

Sharon Lathan

"A romance that transcends time." —*The Romance Studio*

Darcy and Elizabeth embark on the journey of a lifetime

Six months into his marriage to Elizabeth Bennet, Darcy is still head over heels in love, and each day offers more opportunities to surprise and delight his beloved bride. Elizabeth has adapted to being the Mistress of Pemberley, charming everyone she meets and handling her duties with grace and poise. Just when it seems life can't get any better, Elizabeth gets the most wonderful news. The lovers leave the serenity of Pemberley, traveling through the sumptuous landscape of Regency England, experiencing the lavish sights, sounds, and tastes around them. With each day come new discoveries as they become further entwined, body and soul.

What readers are saying:

"Darcy's passion for love and life with Lizzy is brought to the forefront and captured beautifully."

"Sharon Lathan is a wonderful writer… I believe that Jane Austen herself would love this story as much as I did."

"The historical backdrop of the book is unbelievable—I actually felt like I could see all the places where the Darcys traveled."

"Truly captures the heart of Darcy & Elizabeth! Very well written and totally hot!"

978-1-4022-1741-8 • $14.99 US/ $18.99 CAN/ £7.99 UK

My Dearest Mr. Darcy

Sharon Lathan

Darcy is more deeply in love with his wife than ever

As the golden summer draws to a close and the Darcys look ahead to the end of their first year of marriage, Mr. Darcy could never have imagined his love could grow even deeper with the passage of time. Elizabeth is unpredictable and lively, pulling Darcy out of his stern and serious demeanor with her teasing and temptation.

But surprising events force the Darcys to weather absence and illness, and to discover whether they can find a way to build a bond of everlasting love and desire…

Praise for *Loving Mr. Darcy*:

"An intimately romantic sequel to Jane Austen's *Pride and Prejudice*…wonderfully colorful and fun." —*Wendy's Book Corner*

"If you want to fall in love with Mr. Darcy all over again…order yourself a copy." —*Royal Reviews*

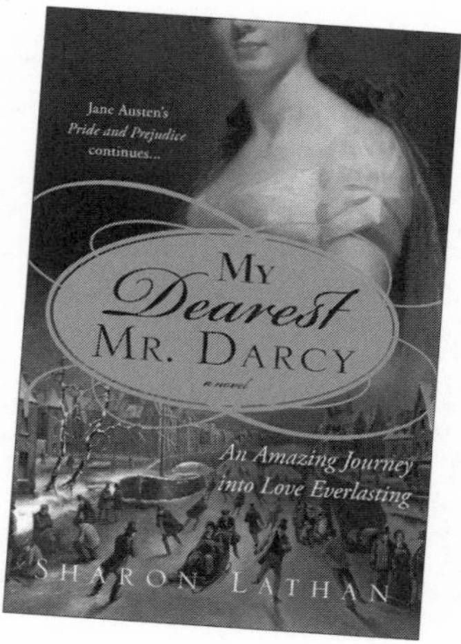

978-1-4022-1742-5
$14.99 US/$18.99 CAN/£7.99 UK

In the Arms of Mr. Darcy

Sharon Lathan

If only everyone could be as happy as they are...

Darcy and Elizabeth are as much in love as ever—even more so as their relationship matures. Their passion inspires everyone around them, and as winter turns to spring, romance blossoms around them.

Confirmed bachelor Richard Fitzwilliam sets his sights on a seemingly unattainable, beautiful widow; Georgiana Darcy learns to flirt outrageously; the very flighty Kitty Bennet develops her first crush, and Caroline Bingley meets her match.

But the path of true love never does run smooth, and Elizabeth and Darcy are kept busy navigating their friends and loved ones through the inevitable separations, misunderstandings, misgivings, and lovers' quarrels to reach their own happily ever afters...

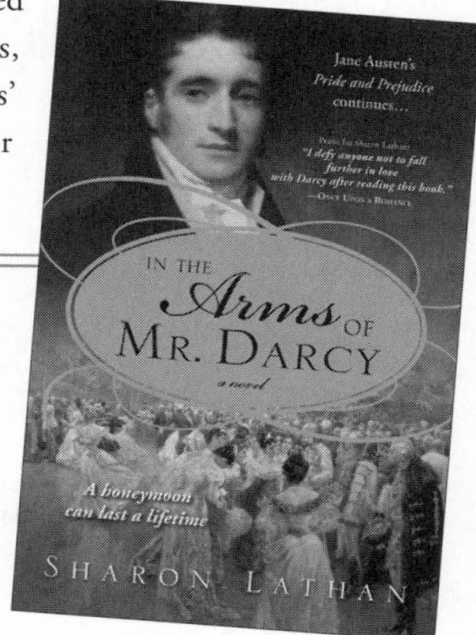

"If you love *Pride and Prejudice* sequels then this series should be on the top of your list!" —*Royal Reviews*

"Sharon really knows how to make Regency come alive." —*Love Romance Passion*

978-1-4022-3699-0
$14.99 US/$17.99 CAN/£9.99 UK

Mr. Darcy Takes a Wife

Linda Berdoll

The #1 best-selling* Pride and Prejudice *sequel

"Wild, bawdy, and utterly enjoyable." —*Booklist*

Hold on to your bonnets!

Every woman wants to be Elizabeth Bennet Darcy—beautiful, gracious, universally admired, strong, daring and outspoken—a thoroughly modern woman in crinolines. And every woman will fall madly in love with Mr. Darcy—tall, dark and handsome, a nobleman and a heartthrob whose virility is matched only by his utter devotion to his wife. Their passion is consuming and idyllic—essentially, they can't keep their hands off each other—through a sweeping tale of adventure and misadventure, human folly and numerous mysteries of parentage. This sexy, epic, hilarious, poignant and romantic sequel to *Pride and Prejudice* goes far beyond Jane Austen.

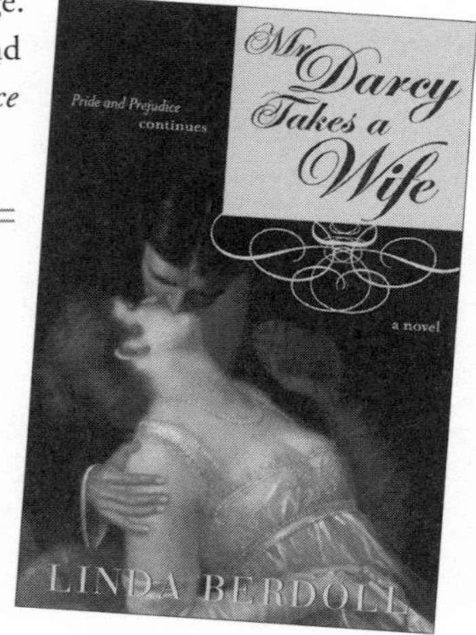

What readers are saying:

"I couldn't put it down."

"I didn't want it to end!"

"Berdoll does Jane Austen proud! ...A thoroughly delightful and engaging book."

"Delicious fun…I thoroughly enjoyed this book."

"My favorite *Pride and Prejudice* sequel so far."

978-1-4022-0273-5 • $16.95 US/ $19.99 CAN/ £9.99 UK

Mr. Darcy's Diary

AMANDA GRANGE

"A gift to a new generation of Darcy fans and a treat for existing fans as well." —AUSTENBLOG

The only place Darcy could share his innermost feelings...

...was in the private pages of his diary. Torn between his sense of duty to his family name and his growing passion for Elizabeth Bennet, all he can do is struggle not to fall in love. A skillful and graceful imagining of the hero's point of view in one of the most beloved and enduring love stories of all time.

What readers are saying:

"A delicious treat for all Austen addicts."

"Amanda Grange knows her subject...I ended up reading the entire book in one sitting."

"Brilliant, you could almost hear Darcy's voice...I was so sad when it came to an end. I loved the visions she gave us of their married life."

"Amanda Grange has perfectly captured all of Jane Austen's clever wit and social observations to make *Mr. Darcy's Diary* a must read for any fan."

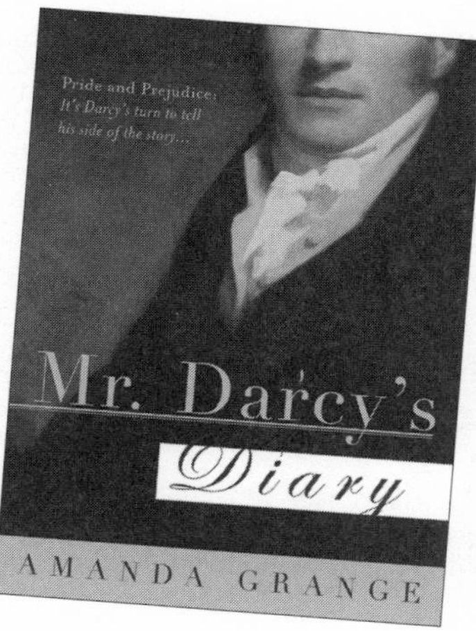

978-1-4022-0876-8 • $14.95 US/ $19.95 CAN/ £7.99 UK

MR. DARCY, VAMPYRE

PRIDE AND PREJUDICE CONTINUES...

AMANDA GRANGE

"A seductively gothic tale..." —Romance Buy the Book

A test of love that will take them to hell and back...

My dearest Jane,

My hand is trembling as I write this letter. My nerves are in tatters and I am so altered that I believe you would not recognise me. The past two months have been a nightmarish whirl of strange and disturbing circumstances, and the future...

Jane, I am afraid.

It was all so different a few short months ago. When I awoke on my wedding morning, I thought myself the happiest woman alive...

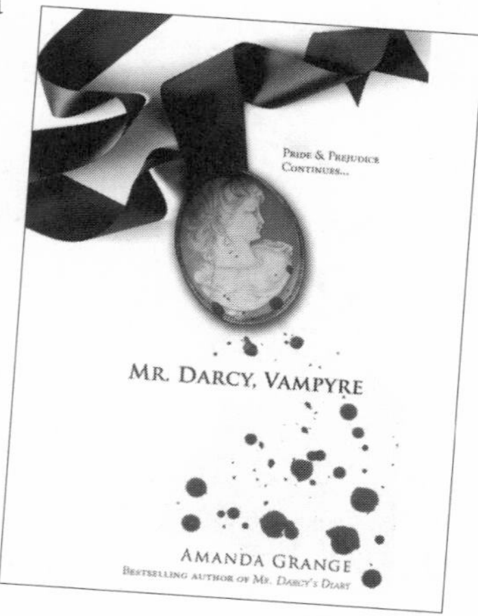

978-1-4022-3697-6

$14.99 US/$18.99 CAN/£7.99 UK

"Amanda Grange has crafted a clever homage to the Gothic novels that Jane Austen so enjoyed." —*AustenBlog*

"Compelling, heartbreaking, and triumphant all at once." —*Bloody Bad Books*

"The romance and mystery in this story melded together perfectly... a real page-turner." —*Night Owl Romance*

"Mr. Darcy makes an inordinately attractive vampire.... *Mr. Darcy, Vampyre* delights lovers of Jane Austen that are looking for more." —*Armchair Interviews*

Wickham's Diary

Amanda Grange

Jane Austen's quintessential bad boy has his say...

Enter the clandestine world of the cold-hearted Wickham...

...in the pages of his private diary. Always aware of the inferiority of his social status compared to his friend Fitzwilliam Darcy, Wickham chases wealth and women in an attempt to attain the power he lusts for. But as Wickham gambles and cavorts his way through his funds, Darcy still comes out on top.

But now Wickham has found his chance to seduce the young Georgiana Darcy, which will finally secure the fortune—and the revenge—he's always dreamed of...

Praise for Amanda Grange:

"Amanda Grange has taken on the challenge of reworking a much loved romance and succeeds brilliantly." —*Historical Novels Review*

"Amanda Grange is a writer who tells an engaging, thoroughly enjoyable story!" —*Romance Reader at Heart*

Available April 2011
978-1-4022-5186-3
$12.99 US

A Darcy Christmas

Amanda Grange, Sharon Lathan, & Carolyn Eberhart

A Holiday Tribute to Jane Austen

Mr. and Mrs. Darcy wish you a very Merry Christmas and a Happy New Year!

Share in the magic of the season in these three warm and wonderful holiday novellas from bestselling authors.

Christmas Present
By Amanda Grange

A Darcy Christmas
By Sharon Lathan

Mr. Darcy's Christmas Carol
By Carolyn Eberhart

978-1-4022-4339-4
$14.99 US/$17.99 CAN/£9.99 UK

Praise for Amanda Grange:

"Amanda Grange is a writer who tells an engaging, thoroughly enjoyable story!"
—*Romance Reader at Heart*

"Amanda Grange seems to have really got under Darcy's skin and retells the story with great feeling and sensitivity."
—*Historical Novel Society*

Praise for Sharon Lathan:

"I defy anyone not to fall further in love with Darcy after reading this book."
—*Once Upon a Romance*

"The everlasting love between Darcy and Lizzy will leave more than one reader swooning." —*A Bibliophile's Bookshelf*